SILVER
P·I·G·S

SILVER P·I·G·S

A Novel by

LINDSEY DAVIS

CROWN PUBLISHERS, INC.

New York

Published by Crown Publishers, Inc., 201 East 50th Street, New York, New York 10022

Originally published in Great Britain by Sidgwick & Jackson Limited

CROWN is a trademark of Crown Publishers, Inc.

Manufactured in the United States of America

Library of Congress Cataloging-in-Publication Data

Davis, Lindsey.
    Silver pigs : a novel / by Lindsey Davis.
        p.   cm.
    1. Rome—History—Vespasian, 69-79—Fiction.   I. Title.
PR6054.A8925S55   1989
823'.914—dc19

89-1139

For Richard

Mona

Eboracum (York)
[LEGIO IX]

BRITANNIA

Viroconium
(Wroxeter)
Lindum
(Lincoln)
LEGIO
[XX]

Glevum
(Gloucester)
Abona
LEGIO II
THE
FRONTIER
ROAD

Sabrina Aes.

Vebiodunum
Aquae Sulis
(Bath)

Isca Dumnoniorum
(Exeter)
Durnovaria
(Dorchester)

Londinium

Rutupiae
(Richborough)
Dubris (Dover)

OCEANUS BRITANNICUS

Fretum
Gallicum

Gesoriacum
(Boulogne)

GERMANIA
INFERIOR

Rhenus Fl.

GERMANIA

GALLIA BELGICA

GALLIA
LUGDUNENSIS

Argentoratum
(Strasbourg)

GERMANIA
SUPERIOR

RHAETIA

NORICUM

AQUITANIA

Lugdunum
(Lyons)

GALLIA NARBONENSIS

R. Rhone
(Rhodanus)

ALPES

GALLIA
CISALPINA

ILLYRICUM

HISPANIA
TARRACONENSIS

Massilia
(Marseilles)

ITALY

ROME
Ostia

MARE   INTERNUM

SARDINIA

MAURETANIA

NUMIDIA   AFRICA

SICILIA

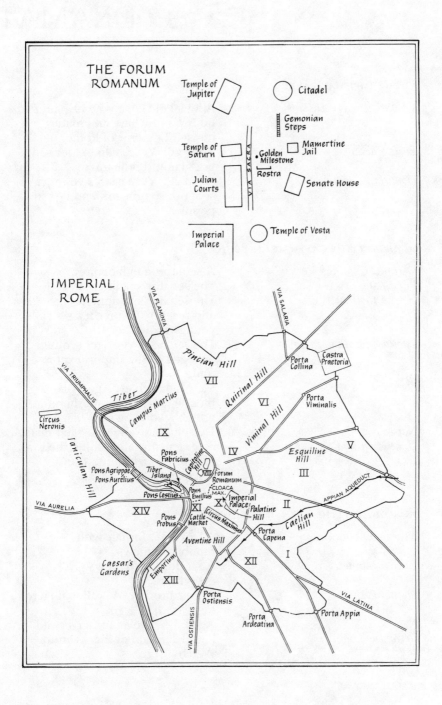

THE FORUM
ROMANUM

Temple of
Jupiter

◯ Citadel

▦ Gemonian
Steps

Temple of
Saturn

• Golden
Milestone

▢ Mamertine
Jail

↳ Rostra

Julian
Courts

▢ Senate House

Imperial
Palace

◯ Temple of Vesta

IMPERIAL
ROME

VIA FLAMINA

VIA SALARIA

VIA TRIUMPHALIS

Tiber

Pincian Hill

VII

Porta
Collina

Castra
Praetoria

Quirinal Hill

VI

Porta
Viminalis

Circus
Neronis

Campus Martius

IX

Viminal Hill

IV

V

Janiculan Hill

Pons
Fabricius

Tiber
Island

Capitoline Hill

VIII

Forum
Romanum

*Esquiline
Hill*

III

Pons Agrippae
Pons Aurelius

CLOACA
MAX.

Pons
Emilius

APPIAN AQUEDUCT

VIA AURELIA

Pons Cestius

XI

X

Imperial
Palace

II

XIV

Pons
Probus

Cattle
Market

Circus Maximus

Palatine
Hill

*Caelian
Hill*

Caesar's
Gardens

Emporium

XIII

Aventine Hill

Porta
Capena

I

XII

VIA LATINA

Porta
Ostiensis

VIA OSTIENSIS

Porta
Ardeatina

Porta Appia

 DRAMATIS

AT THE IMPERIAL PALACE

Vespasian Augustus:	A jovial old cove who has jumped up from nowhere and made himself Emperor of Rome.
Titus Caesar:	Aged 30. Vespasian's elder son; popular and brilliant.
Domitian Caesar:	Aged 20. Vespasian's younger son; not so brilliant, and not so popular.

IN *REGIO I* (THE CAPENA GATE SECTOR)

Decimus Camillus Verus:	A senator (a millionaire).
Julia Justa:	The senator's noble wife.
Helena Justina:	The senator's daughter. Aged 23 and recently divorced: a sensible young woman.
Publius Camillus Meto:	The senator's younger brother; engaged in the import/export trade.
Sosia Camillina:	Meto's daughter. Aged 16. Blonde, beautiful, and therefore not obliged to be sensible.
Naïssa:	Helena Justina's wide-eyed maid.
Gnaeus Atius Pertinax:	A junior official, holding the rank of aedile (special interest: discipline).

IN *REGIO XIII* (THE AVENTINE SECTOR)

Marcus Didius Falco:	A private informer with republican views.
Falco's Mother:	A mother; with views on everything.
Didius Festus:	Falco's brother. A National Hero (deceased).
Marcia:	Aged 3. Falco's brother's child.
Petronius Longus:	Patrol Captain of the Aventine Watch.

viii

PERSONAE ✑

Lenia:	A laundress.
Smaractus:	A property speculator; also the owner of a gladiators' training school.

Astia:	A drayman's floosie.
Julius Frontinus:	A captain in the Praetorian Guard.
Glaucus:	A Cilician. Proprietor of a respectable gymnasium: an unusual character.
A hot-wine waiter:	(Pungent).
A watchman:	(Drunk).
A gardener's horse:	(Disposition unknown).

IN BRITAIN

Gaius Flavius Hilaris:	Imperial procurator in charge of finance; whose brief includes the silver mines.
Aelia Camilla:	The procurator's wife, youngest sister of the senator Camillus Verus and his brother Publius.
Rufrius Vitalis:	An ex-centurion of the Second Augustan Legion, living in retirement at Isca Dumnoniorum.
T. Claudius Triferus:	(A Briton). Holder of the contract to manage the Imperial silver mine at Vebiodunum in the Mendip Hills.
Cornix:	A sadist. Foreman in charge of slaves at the Imperial silver mine.
Simplex:	Medical officer to the Second Augustan Legion at Glevum (special interest: surgery).

ix

Introduction

Rome: AD 70.

A city in confusion, as the death of Nero ended the ruling dynasty founded by Augustus Caesar.

A city which governed a vast Empire: most of Europe, North Africa and parts of the Middle East. The Emperor Claudius (aided by an unkown young general called Vespasian) had even gained a foothold in a wild location which Romans regarded with unrelieved horror: Britain! Thirty years later it was Vespasian who had emerged triumphant from the struggle for power after Nero.

This had cost Rome a bitter civil war. The Empire was in chaos. The Treasury was bankrupt. Vespasian urgently needed to convince his critics that he and his two sons, Titus and Domitian, represented the best hope of good government and peace.

Meanwhile in Britain, which was slowly recovering from Queen Boudicca's Rebellion, Nero's slack administration had taken its toll. Important mineral rights were leased out to local contractors, including management of the main imperial silver mine in the Mendip Hills. The mines were badly run: four stolen ingots franked at Charterhouse in the First Century AD have been discovered hidden beneath a cairn of stones. Who stole them and hid them so carefully, then never returned? And how did this faraway local fraud affect the new Emperor Vespasian, struggling to maintain his position in Rome?

Marcus Didius Falco – who disapproved of Emperors but who served the state in his own private way – knew the truth . . .

PART I

ROME
Summer–Autumn, AD 70

I

When the girl came rushing up the steps, I decided she was wearing far too many clothes.

It was late summer. Rome frizzled like a pancake on a griddle-plate. People unlaced their shoes but had to keep them on; not even an elephant could cross the streets unshod. People flopped on stools in shadowed doorways, bare knees apart, naked to the waist – and in the backstreets of the Aventine Sector where I lived, that was just the women.

I was standing in the Forum. She was running. She looked overdressed and dangerously hot, but sunstroke or suffocation had not yet finished her off. She was shining and sticky as a glazed pastry plait, and when she hurtled up the steps of the Temple of Saturn straight towards me, I made no attempt to move aside. She missed me, just. Some men are born lucky; others are called Didius Falco.

Close at hand, I still thought she would be better off without so many tunics. Though don't misunderstand me. I like my women in a few wisps of drapery: then I can hope for a chance to remove the wisps. If they start out with nothing I tend to get depressed because either they have just stripped off for someone else or, in my line of work, they are usually dead. This one was vibrantly alive.

Perhaps in a fine mansion with marble veneers, fountains, garden courtyards deep in shade, a leisured young lady might keep cool, even swaddled in embroidered finery with jet and amber bangles from her elbow to her wrist. If she ran out in a hurry she would instantly regret it. The heat haze would melt her. Those light robes would stick to all the lines of her slim figure. That clean hair would cling in tantalizing tendrils against her neck. Her feet would slip against the wet soles of her sandals, runnels of sweat dash down her warm throat into interesting crevices under all that fancy bodicework . . .

'Excuse me –' she gasped.

3

'Excuse *me*!'

She veered around me; I sidestepped politely. She dodged; I dodged. I had come to the Forum to visit my banker; I felt glum. I greeted this smouldering apparition with the keenness of a man who needs troubles taking off his mind.

She was a slight thing. I liked them tall, but I was prepared to compromise. She was wickedly young. At the time I lusted after older women – but this one would grow up, and I could certainly wait. While we sashayed on the steps, she glanced back, panic-struck. I admired her shapely shoulder, then squinted over it myself. Then I had a shock.

There were two of them. Two ugly lumps of jail-fodder, jellybrained and broad as they were high, were pushing through the crowds towards her, just ten paces off. The little lass was obviously terrified.

'Get out of my way!' she pleaded.

I wondered what to do. 'Manners!' I chided thoughtfully, as the jellybrains came within five paces.

'Get out of my way *sir*!' she roared. She was perfect!

It was the usual scene in the Forum. We had the Record Office and Capitol Hill hard above us on the left; to the right the Courts, and the Temple of Castor further down the Sacred Way. Opposite, beyond the white marble rostrum, stood the Senate House. All the porticos were crammed with butchers and bankers, all the open spaces filled with sweaty crowds, mainly men. The piazza rang with the curses of strings of slaves crisscrossing like a badly organized military display. The air simmered with the reek of garlic and hair pomade.

The girl pranced to one side; I slid the same way.

'Need directions, young lady?' I asked helpfully.

She was too desperate to pretend. 'I *need* a district magistrate.' Three paces: options fast running out . . . Her face changed. 'Oh *help me*!'

'My pleasure!'

I took charge. I hooked her away by one arm as the first of the jellybrains lunged. Close to they looked even larger, and the Forum was not an area where I could count on any support. I planted the sole of my boot on the first thug's breastbone, then vigorously straightened my knee. I felt my leg crunch, but the draught-ox staggered into his evil friend so they teetered backwards like faltering acrobats. I looked around frantically for a diversion to cause.

The steps were crowded with the usual illegal touts and over-

4

priced market stalls. I considered upending some melons but smashed fruit meant a diminished livelihood for their market gardener. I had a diminished livelihood myself so I settled on the tasteful copperware. Tilting it with my shoulder, I keeled over a complete stall. The stallholder's thin cry was lost as bouncing flagons, ewers and urns sped at a denting pace down the Temple steps, followed by their despairing owner and numbers of righteous passers-by – all hoping to stroll home with a nice new fluted fruitbowl under one arm.

I grabbed the girl and hared up the Temple steps. Scarcely pausing to admire the dignified beauty of the Ionic portico, I pulled her through the six columns and into the inner sanctum. She squeaked; I kept going at speed. It was cool enough to make us shiver and dark enough to make me sweat. There was an old, old smell. Our footsteps rang fast and sharp on the ancient stone floor.

'Am I allowed in here?' she hissed.

'Look pious; we're on our way!'

'But we can't get out!'

If you know anything about temples you will realize they have a single imposing entrance at the front. If you know anything about priests, you will have noticed they usually have a discreet little door for themselves somewhere at the back. The priests of Saturn did not disappoint us.

I brought her out on the racecourse side, and set off south. The poor girl had wriggled out of the arena straight into a lion pit. I cantered her through dark alleys and pungent back doubles to home ground.

'Wherever are we?'

'Aventine Sector, Thirteenth District. South of the Circus Maximus, heading for the Ostia Road.' As reassuring as a shark's grin to a flounder. She would have been warned about places like this. If her loving old nurses knew what they were doing, she had been warned about fellows like me.

I slowed down after we crossed the Aurelian Way, partly because I was on secure home ground, but also because the girl was ready to expire.

'Where are we going?'

'My office.'

She looked relieved. Not for long: my office was two rooms on the sixth floor of a dank tenement where only the dirt and dead bedbugs were cementing together the walls. Before any of my neighbours could price up her clothing I wheeled her off

5

the mudtrack that passed for a highroad, and into Lenia's distinctly low-class laundry.

Hearing the voice of Smaractus my landlord, we wheeled smartly back out.

II

Fortunately he was leaving. I stowed the girl in a basketweaver's portico while I crouched down behind her and fiddled with the straps of my left boot.

'Who is it?' she whispered.

'Just a blotch of local slime,' I told her. I spared her my speech about property-magnates as parasites on the poor, but she took the point.

'He's your landlord!' Smart!

'He gone?'

She confirmed it. Taking no chances, I asked, 'Five or six skinny gladiators at his heels?'

'All black eyes and dirty bandages.'

'Come on then!' We pushed through the wet garments Lenia was allowing to dry out in the street, turning our faces away as they flapped back at us, then went in.

Lenia's laundry. Steam billowed out to flatten us. Washerboys stamped the clothes, sploshing up to their cracked little knees in hot tubs. There was a great deal of noise – slapping the linen, thumping and pounding it, clanging cauldrons – all in a close, echoing atmosphere. The laundry took up the whole ground floor, spilling out into the courtyard at the back.

We were greeted with derision by the slipshod proprietress. Lenia was probably younger than me, but she looked forty, with a gaunt face and a slack stomach that rolled over the edge of the basket she was carrying. Wisps of frizzled hair escaped from a colourless ribbon around her head. She cackled with throaty laughter when she saw my honeycake.

'Falco! Does your mother let you play with little girls?'

'Ornamental eh?' I adopted a suave expression. 'Bargain I picked up in the Forum.'

'Don't chip her pretty glaze!' Lenia scoffed. 'Smaractus left a hint: pay up, or his fisherboys will be poking their tridents up your delicate parts.'

7

'If he wants to wring out my arm-purse, he should render a written account. Tell him – '

'Tell him yourself!'

Lenia, whose instinct must have been to favour me, kept well clear of my tussle with the landlord. Smaractus paid her certain attentions which at present she was resisting because she liked her independence, but as a good businesswoman she kept her options open. He was foul. I thought Lenia was mad. I had told her what I thought; she had told me whose business I could mind.

Her restless gaze flickered again towards my companion.

'New client,' I boasted.

'*Really!* She paying you for the experience or you paying her for the treat?'

We both turned to survey my young lady.

She wore a fine white undertunic fixed along the sleeves with blue enamel clasps, and over it a sleeveless gown so generous in length it was bunched up over her girdle of woven gold threads. Apart from the wide bands of patterned embroidery at her neck, and hem, and in broad stripes down the front, I could tell from the narrowing of Lenia's watery eyes we were admiring a quality cloth. My goddess had wire hoops threaded with tiny glass beads in each neat little ear, a couple of chain necklaces, three bracelets on her left arm, four on her right, and various finger rings in the form of knots, serpents or birds with long crossed beaks. We could have sold her girlish finery for more than I earned last year. It was best not to consider how much a brothel keeper might pay us for the pretty wench.

She was blonde. Well, she was blonde that month, and since she was hardly from Macedonia or Germany, dye must have helped. It was cleverly done. I would never have known, but Lenia informed me afterwards.

Her hair had been curled into three soft fat ringlets tied in a clump with a ribbon at the nape of her neck. The temptation to untie that ribbon niggled me like a hornet bite. She painted her face of course. All my sisters turned themselves out spanking with colour like newly gilt statues, so I was used to that. My sisters are amazing, but blatant works of art. This was much more subtle, invisibly achieved, except that running in the heat had left one eye very faintly smudged. Her eyes were brown, set wide apart, and sweetly without guile.

Lenia tired of looking long before I did.

'Cradle snatcher!' she told me frankly. 'Tinkle in the bucket before you take her up!'

This was not a request for a medical sample because cradle snatching made Lenia diagnose me as unwell; it was a straight hospitable offer, with business overtones.

I shall have to explain about the bucket and the bleach vat.

A long time afterwards I described all this to someone I knew well, and we discussed what launderers use for whitening cloth.

'Distilled woodash?' my companion suggested doubtfully.

They do use ash. They also use carbonate of soda, fuller's earth, and pipeclay for the brilliant robes of election candidates. But the pristine togas of our magnificent Empire are effectively bleached with urine, obtained from the public latrines. The Emperor Vespasian, never slow to light on brisk new ways of squeezing out cash, had slapped a tax on this ancient trade in human waste. Lenia paid the tax, though on principle she increased her supply for nothing whenever she could.

The woman I had been telling the story to commented, in her cool way, 'I suppose in the salad season, when everyone's eating beetroot, half the togas in the Forum are a delicate hue of pink? Do they rinse it out?' she enquired.

I shrugged in a deliberately vague way. I would have skipped this unsavoury detail but as it turned out eventually, Lenia's bleach vat was critical to the tale.

Since I lived six floors up in a block that was no better equipped than any other slum in Rome, Lenia's bucket had long been my welcome friend.

Lenia offered my visitor, not unkindly, 'Girlies go behind the carding rails, dear.'

'Lenia, don't embarrass my dainty client!' I was blushing on her behalf.

'Actually I left home rather suddenly – '

Dainty but desperate, my client shot behind the rods where the dried clothes were hung on poles through the shoulders to be scratched down with teasels to bring up the nap. While I waited, I topped up my usual bucket and talked to Lenia about the weather. As one does.

After five minutes I ran out of weather.

'Get lost, Falco!' a carding-girl greeted me as I peered around the rails. No sign of my client.

Had she been less attractive, I might have let her go. She was extremely attractive – and I saw no reason to part with that sort of innocence to anybody else. Cursing now, I barged past the giant screw clothes-presses and out to the laundry yard.

There was a furnace heating the well water used in the wash. There were garments spread over wicker frames above braziers of burning sulphur, which through some mysterious chemistry smokes in additional whiteness. There were several youths scoffing at my fury, and there was a dreadful smell. There was no client. I hopped over a handcart and set off fast down the lane.

She had scampered past the dyer's lampblack ovens, braved the midden, and was halfway along the poultry cages where some footsore geese and a drooping cerise flamingo rested for market the next day. As I approached she pulled up short, her way blocked by a ropemaker, who was unbuckling his belt from his eighteen stone girth, to ease the task of raping her with that casual brutality which passed in these parts for appreciation of the female form. I politely thanked the ropemaker for looking after her, then before either of them could haggle I brought her back.

This was one client whose contract would need to be enforced by tying her to my wrist with a long piece of string.

III

After the hum of the Forum and the hurly-burly of the Roman squares, the Falco apartment was blessedly still, though faint noises rose from the street below and occasional birdsong could be heard across the acres of red tiled roofs. I lived right at the top. We arrived, as did all comers, wearily gasping for breath. The girl stopped to read my ceramic fingerplate. A fingerplate was unnecessary since no one climbs six flights unless they know who lives upstairs, but I had taken pity on a travelling salesman who flogged up to persuade me it would help business to advertise. Nothing helps my business, but never mind.

'M Didius Falco. M for Marcus. Shall I call you Marcus?'

'No,' I said.

We went in.

'More steps, less rent,' I explained wryly. 'I lived on the roof until the pigeons complained I was lowering the tone of their pantiles . . .'

I lived halfway to the sky. The girl was entranced. Used only to desirable spreads at ground floor level, with their own gardens and access to the aqueducts, she probably missed the disadvantages of my eagle's nest. I dreaded that the foundations would collapse and six layers of habitation collapse in a puff of plaster dust, or that one blazing night I would sleep through the fire watchers' alarm and fry in my own fat.

She made a beeline for the balcony. I gave her a moment and then went out to join her, genuinely proud of my view. The view, at least, was fabulous. Our block stood high enough on the Aventine to see over its neighbours towards the Probus Bridge. You could spy for miles, out across the river and the Transtiberina Sector to the Ianiculan Mount and the west coast countryside. It was best at night. Once the delivery carts stopped their racket, sounds became so intense you could hear the water lapping on the Tiber's banks, and the Emperor's

11

sentries grounding their spears behind you on Palatine Hill.

She breathed deeply of the warm air, rich in city smells – cookshops and chandleries, and the aromatic waft from the stone pines in the public gardens on Pincian Hill.

'Oh I wish I lived somewhere like this – ' She must have seen my face. 'Condemned as a pampered brat! You suppose I don't realize you have no water, no winter heat and no proper oven so you have to carry in your meals from a hot pie shop – ' She was right, I had supposed that. Dropping her voice, she sprang on me, 'Who are you?'

'You read it: Didius Falco,' I said, watching her. 'I'm a private informer.'

She considered this. For a moment she was uncertain, then she became quite excited: 'You work for the Emperor!'

'Vespasian hates informers. I operate for sad middle-aged men who think their wicked wives are sleeping with charioteers, and even sadder ones who know their wives are sleeping with their nephews. Sometimes for women.'

'What do you do for the women – or is it indiscreet to ask?'

I laughed. 'Whatever they pay for!'

I left it at that.

I went inside and tidied away various items I preferred her not to see, then I set about preparing my evening meal. After a time she followed me in and inspected the bleak hole Smaractus rented me. For the price it was an insult – but I rarely paid his price.

There was an outer room in which a dog might just turn round, if he was a thin dog with his tail between his legs. A wonky table, a slanty bench, a shelf of pots, a bank of bricks I used as a cooking stove, a gridiron, winejars (empty), rubbish basket (full). One way out to the balcony for when you got tired of stamping on the cockroaches indoors, plus a second opening behind a curtain in bright, welcoming stripes – this led to the bedroom. Sensing it perhaps, she did not ask.

'In case you're used to all-night banquets that run through seven courses from eggs in fish pickle sauce to frozen sorbets dug out of snow pits, I warn you on Tuesdays my cook goes to see his granny.' I had no cook, no slaves at all. My new client was beginning to look unhappy.

'Please don't trouble. I can eat when you take me home – '

'You're going nowhere yet,' I said. 'Not until I know what I'm taking you back to. Now eat!'

We had fresh sardines. I would have liked to provide something more exciting, but sardines were what the woman who

12

took it upon herself to leave my meals had left. I made a cold sweet sauce to liven up the fish: honey, with a dash of this, a sprinkle of that, the normal sort of thing. The girl watched me do it as if she had never seen anybody grinding lovage and rosemary in a mortar in her life. Perhaps she never had.

I finished first, then leaned my elbows on the edge of the table while I gazed at the young lady with a frank and trust-worthy face.

'Now, tell your Uncle Didius all about it. What's your name?'

'Helena.' I was so busy looking frank, I missed the flush on her own face that ought to have told me the seed pearl in this oyster was a fake.

'Know those barbarians, Helena?'

'No.'

'So they grabbed you where?'

'In our house.'

I whistled slowly. That was a surprise.

Remembering made her indignant, which made her more talkative. They had snatched her in broad daylight.

'They clanged the bell as bold as brass, barged past the porter, burst through the house, pulled me out to a carrying chair and raced down the street! When we got to the Forum the crowds slowed them, so I jumped out and ran away.'

They had threatened her enough to keep her quiet, though clearly not enough to quash her spirit.

'Any idea where they were taking you?'

She said not.

. 'Now don't be worried!' I reassured her. 'Tell me, how old are you?'

She was sixteen. O Jupiter!

'Married?'

'Do I look like a person who is married?' She looked like a person who soon should be!

'Papa any plans? Perhaps he has his eye on some well-bred army officer, home from Syria or Spain?'

She seemed interested in the concept, but shook her head. I could see one good reason for kidnapping this beauty. I improved on my trustworthy look. 'Any of papa's friends been ogling you too keenly? Has your mother introduced you to any spruce young sons of her childhood friends?'

'I haven't a mother,' she interrupted calmly.

There was a pause while I wondered at her odd way of putting it. Most people would say 'My mother's dead', or whatever. I worked out that her noble mama was in excellent heath, probably found in bed with a footman and divorced in disgrace.

'Excuse me – professional question – any special admirer your family knows nothing about?'

Suddenly she burst into giggles. 'Oh do stop being so silly! There's nobody like that!'

'You're a very attractive young lady!' I insisted, adding quickly, 'Though of course you're safe with me.'

'I see!' she remarked. This time those huge brown eyes suddenly danced in high spirits. I realized with astonishment that I was being teased.

Some of it was bluff. She had been badly frightened and now she was trying to be brave. The braver she was, the sweeter she looked. Her beautiful eyes were gazing into mine, brimming with mischief and causing serious troubles of my own . . .

Just in time, footfalls dragged to a halt outside, then my door was battered with that casual arrogance that could only mean a visit from the law.

IV

The law settled his breathing-rate after the stairs.

'Do come in,' I said mildly. 'It's not locked.'

He was in. He collapsed at the other end of my bench. 'Have a seat,' I offered.

'Falco, you villain! This is an improvement!' He gave me a slow grin. Petronius Longus, patrol captain of the Aventine watch. A big, placid, sleepy-looking man with a face people trusted – probably because it gave so little away.

Petronius and I went back a long time. We joined the army on the same day, finding each other in the queue to take the oath to the Emperor, and finding too that we had been brought up only five streets apart. We were tent mates for seven years and when we came home we had another thing in common: we were veterans of the Second Augustan Legion in Britain. Not only that, we were veterans of the Second at the time of Queen Boudicca's Revolt against Rome. So because of the Second's abysmal performance, we both left the army eighteen years early and we both had something we never wanted to talk about.

'Poke your eyes back in,' I told him. 'Her name's Helena.'

'Hello, Helena. What a pretty name! Falco, where did you find that?'

'Running a foot race round the Temple of Saturn.' I had chosen to answer with such simple honesty because there was a slim chance Petronius already knew. Besides, I wanted the girl to believe she was dealing with a man who told the truth.

I introduced the watch captain to my dazzling client: 'Petronius Longus, district patrolman; the best.'

'Good evening, sir,' she said.

I guffawed bitterly. 'Take a job in local government, women will call you "sir"! Sweetheart, there's no need to overdo it.'

'Take no notice of this tricky character,' Petronius scoffed in

15

his easy way, smiling at her with an interest I did not altogether like.

She smiled back at him, so I clipped tersely, 'We men want to gossip with a wine jug; go into the bedroom and wait for me.'

She shot me a look, but she went. That's the benefit of a liberal education, this little girl knew she lived in a man's world. Besides, she had pretty manners and it was my house.

'Nice!' approved Petronius, in a low voice.

He has a wife, who for some reason adores him. He never refers to her, but must care about her; he's the type who would. They have three daughters, and like a good Roman father he is utterly sentimental about his girls. I could see a day coming when the Tullianum jail would be crammed with frightful young sprogs who had cast their beady eyes at Petro's girls.

I produced two winecups which looked clean, though I polished up Petro's on the hem of my tunic before I clonked them on the table. In the hole under a floorboard that passed for my winecellar I had some smoked Spanish poison that was a gift from a grateful client, some new dusky red that tasted as if it had been robbed from an Etruscan tomb, and a well-aged amphora of decent white Setinum. Since Petro's visit was so awkwardly timed, I wavered over acting casual and just serving the Etruscan, but in the end I settled for the Setinum because we were old friends and anyway I fancied some myself.

As soon as he tasted it, he knew he was being bribed.

He said nothing. We drained several cups. The time came when a chat seemed unavoidable.

'Listen,' he broached. 'There's a hue and cry for a little gold-hemmed skirt who was lifted from a senator's house this morning, don't ask me why – '

'Want me to keep an eye out?' I suggested, perking up cheerily, though I could see he was not deceived. 'Heiress, is she?'

'Shut up, Falco. She was spotted later in the clutch of some slavering ghoul whose description uncannily fits yours. Her name is Sosia Camillina, she's strictly off limits, and I want her put back where she came from before we have some praetor's pet helpers crawling all over my patch passing rude remarks on the way I run the markets . . . That her in there?' He nodded at the bedroom doorway.

I owned up meekly. 'Imagine it must be.'

I liked him; he was good at his job. We both knew he had found his lost kitten.

16

I explained about her in a way that laid a great deal of emphasis on my gallant role as rescuer of frantic nobility, and (in view of Petro's earlier remark) less on me wrecking market stalls. It seemed best not to place him in any awkward dilemmas.

'I'll have to take her back,' Petro said. He was nicely drunk.

'I'll take her,' I promised. 'Do me a favour. If you go it's *Thanks for doing your duty, officer*; for me they may stretch to a small reward. Split?'

Lubricated by a good wine, my crony Petronius becomes a gentleman. Not many men are so considerate of the profit and loss columns of M Didius Falco's personal accounts.

'Oh . . .' He tipped his cup wryly. 'This will do me. Give me your word.'

I gave him my word and the rest of the Setinum, then he went away happy.

I had no real intention of giving her back.

Well . . . not yet.

V

I whipped into the bedroom, dangerous with annoyance. The curtain zinged along its rod. The little lost person jumped up guiltily, spilling my private notebooks onto the floor.

'*Give me those!*' I roared. Now I was really furious.

'You're a poet!' She was stalling for time. 'Is "Aglaia the White Dove" about a woman? I suppose they are all about women, they're rather rude . . . I'm sorry. I was interested . . .'

Aglaia was a girl I knew, neither white nor the least bit like a dove. Come to that, Aglaia was not her name.

Bright eyes was still giving me that vulnerable look, but to rather worse effect. The loveliest women lose their gloss once you notice they are lying through their teeth.

'You're about to hear something considerably ruder!' I snapped. '*Sosia Camillina?* So why the false travel pass?'

'I was frightened!' she protested. 'I didn't want to say my name, I didn't know what you wanted – ' I let it pass; neither did I.

'Who's Helena?'

'My cousin. She went to Britain. She got divorced – '

'Extravagance, or mere adultery?'

'She said it was too complicated to explain.'

'Ah!' I cried bitterly. I had never been married but I was an expert in divorce. 'Adultery! I've heard of women being exiled to islands for immoral behaviour, but exile to Britain seems a bit bleak!'

Sosia Camillina looked curious. 'How can you tell?'

'I've been there.'

Because of the rebellion I sounded terse. She would have been six years old at the time. She did not remember the great British Revolt and I was not starting history lessons now.

Suddenly she demanded: 'Why did your friend call you a tricky character?'

'I'm a republican. Petronius Longus thinks that's dangerous.'

18

'*Why* are you a republican?'

'Because every free man should have a voice in the government of the city where he has to live. Because the senate should not hand control of the Empire for life to one mortal, who may turn out insane or corrupt or immoral – and probably will. Because I hate to see Rome degenerate into a madhouse controlled by a handful of aristocrats manipulated by their cynical ex-slaves, while the mass of its citizens cannot earn a decent living . . .' Impossible to tell what she made of all that. Her next inquiry was stubbornly practical.

'Do private informers earn a decent living?'

'Taking every legal opportunity, they grab enough to keep alive. On good days,' I said, 'there may be tucker on the table to give us the energy to rave at the injustice of the world – ' I was well away now. I had matched Petronius levelly with the wine.

'Do you think the world is unjust?'

'I know it, lady!'

Sosia stared at me gravely, as if she were saddened that the world had treated me so hard. I stared back. I was none too overjoyed myself.

I felt tired. I went out into the living room and after a moment the girl came too.

'I need to go to the lavatory again.'

I was seized by the wild anxiety of a man who brings home a puppy because it looks so sweet, then realizes that on the sixth floor he has problems. No need to panic. My apartment was spartan, but my way of life hygienic.

'Well,' I teased. 'There are several alternatives. You can pop downstairs and try to persuade Lenia to open up the laundry after hours. Or you can run along the street to the big public convenience – but don't forget to take your copper to get in because six flights is a long way to come back for it – '

'I suppose,' snapped Sosia haughtily, 'you and your men friends pee off the balcony?'

I looked shocked. I was, mildly. 'Don't you know there are laws against that?'

'I had not imagined,' sneered Sosia, 'you would worry about the public nuisance laws!' She was getting the measure of the establishment I ran. She had already got the measure of me.

I crooked my finger. She followed me back into the bedroom where I introduced her to the arrangements which I modestly used myself.

19

'Thank you,' she said.

'Don't mention it,' I returned.

I peed off the balcony just to prove my independence.

This time when she came back I was brooding. I seemed to be struggling more than usual with the background to this kidnap. I could not decide whether I had missed the point, or whether in fact I knew all there was to know. I wondered if the senator she belonged to was politically active. Sosia might have been snatched to influence his vote. Oh gods, surely not! She was far too beautiful. There must be more involved than that.

'Are you taking me home?'

'Too late. Too risky. I'm too drunk.' I turned away, wandered across the bedroom and collapsed onto my bed. She stood in the doorway like a leftover fishbone.

'Where am I going to sleep?'

I was almost as drunk as Petronius. I was lying flat on my back, nursing my notebooks. I was incapable of anything more than feeble gestures and silliness.

'Against my heart, little goddess!' I exclaimed, then flung my arms wide, very carefully, one at a time.

She was frightened.

'All right!' she retorted. She was a stalwart little piece.

I grinned at her weakly, then flopped back into my previous position. I was pretty frightened myself.

I was right though. It was too great a risk to step out of doors with anyone so precious. Not after nightfall. Not in Rome. Not through those pitch-black streets full of burglars and buggery. She was safer with me.

Was she safe? somebody asked me afterwards. I avoided answering. To this day I don't know, really, whether Sosia Camillina was safe with me that night or not.

To Sosia I said gruffly, 'Guests take the reading couch. Blankets in the wooden box.'

I watched her construct an elaborate cocoon. She made a terrible job of it. Like a tentful of legionary recruits, eight lackadaisical lads wearing scratchy new tunics who had never made up a camp bed before. She fidgeted round the couch for ages, tucking in far too many covers far too tight.

'I need a pillow,' she complained finally in a small, serious voice, like a child who could only sleep if she followed a fixed nightly routine. I was blissful with wine and excitement; I did

20

not care whether I had a pillow or not. I hooked one hand behind my head then flung her mine, wide, but she caught it.

Sosia Camillina inspected my pillow as though it might harbour fleas. Another charge of resentment against the nobility. Possibly it did, but any wildlife was tightly sewn inside a cheerful red and purple cover inflicted on me by my mama. I did not care to have snooty chits of girls casting aspersions on my household goods.

'It's perfectly clean! Use it and be grateful.'

She laid the pillow very neatly at the end of her bed. I blew out the light. Private informers can be gentlemen when they are too drunk for anything else.

I slept like a babe. I have no idea whether my visitor did the same. Probably not.

VI

The senator Decimus Camillus Verus lived in the Capena Gate Sector. The Capena Gate was the district next but one to mine, so I walked. On the way I passed my youngest sister Maia and at least two little roughnecks off our family tree.

Some informers give the impression we are solitary men. Perhaps that was where I went wrong. Every time I was surreptitiously trailing some adulterous clerk in a shiny tunic, I looked up to find one of these midgets wiping his nose on his arm and bawling my name across the street. I was a hobbled donkey in Rome. I must have been related to most people between the Tiber and the Ardeatine Gate. I had five sisters, the poor girl my brother Festus never found the time to marry, thirteen nephews and four nieces, with several more visibly on the way. That excludes what lawyers call my heirs of the fourth and fifth degree: my mother's brothers, and my father's sisters, and all the second cousins of the first marriage children of the stepfathers of my grandfather's aunts.

I had a mother too, though I tried to ignore that.

I waved back at the roughnecks. I keep them sweet. One or two of them are. Anyway, I use these artful urchins to trail the adulterers when I slope off to the races instead.

Decimus Camillus owned a freehold mansion on his own square of land among quiet domestic streets. He had purchased the right to draw water direct from the old Appian aqueduct nearby. He felt no financial necessity to lease his frontage out as shops, nor his upper storey as lodging rooms, though he did share his desirable plot with the owner of an identical house next door. From which I deduced that this senator was by no means extravagantly rich. Like the rest of us, the poor muffin was struggling to keep up the way of life appropriate to his rank. The difference between him and most of us being that to qualify for the senate Decimus Camillus Verus must be a millionaire.

22

Since I was visiting a million sesterces I risked my throat under a barber's razor. I wore a worn white toga with the holes folded out of sight, a short clean tunic, my best belt with the Celtic buckle, and brown boots. A free citizen, his importance signalled by the length of his train of slaves – in my case, none.

There were spanking new escutcheon plates on the senator's doorlocks, but a hangdog porter with a badly bruised cheekbone looked through his grille and opened up as soon as I pulled at the rope on the big copper bell. They were expecting someone. Probably the same someone who socked the porter yesterday and carried off the girl.

We crossed a black and white tiled hall, with a spluttery fountain and faded cinnabar paint. Camillus was a diffident man in his fifties who lurked in a library among a mass of paperwork, a bust of the Emperor, and one or two decent bronze lamps. He looked normal, but he wasn't. For one thing, he was polite.

'Good morning. How can I help you?'

'The name's Didius Falco. Credentials, sir.' I bowled him one of Sosia's bracelets. It was British jet, the stuff they ship down from the northeast coast, carved in interlocking pieces like whale's teeth. She had told me her cousin sent it. I knew the style from my army days, but they were rare in Rome.

He inspected it gently.

'May I ask where you obtained this?'

'Off the arm of a decorative party I rescued yesterday from two thieving hulks.'

'Is she hurt?'

'No, sir.'

He had heavy eyebrows above decently spaced eyes that looked at me directly. His hair bristled straight up from his head even though it was not particularly short, giving him a cheerful, boyish look. I saw him brace himself to ask what I wanted. I put on my helpful face.

'Senator, would you like me to bring her back?'

'What are your terms?'

'Any idea who took her, sir?'

'None.' If I had realized he was lying, I should have admired the brisk way the man spoke. As it was, I liked his insistence. 'Your terms please?'

'Just professional curiosity. I've tucked her away somewhere safe. I'm a private informer. A watch captain called Petronius Longus in the Thirteenth will vouch for me – '

23

He reached for his inkpot and made some notes across the corner of a letter he had been reading. I liked that too. He intended to check.

I suggested, without pressure, that if he was grateful he might hire me to help. He looked thoughtful. I outlined my rates, adding something for his rank since it would all take slightly longer if I had to keep calling him 'sir'. He showed some reluctance, which I reckoned was because he did not want me hanging round the girl, but eventually we agreed I would advise him on household security and keep an ear to the ground about the kidnappers.

'You may be right about keeping Sosia Camillina out of sight,' he said. 'Is your hideout respectable?'

'Supervised by my own mother, sir!' True: she scoured my rooms regularly for evidence of loose women. Sometimes she found it, sometimes I hustled them out in time.

This senator was no idiot. He decided someone had to come back with me to make sure the wench was safe. I advised him against that. I had seen some greasy meatballs in the cookshop opposite, watching visitors to his home. There was nothing to say they were connected with Sosia, they could have been casual burglars who had picked an unlucky day to size up a future break-in. Since he was walking me round his property anyway, we went to look.

On the front door they had a sound wooden lock with a six inch, three-toothed iron rotary key, plus four brass bolts, an inspection grille with a natty little slider, and a great holm oak beam inside to sling across on two well-bedded cradles at night. The door porter lived in a cubbyhole at the side.

'Adequate?' remarked the senator.

I gave him a long look, including the dozy sprite they used as a doorman – the slack-mouthed strip of wind who had let Sosia's abductors walk in.

'Oh yes, sir! A wonderful system, so let me offer some advice: use it!' I could see he took the point.

I made him peer through the grille to inspect the two loafers in the cookshop.

'Those peepers saw me come. I'll hop out over your back wall; give me a chance to survey the rear of the house. Send a slave to the local lockup and get them arrested for causing a breach of the peace.'

'But they are not – '

'They will be,' I told him. 'When the praetor's posse starts arresting them.'

He was persuaded. The leaders of the Empire are so easily led.

The senator spoke to his doorman, who looked annoyed but ambled off on the errand. I made Camillus Verus show me his upstairs accommodation, then when we came down ten minutes later I looked out again and saw the two loafers from the cookshop with their arms up their backs, being marched off down the street by a brisk group of soldiers.

Reassuring to discover that when a citizen of substance complains to a magistrate the response is so prompt!

With all that cast iron work on the front door, at the back they had seven different entrances to the garden, with nary a decent lock among them. The kitchen door opened when I tried my own home latch-lifter. None of the windows had bars. A balcony around the upper storey offered access to the entire house. Their elegant smoky blue dining room possessed flimsy folding doors which I forced with an edging tile from a flower-bed, while the senator's secretary watched. He was a thin Greek slave with a hooked nose and the air of superiority with which Greek secretaries are embalmed at birth. I dictated instructions at length.

I decided I enjoyed dictating. I also enjoyed the look on the Greek's face when I grinned goodbye, clambered onto a sundial, found a toehold on a knot of ivy, and hoisted myself up the sheer dividing wall to see about the house next door.

'Who lives there?'

'The master's younger brother.'

As a younger brother myself I noted with pleasure that Camillus junior had sense. He had fixed up every window with solid slatted shutters, all painted in dark malachite green. Both houses had been faced in standard lava blocks, with their upper floors supported on skinny pillars hewn from a very ordinary grey stone. The architect had been lavish with his shaped terracotta gable ends, but by the time he came to stock the grounds with the customary statues of graceful nymphs in their underwear, his contingency funds ran out. The gardens were furnished with meagre sticks of trellis, though their plants burgeoned with health. It was the same building contract on both sides of the wall. Hard to say why the senator's house bore an approachable, easygoing smile while his brother's felt formal and cold. I was glad Sosia lived in the house with the smile.

I gazed at the brother's house for a long time, not quite sure what I was looking for. Then, with a wave to the Greek, I walked along the top of the divider to the far end. I jumped nonchalantly off.

I got covered in dust and twisted my knee, landing in the alley behind the senator's garden wall. Hercules knows why I did it, there was an entry for delivery carts with a perfectly good gate.

VII

As I walked towards home the streets became more clamorous, with traders' cries, hoofbeats and harness bells. A small black dog, his fur clinging in spiked clumps, barked madly at me as I passed a baker's shop. When I turned back to swear at him, my head bonked against a sequence of jugs that had been hung on a rope by a potter whose idea of advertisement was to show his work could take a bashing; luckily my head was also strong. In the Ostia Road I was buffeted by bodkinsellers and footmen in crimson livery, but I managed to get my own back by squashing the toes of several slaves. Three streets from home I glimpsed my mother buying artichokes with the purse-lipped look that means she is thinking about me. I ducked behind some barrels of winkles and then backtracked to avoid finding out whether this was true. She did not appear to have seen me. Things were going well: friends with a senator, open-ended contract, and best of all, Sosia.

I was brought up sharp from this reverie by two bullyboys whose greeting made me grunt with pain.

'Whoops!' (cried I). 'Look lads, it's all been a mistake. Tell Smaractus my rent's with his accountant –' I failed to recognize either, but Smaractus rarely keeps his gladiators long. If they can't run away they inevitably die in the ring. If they don't make it that far they perish from starvation, since Smaractus' idea of a training diet is a handful of pale yellow lentils in lashings of old bathwater. I assumed these were my landlord's latest bruisers from the gym.

My assumption was awry. By now my head was being gripped under the first bullyboy's elbow. The second put his face down to grin at me; I had a sideways view of the cheek-guards of the latest design of helmet and a familiar scarlet neckerchief under his chin. These beggars were army. I considered coming the old soldier but in view of my legion's record, a dropout from the Second Augusta was unlikely to impress.

'Guilty conscience?' (cried the sideways face). 'Something else to worry you – Didius Falco, you're under arrest!'

Arrest by the boys in red felt familiar, like being tickled for cash by Smaractus. The biggest of these two big lads was attempting to squeeze out my tonsils with the racy efficiency of a cook's boy podding peas with his thumb. I would have asked him to stop but I was speechless with admiration for his technique . . .

VIII

A social at-home in a guardpost, courtesy of an aedile called Atius Pertinax. I was expecting to be hauled off to prison, the Tullianum, or even the Mamertine if my luck had completely run out. Instead, they trooped me all the way back east into the First. This startled me, since until that morning I had never done business in the Capena Gate Sector. I was astonished that I had offended the authorities in quite so short a time.

If there is one class of person I hate above all others, it is aediles. For the benefit of provincials let me say that in Rome the praetors govern law and order, senior senators elected six at a time, who divide the fourteen districts between them. Each has a junior to do all the legwork – these aediles, brash young politicians in their first public posts, filling time before the better jobs that bring in bigger bribes.

Gnaeus Atius Pertinax was typical of the breed, a short-haired pup yapping up the political ladder, nagging butchers to sweep clean their shopfronts, and beating the hell out of me. I had never seen him before. In retrospect I remember no more than a washed-out grey streak, half hidden by a shaft of dazzling sunlight. The greyness may be lost recollection. I think he had light eyes and a stiff nose. He was in his late twenties (just younger than me), his tight nature reflected in a constipated face.

There was an older man, no purple on his clothes – not a senator – who sat on the sidelines and said nothing. A bland unremarkable face and a bald unremarkable head. In my experience, men who sit in corners are the ones to watch. But first, pleasantries with Pertinax.

'Falco!' he commanded, after brisk preliminaries established who I was. 'Where's the girl?'

I had a serious grudge against Atius Pertinax, though I did not know it yet.

I was wondering how to answer in a way that would be rude

29

enough, when he ordered his sergeant to encourage me. I pointed out I was a freeborn citizen and that laying a fist on a citizen was an affront to democracy. It turned out neither Pertinax nor the bullyboys were students of political science: they set about affronting democracy without a qualm. I had the right of appeal directly to the Emperor but I decided there was not much future in that.

If I had thought Pertinax was being so violent out of affection for Sosia, it might have been easier to bear, but we shared no fellow feeling. The whole event troubled me. A senator might well have second thoughts, cancel our contract and report me to the magistrate, yet Decimus Camillus had looked a soft touch and he knew (more or less) where his missing miss was. So I braved it out, bruised but proud.

'I shall return Sosia Camillina to her family when they ask me, and do your worst, Pertinax – I shall return her to no one else!'

I saw his eyes travel to the middle ranker in the corner. The man had a lean, sad, tolerant smile.

'Thank you,' this one said. 'My name is Publius Camillus Meto. I am her father. Perhaps I can ask you now.'

I closed my eyes. It was quite true – nobody had actually told me the senator's relationship to Sosia. This must be his younger brother, the man who lived in the frosty house next door. So my client was only her uncle. All the rights of ownership would lie with her papa.

In response to further questioning, as they say, I agreed to take her father and his pleasant friends to fetch her.

Back at the laundry Lenia popped out, intrigued by the uncoordinated tramping of large numbers of feet. Seeing me under arrest caused no surprise.

'Falco? Your mother says – *Oh!*'

'Out of the way, you filthy old bladder!' shouted the aedile Pertinax, flinging her to one side.

To spare him the indignity of being fruit-pressed to a pulp by a woman, I interceded gently: 'Not the time, Lenia!'

After twenty years of wringing out heavily wet togas, she possessed deceptive strength. He could have been badly damaged. I wish that he had been. I wish I had held him down for Lenia while she did it. I wish I had damaged him myself.

By then the momentum of our arrival had carried us up the stairs. Their visit was brief. When we all burst into my apartment, Sosia Camillina was not there.

IX

Pertinax was furious. I felt depressed. Her father looked weary. I offered to help him find her: I saw him snap.

'Stay away from my daughter, Falco!' he cried angrily.

Understandable. He could probably guess my interest. Keeping layabouts away from a daughter like that must occupy a lot of his time. I murmured, in a responsible tone:

'So I'm off the case – '

'You were never on it, Falco!' the aedile Pertinax crowed.

I knew better than to argue with a touchy politician. Especially one with such a pained face and pointy nose.

Pertinax let his men rummage through my apartment for evidence. They found nothing: even the sardine plates had been washed, though not by me. Before they left, they rearranged my furniture into handy cordwood sticks. And when I protested, one of them smashed me in the face so hard he all but broke my nose.

If Atius Pertinax wanted me to think him a frowsty lout with the habits of a gutter rat, he was halfway home.

As soon as they had gone, Lenia rushed upstairs to see whether she could inform Smaractus that one of his tenants had expired. My wrecked belongings stopped her short.

'Juno! Your room – and your face, Falco!'

The room was nothing special, but I had once been proud of my face.

'I needed a new table,' I groaned wittily. 'You can buy wonderful ones nowadays. Decent slice of maple six feet across, bolted on a simple marble stand, just right with my bronze candelabrum – ' I used to light my room with a tallow-dipped rush.

'Fool! Your mother says – '

'Spare me,' I said.

'Suit yourself!' She flounced off with her *I'm just the baggage who takes messages* face.

Things were not going so well. Still, my brain was not completely pulverized. I was too keen on good health to ignore a message from my ma. No need to trouble Lenia; I knew what it would be. And regarding my lost moppet with the mellifluous brown eyes, I did have an idea where she was.

News travels fast in the Aventine. Petronius turned up, fussing and none too pleased, while I was still exclaiming in agony as I bathed my face.

'Falco! Keep your filthy-mannered civic friends off my patch–' He whistled. Then at once took the black pottery jug from my shaking hand and poured for me himself. It was like old times, after a bad night's brawling outside the centurions' dining club in Isca Dumnoniorum. At twenty nine it hurt much more than when we were nineteen.

After a while he propped up what remained of my bench on two bricks from my stove, then sat me down.

'Who did this to you, Falco?'

I managed to tell him, using only the left half of my mouth. 'An overexcited aedile called Atius Pertinax. I'd like to open him out like a spatchcock chicken, completely boned, on a very hot grill!'

Petronius growled. He hates aediles even more than I do. They get in his way, they upset local loyalties, they take all the credit, then leave him to tidy up their mess.

He prised up my loose floorboard and brought me some wine, but it stung me too much, so he drank it himself. We both hate waste.

'You all right?' I nodded, and let him do the talking. 'I've been checking on the Camillus family. The senator's daughter is away on travel leave. There are two sons, one doing his year in the army in Germany, one bashing a desk – wiping the governor's nose in Baetican Spain. Your little girlfriend is some hushed up indiscretion of the senator's brother. He's not married – don't ask me how he gets away with that! According to the Censor's office Sosia was recorded as the child of one of his slaves, acknowledged then adopted by him. Could just be her father is a decent type. Or could be her mother was someone more important than he can say.'

'Met him,' I squeezed out like a sour pip. 'Bit thin-lipped. Why not in the senate too?'

'Usual story. Family could only buy in the political votes

once: elder son was put into purple stripes, younger foisted into commerce instead. Lucky old commerce! Is it true that you've lost her?'

I tried to grin. What a failure. Petro winced.

'She's not lost. Come with me, Petro. If she's where I think, I need your support . . .'

Sosia Camillina was where I thought.

X

Petro and I ducked down a tiled entry between a cutler's and a cheese shop. We took the stairs before the elegant ground floor apartment that was occupied by the idle ex-slave who owned the whole block (and several other blocks too; they know how to live). We were in a flaky grey building behind the Emporium, not far from the river but not so near that it flooded in the spring. It was a poor neighbourhood, but there were green creepers wound round all the pillars on the street side, sleek cats asleep in windowboxes, summer bulbs brightening the balconies; someone always kept the steps swept here. It seemed to me a friendly sort of place, but I had known it a long time.

On the first floor landing we banged at a brick-red door, which I had under pressure painted myself, and were admitted by a tiny waif of a slave. We found our own way to the room where I knew everyone would be.

'Hah! Wine shops all closed early?'

'Hello, Mother,' I said.

My mother was in her kitchen, supervising her cook, which meant the cook was nowhere in sight but ma was doing something rapid to a vegetable with a sharp knife. She works on the principle that if you want anything done properly, do it yourself. All around were other people's children, with their steely jaws clamped into loaves and fruit. When we arrived, Sosia Camillina sat at the kitchen table gorging a piece of cinnamon cake with a gusto that told me she was already well at home, as people in my parents' house tend to be.

Where was my father? Best not to enquire. He went out to a game of draughts when I was seven. Must be a long game, because he still hasn't come home.

I kissed my mother's cheek like a dutiful son, hoping Sosia would notice, and was whacked with a colander for my trouble.

34

Ma greeted Petronius with an affectionate smile. (Such a good boy; such a hard-working wife; such a regular well-paid job!)

My eldest sister Victorina was there. Petronius and I both withdrew into ourselves. *I* was terrified Victorina would call me Trouble in front of Sosia. I could not imagine why *he* looked so worried.

'Hello, Trouble,' said my sister, then to Petronius, 'Hello, Primrose!'

She was married now to a plasterer, but in some ways she had not changed since she tyrannized the Thirteenth when we were small. Petronius had not known the rest of us in those days, but like everyone for miles around he knew our Victorina.

'How's my favourite nephew?' I asked, since she was holding her latest pug-faced progeny. He had the wrinkled face and tearful gaze of a hundred-year-old man. He stared at me over her shoulder with visible contempt: barely crawling yet, but he could recognize a fraud.

Victorina shot me a tired look. She knew my heart belonged to Marcia, our three-year-old niece.

My mother sedated Petronius with a casket of raisins while she extracted impertinent facts about his relations with his wife. I managed to get hold of a melon slice, but Victorina's infant seized the other end. He had the grip of a Liburnian wrestler. We struggled for some minutes, then I gave way to the better chap. The wretch hurled the melon onto the floor.

Sosia watched everything with immense, solemn eyes. I suppose she had never been anywhere where there was so much going on in such good-humoured chaos.

'Hello, Falco!'

'Hello, Sosia!' I smiled, in tones that were meant to lap her body in liquid gold. My sister and mother exchanged a derisory glance. I put one foot on the bench beside Sosia and gazed down with a simmering leer until my mother noticed.

'Get your boot off my bench!'

I took my boot off the bench.

'Little goddess, you and I need a private talk.'

'Whatever you need,' ma informed me, 'can be discussed right here!'

Grinning more than I thought necessary, Petronius Longus sat down at the table and leaned his chin on his hands while he waited for me to begin. Everyone knew that I had no idea what I wanted to say.

On several occasions before that, indignant females had described to me the expression on my mother's face when she met some painted madam with a scented skirt in my rooms. Sometimes I never saw them again. In fairness to my mother, my conquests had included bad mistakes.

'What's going on here?' my mother had rapped at Sosia when she discovered her during my enforced chat with Pertinax.

'Good morning,' responded Sosia. My mother sniffed. She strode to the bedroom, flung aside the curtain, and weighed up the situation with the camp bed.

'*Well!* I can see what's going on! Client?'

'I am not allowed to say,' Sosia said.

My mother replied that she would be the judge of what was allowed. Then she sat Sosia down and gave her something to eat. She has her methods. Pretty soon she had wormed out the whole tale. She demanded what Sosia's noble mama would think, so Sosia unwisely mentioned having no noble mama. My own sweet parent was appalled.

'Right! You can come with me!' Sosia murmured that she felt safe enough. Mother gave her a sharp look; Sosia went with my mama.

Now Petronius, bless him, weighed in to help me out.

'Time we took you home, little lady!'

I told Sosia how the senator had engaged me. From which she assumed rather too much.

'So he explained? I thought Uncle Decimus was being over-cautious at first –' She stopped, then rounded on me accusingly, 'You don't know what I'm talking about!'

'Tell me then,' I said very gently.

She was deeply troubled. Her great eyes flew towards my mother. People always trust my mother. 'I don't know what to do!' she pleaded.

My mother answered huffily, 'Don't look at me, I never interfere.'

I snorted at this. Ma ignored it, but even Petro had let slip a stifled guffaw of amusement.

'Oh, tell him about your bank box, child. The worst he can do is steal it,' mother said. Such wonderful faith! I suppose you can't blame her. My elder brother Festus for some peculiar reason made himself a military hero. I can't compete with that.

'Uncle Decimus is hiding something very important in my bank box in the Forum,' Sosia muttered guiltily. 'I'm the only person who knows the number to open the box. Those men were taking me there.'

I stared at her with a set face, making her suffer. In the end I turned man-to-man to Petronius. 'What do you think?' I had no doubt of his answer.

'Stroll along and look!'

Sosia Camillina was behaving very meekly, but she did pipe up to warn us we should need to take a handcart to carry the loot.

XI

The Forum was cooler and quieter than when I was here with Sosia before, especially in the long colonnade where money-changers offered safe deposits for nervous citizens. The Camillus family banked with a grinning Bithynian who had invested unhealthily in excess body fat. Sosia whispered a number to identify her property; happyface unlocked her box. It was a large box, although what was inside turned out to be comparatively small.

The box lid fell back. Sosia Camillina stood to one side. When Petro and I peered in, her savings were even less impressive than mine. Her uncle hired her this strongbox as a sensible discipline, but she owned no more than ten gold coins and a few decent pieces of jewellery that her aunt thought she was too young yet to wear. (It was a point of view. She was old enough for me.)

Our object of enquiry was folded up in felt and roped around with hemp. Since the banker was watching us with frank Bithynian curiosity, Petronius gave me a hand to drag it out unwrapped. It seemed impossibly heavy. It was lucky we had borrowed a handcart from my brother-in-law the plasterer, who was out of work as usual. (My brother-in-law was not out of work because all the walls in Rome were sound and smooth. It was because people in Rome would rather look at bare slats than employ a boss-eyed, bone idle swine like him.) We staggered off with our trolley creaking under the weight. Petro let me do most of the work.

'Don't hurt yourself!' Sosia had the grace to exclaim.

Petronius winked at her. 'Not as puny as he looks. Does secret weight training in a gladiators' gym. Use your muscles, blossom – '

'You must tell me some time,' I gasped in retaliation, 'why my sister Victorina calls you Primrose!'

He said nothing. But he blushed, I swear he did.

38

Fortunately Rome is a sophisticated city. Two men with a girl and a handcart can crawl into a wine shop without causing comment. We moved down a shady side street and plunged indoors. I bagged a table in a dark corner while Petro laid on some hot pies. It took both of us to raise the precious object up onto the table with a thud. Cautiously we peeled back the felt.

'Shades of Hades!' Petronius let out.

I could see why Uncle Decimus did not want this new baby announced in the *Daily Gazette*.

Sosia Camillina had no idea what it was.

Petro and I knew. Both of us felt slightly sick. Petro, with his iron stomach, nevertheless leaned back on his joint-stool and snapped his teeth into a vegetable pie. Rather than surrender to unhappy memories, I bit into one too. Mine was basically rabbit, with chicken livers and, I think, juniper – not bad. There was a plate of pork titbits; we let Sosia chew on those.

'That lonely hole of a customs post,' Petro reminisced in horror. 'Stuck on the Sabrina Estuary the wrong side of the frontier. Nothing to do but count the coracles floating in the mist, and keep one eye open in case the dark little men came over the river on a raid. Oh dear gods, Falco, remember the rain!'

I remembered the rain. The long, drear rain in southwest Britain is unforgettable.

'Falco, whatever is it?' Sosia hissed.

I said, relishing the drama, 'Sosia Camillina, this is a silver pig!'

XII

It was an ingot of lead.

It weighed two hundred Roman pounds. I tried to explain once to a woman I knew, how heavy that was:

'Not a lot heavier than you. You're a tall girl, quite a solid piece. A bridegroom could just about heave you over his threshold and not lose his silly smile . . .' The wench I was insulting happened to be a substantial armful, though by no means overweight. It sounds unkind, but if you've ever tried picking up a well fed young lady you'll appreciate the comparison was fairly exact. In fact, lifting this dense grey slab before we knew what we were doing had left two of us with bad backs.

Petronius and I gazed at the silver pig like an old, and not entirely convenient, friend.

'Whatever is it?' Sosia demanded. I told her. 'Why do you call them pigs?'

I explained that when precious ore is being refined, molten metal runs away from the furnaces into a long channel where moulds for the ingots lead off down each side, like sucking piglets beside their mother sow. Petronius stared at me sceptically while I said this. Sometimes Petro seems amazed by the things I claim to know.

This valuable porker was a long dull block of metal, about twenty inches long by five wide and four deep, slightly bevelled at the sides, with the Emperor's name and the date on one long edge. It looked nothing, but a man who tried to carry it would soon find himself bent double. Twenty-four ladles of molten ore to each standard mould, not quite too heavy to handle, but difficult to steal. Worth it though, if you could. The silver yield from Mendips ore is remarkably high, on average a hundred and thirty ounces to the ton. I wondered whether the silver had already been extracted from the bauble on the table.

The government claims a monopoly of precious ore.

40

Wherever it came from, this belonged in the Mint. We rolled it, and banged it topside up, looking for an official stamp.

It was stamped all right: *T CL TRIF*, some new piece of nonsense, not once but four times, then *EX ARG BRIT* – the old familiar mark we half hoped and half dreaded to find. Petronius groaned.

'Britain; a perfect signature! Someone must be sweating.'

An uncomfortable feeling struck us both at the same time.

'Better move,' Petro suggested. 'Shall I tidy this away? Our usual place? You take the girl?'

I nodded.

'Falco, what's happening?' Sosia demanded excitedly.

'He's putting the silver pig somewhere smelly where felons will be too sensitive to look,' I said. 'You're going home. And I need an urgent chat with your Uncle Decimus!'

XIII

I took Sosia Camillina home in a sedan chair. There was room for two; she was a diminutive scrap and I could so rarely afford enough to eat that the bearers let us both ride. I stayed silent for a long time, so once she worked out I was no longer disgruntled with her, she chattered. I listened without listening. She was too young to sit in peace after a surprise.

I was beginning to be annoyed with the entire Camillus family. Nothing any of them ever said was true or complete, unless it turned into something I preferred not to hear. My open-ended contract had led me down a cul-de-sac.

'Why are you so quiet?' Sosia demanded suddenly. 'Are you wishing you could steal the silver pig?' I said nothing. Naturally I was wondering how that might be arranged. 'Do you *ever* have any money, Falco?'

'Sometimes.'

'What do you do with it?'

I told her I paid the rent.

'I see!' she commented gravely. She was looking up at me with those great unsettling eyes. Her expression saddened into melting reproach for my aggressiveness. I wanted to suggest it was a bad idea to turn a look like that on men with whom she found herself alone, though I said nothing because I foresaw difficulties explaining why.

'Didius Falco, what do you really do with it?'

'I send it to my mother.' My tone of voice left her unsure whether I meant it, which was how I liked a woman to be left.

At that time I thought a man should never tell women what he does with his money. (Those days were the days, of course, before I was married and had this issue placed in true perspective by my wife.)

What I *really* did with my money in those days was that sometimes I paid the rent. (More often not.) Then, after deducting unavoidable expenses, I sent half to mama; I gave the rest to the young woman my brother never found the time to marry before he was killed in Judaea, and the child he never even discovered he had.

None of that was any business of a senator's niece.

I dumped the girl on her relieved aunt.

Senators' wives, in my scheme, fall into three types. The ones who sleep with senators, but not the senators who married them; the ones who sleep with gladiators; and a few who stay at home. Before Vespasian, the first two types were everywhere. There were even more afterwards, because when Vespasian became Emperor, while he and his elder son were out in the east, his young puppy Domitian lived in Rome. Domitian's idea of becoming a Caesar was seducing senators' wives.

The wife of Decimus Camillus fell into my third type: she stayed at home. I knew that already, otherwise I would have heard of her. She was what I expected: glossy, tense, perfect manners, jingling with gold jewellery – a well-treated woman with an even better-kept face. She glanced first at Sosia, then her shrewd black eyes flicked over me. She was just the sort of sensible matron a bachelor would be lucky to find when he was presented with an illegitimate child he felt unable to ignore. I could see why the nifty Publius parked his Sosia here.

Julia Justa, the senator's wife, took back her lost niece without fuss. She would ask her questions later, once the household settled down. Just the sort of decent, deserving woman who has the unhappy luck to be married to a man who dabbles in illegal currency. A man so inept, he hires his own informer to expose him.

I made my way to the library and marched in on Decimus unannounced.

'Surprise! A senator who collects not grubby Greek antiques but ingots engraved artistically by the government! You're in enough trouble, sir, why hire me as well?'

He had a shifty expression for a moment, then he seemed to straighten up. I suppose a politician gets used to people calling him a liar.

'Dangerous ground, Falco. When you calm down – '

I was perfectly calm. Furious, but lucid as glass.

'Senator, the silver pig must be stolen; I don't rate you as a thief. For one thing,' I sneered, 'if you had gone to the trouble of stealing British silver, you would take much more care of your loot. What's your involvement?'

'Official,' he said, then had second thoughts. That was just as well, since I didn't believe him. 'Semi-official.'

I still didn't believe him. I choked back a laugh. 'And semi-corrupt?'

He brushed my bluntness aside: 'Falco, this has to be in confidence.' The stale crust of this family's confidence was the last thing I welcomed. 'The ingot was found after a scuffle in the street and handed in to the magistrate's office. I know the praetor for this Sector; he's a man I dine with and his nephew gave a posting to my son. We discussed the ingot, naturally.'

'Ah, *just among friends!*'

Whatever he had done, to a man of his station I was being unacceptably rude. His patience surprised me. I watched him closely; he was just as intently observing me. I would suspect he wanted a favour, had he been a different class of man.

'My daughter Helena took a letter to Britain – we have relatives there. My brother-in-law is the British secretary of finance. I wrote to him – '

'*All in the family*; I see!' I scoffed again. I had forgotten how clannish these people can be: little pockets of reliable friends sewn into every province from Palestine to the Pillars of Hercules.

'Falco, please! Gaius – my brother-in-law – conducted a skeleton audit. He discovered there had been a steady wastage from the British mines at least since the Year of the Four Emperors. Theft on a grand scale, Falco! Once we heard that, we wanted our evidence secure; my friend the praetor asked my help. Using Sosia Camillina's bank box was, I regret to say, my own bright idea.'

I told him our new hideout. He looked ill. Petro had taken the silver pig to Lenia's laundry. We would be banking it in her vat of bleaching pee.

The senator made no comment on either our snaffling his exhibit or its pungent hiding place. What he offered me was much more dangerous.

'Are you busy at the moment?' I was never busy. As an informer I was not that good. 'Look Falco, are you interested in helping us? We can't trust the official machine. Someone must already have talked.'

'What about here?' I interrupted.

'I never mentioned the ingot here. I took Sosia to bank it without telling her why, then forbade her to talk.' He paused. 'She's a good child.' I gestured wry acknowledgement. 'Falco,

I admit we were careless before we grasped the implications, but if the praetor's organization leaks we can't take further risks. Your face seems to fit this job – semi-official and semi-corrupt – '

Sarcastic old beggar! I realized the man had a quietly wicked streak. He was shrewder than he liked to appear. He certainly knew what preoccupied me. He ran one hand over that upright bush of hair, then said awkwardly:

'I had a meeting today at the Palace. I can't say more than that, but with the Empire to reconstruct after Nero and the civil war those ingots are sorely needed by the Treasury. In our talks your name came up. I understand you had a brother – ' My face really set. 'Excuse me!' he exclaimed abruptly in that concerned way the occasional aristocrat has, which I never entirely trust. It was an apology; one I ignored. I would not have these people discussing my brother. 'Well, would you want the job? My principal will honour your usual rates; I gather you inflated them for me! If you find the missing silver, you can expect a substantial bonus.'

'I'd like to meet your principal!' I snapped. 'My idea of a bonus may not be the same as his.'

Decimus Camillus snapped straight back: 'My principal's idea of a bonus is the best you will get!'

I knew it meant working for some snooty secretariat of jumped-up scribes who would slash my expenses given half a chance, but I took the job. I must have been mad. Still, he was Sosia's uncle, and I felt sorry for his wife.

There was something odd about this case.

'By the way, sir, did you set a slick lynx called Atius Pertinax on my tail?'

He looked annoyed. 'No!'

'Has he ties with your family?'

'No,' he chipped in impatiently, then checked. Nothing was simple here. 'A slight connection,' he corrected himself, and by now his expression had deliberately cleared. 'Business links with my brother.'

'Did you tell your brother that Sosia was with me?'

'I had no opportunity.'

'Someone did. He asked Pertinax to arrest me.'

The senator smiled. 'I do apologize. My brother has been frantically worried about his daughter. He'll be delighted you brought her home.'

Tidily cleared up. Petronius Longus had said my description was known, so an aedile might track me down. Pertinax and

Publius assumed I was a villain. Big brother Decimus had omitted to mention to little brother Publius the fact that he hired me. I was not surprised. I come from a large family myself. There were lots of things Festus had never remembered to tell me.

XIV

This silver leak was a clever scheme! The British mines, which in my day were guarded so cautiously by the army, had apparently been tapped off as neatly as those illegal standpipes plugged in by private citizens all along the Claudian aqueduct; silver bars sparkling all the way to Rome like the crystal waters of the Caerulean Spring. I wished Petro and I had done it ten years before.

Passing the Capena Gate lockup, I nipped in to see the loafers from the cookshop whom I had seen being arrested that morning for spying on the senator. I was out of luck. Pertinax had let them go – no evidence to hold them, he maintained.

I gazed at the duty guard with my world-weary fellow comrade sigh.

'Typical! Did he bother to question them?'

'Few friendly words.'

'Brilliant! What about this Pertinax?'

'Knows it all!' the squaddie complained. We were both acquainted with the type. We exchanged a painful look.

'Is he just inefficient, or would you say it was something else?'

'I'd say I don't like him – but I say that about them all.'

I grinned. 'Thank you! Look,' I cajoled frankly, 'what's the word on an ingot of government lead? This is unofficially official, if you understand what I mean.' This was a lark. I didn't understand what I was saying myself.

He insisted he was under strict orders to say nothing. I chinked some coinage his way. Never fails.

'A drayman handed it in last week; turned up hoping for a reward. The magistrate himself came down to look. The drayman lives . . .' (Another magic chink.) 'In a river booth on the Transtiberina bank, at the sign of the Turbot, near the Sulpician Bridge . . .'

I found the booth, but not the drayman. Three days after his horse stumbled over the silver pig in the dark, he was dredged out of the Tiber by two men fishing from a raft. They took him to Tiber Island, the medical hospice at the Temple of Aesculapius. Most of their patients die. It didn't worry the drayman; he was already dead.

Before leaving the island I leaned on the parapet of the old Fabrician Bridge and did some hard thinking. Someone approached in that all too casual way, the way that is never casual at all.

'You Falco?'

'Who wants to know, princess?'

'My name's Astia. You asking about the man who was drowned?'

I guessed Astia was the drayman's floosie. She was a thin, bleached waterfront shrimp with a tired, hard waterfront face. Best to know where you are: 'You his woman?' I asked her straight out.

Astia laughed bitterly. 'Not any longer! You with the Praetorians?' she spat at me.

I played down my astonishment. 'Life's too short!' I waited after that. It was the only thing to do, since I had no idea what I was waiting for. She seemed to consider whether I could be trusted, then after a moment, out it spilled.

'They came here afterwards. They didn't care about him, they only wanted information.'

'Tell them anything?'

'What do you think! He was good to me when he had any money . . . I went to the Temple; I buried him myself. Falco, he may have been found in the river, but I know he didn't drown. They told me at the Temple he must have tipped in when he was drunk. But when he was drunk – ' that was probably quite often, but I had more tact than to ask – 'he used to lie down in the cart and let the horse walk him home.'

'Anyone find the cart?'

'Left in the Cattle Market Forum, minus the horse.'

'Hmm. What did the Guards want, princess?'

'He had found something valuable. He wouldn't tell me what, but it frightened him. He handed it in at the nearest lockup instead of selling it himself. The Guards knew he found it. They didn't know what he had done with it.' So it was not the Guards who snatched young Sosia. Unlikely anyway; she would not have escaped so easily – she might never have escaped at all.

48

'I'll have to speak to them. Any chance of a name?' Astia knew very little. Their captain, she told me, was called Julius Frontinus. As a member of an élite regiment, he undoubtedly possessed the full three names of a substantial man, but two were enough for me to pin him down. For the first time in my life I volunteered to face an interview with the Emperor's Praetorian Guards.

XV

The Praetorian Camp was on the far side of the city. I walked slowly. I was expecting when I got there to be crushed like an eggshell beneath a Guard's heavy boot . . .

I recognized Frontinus at once. He wore an enamelled breast-plate and a great silver buckle on his belt, but he had once learned his alphabet sharing a stool under the primary school awning at the corner of our street, side by side with a curly-haired rogue called Didius Festus. To Julius Frontinus, there-fore, I was a national hero's baby brother and since he could no longer take Festus to a tavern and get him joyously drunk – because Festus was dead in the desert in Judaea – he took me.

It was a discreet, well-run winery, way out in the northeast corner of Rome, near the Viminal Gate, full of soldiers from the city regiments and very businesslike. There was no food. There were no women. There was every kind of liquor, warm and cold, spiced or straight, charged well over the odds, though I was not allowed to pay. On my own I would never have got a foot indoors. With Frontinus, no one gave me a second glance.

We sat among a group of tall, well-padded men who openly overheard but never spoke. Frontinus must have known them; they seemed to know whatever he was going to say. Getting him to say it took a while. When a man like that invites you out drinking it is understood that prior to business there must be ceremonial. Ours, in honour of me and as a pleasure for him, was to discuss heroes and their heroism until we were both maudlin drunk.

After we talked about Festus and before I passed out, I managed to ask some questions. Before Frontinus sent me home in a builder's waggon with a load of ridging tiles, he managed to answer them.

'Whyever did he do it?' Frontinus was still musing. 'First up the town wall at Bethel, so first dead. Nothing to do for the rest of eternity but let his gravestone whiten in the desert sun. Lunatic!'

'Wanted to cash his deposit with the burial club. Couldn't bear losing all those stoppages from his pay. So, patriotic brother, Hail and Farewell!'

It was two years since Festus died, towards the end of Vespasian's Galilean campaign, though so much had happened in the city since then that it seemed much longer. Yet I could not believe he had gone. In some ways I never will. I am still waiting for a message to say Festus has landed back at Ostia so will I please bring him a waggon and some wineskins because he's run out of cash but has met some lads on the boat that he'd like to entertain . . . I shall probably be waiting for that message all my life.

It was good to say his name, but I had had enough. Perhaps it showed. I had drunk enough too, and may have given the impression I was likely to be sick. Despite this, Frontinus refilled our cups. Then he hunched up on the bench, obviously ready to talk.

'Falco – Falco, what's your given name?'

'Marcus,' I admitted. Same as Festus, as Frontinus must have known.

'*Marcus!* Jupiter! I'll call you Falco. How are you knotted up in this, Falco?'

'There's a reward for the silver pigs.'

'Now, laddie, that's not on!' He became wonderfully paternal. 'This is political; leave it to the Guards! Festus would tell you, and as he's not here, you take it from me. Listen, I'll spell it out. After four new heads of state in less than twelve months, Vespasian makes a relaxing change, but some odd types are still after him. You know how it is – they come sidling up when you're off duty, little men with something big to sell – '

'Silver pigs!' Everything fell into place. '*Ex Argentiis Britanniae.* Financing a political plot! Who's behind this?'

'That's what the Guards want to know,' Frontinus told me grimly.

I sensed a movement in the men around him. I said carefully, not looking at any of them, 'Loyalty to the Emperor!'

'If you like . . .' Julius Frontinus laughed.

They pride themselves on loyalty. In their time the Praetorians have physically hoiked new Emperors onto the throne. They crowned Claudius that way, and in the Year of the Four

Emperors even a barbered booby like Otho could snatch the Empire once he swung Praetorian support. To buy them would take a private mint. But someone had braved the British weather to arrange just that.

'When they approached me,' Frontinus said, 'I asked for proof. Stalling for time. They turned up two days afterwards with a hallmarked bar. My troopers were tracking the weevils back to their biscuit when they scarpered and dropped the loot.' Having tried to lift it, I could see why! 'We lost them, and when we went back we had lost the bar too. Once we put spies into the waterfront drinking holes we soon heard of a drayman who was boasting he had found something that would win him a golden thank you from the Emperor himself. Someone less gentle than the Guards obviously heard of him too.'

He gave me a heavy stare. There was a cold, wet patch on my undertunic against the hollow of my chest. It had nothing to do with the drink.

'Vespasian's no fool, Falco. He may have jumped up from nothing, but he did it on clever judgement and guts. We reckoned he must be onto this. And now here you are! You informing for the Palace, sunshine? You on some special payroll to cover Vespasian if the Guards let him down?'

'Not as far as I know, Julius . . .'

I was beginning to realize just how much I didn't know.

XVI

I went back to see the senator next day. After my party with Frontinus it was an afternoon call; let's omit details of my morning. Most of it was spent in bed, though there were spasms of painful activity from time to time. When I arrived at his house the senator had mild indigestion after lunch. I had severe indigestion, though I had not been able to face lunch.

I stormed in. He was beginning to judge my moods by the suddenness of my arrival in his sanctuary. Today I popped up like a playwright's villain, cackling with malice which I was eager to share with an audience. Camillus Verus had the goodness to set aside his paperwork and let me spout my colourful spume.

'No silver bars, but I stubbed my toe on quite a plot! You lied to me, sir; more lies than a sick whore at the Temple of Isis, to much less good purpose, but just as expertly told!'

'Falco! Can I explain?'

No, he owed me a rant at least. My violent excitement held him mesmerized.

'Spare me, senator! I don't touch political work; I don't rate the risk. My mother gave one son to Vespasian in Galilee: I'm her only survivor, and surviving suits me fine!'

He looked tetchy. He considered I was belittling the political aspects. Since I considered *he* was, we were draughtsmen in stalemate.

'You'll see Vespasian assassinated? Oh Falco! Plunge the country back into civil war? Ruin the Empire? More fighting, more uncertainty, more Roman blood spilt on Roman streets?'

'People are paid heavy salaries to protect the Emperor,' I rasped. 'I'm paid with lies and promises!' Suddenly I lost patience. There was no future for me here. They had deceived me; they had tried to use me. Cleverer men than this had mistaken me for a country clown in a farce; cleverer men had

53

discovered the mistake. More quietly, I brought the ridiculous piece of theatre to an end.

'Vespasian doesn't like informers; I don't like Emperors. I thought I liked you, but any poor sprat out of his depth can make a mistake! Good day, sir.'

I stormed out again. He let me go. I had noticed before, Decimus Camillus Verus was a shrewd man.

I was striding angrily across the hall with its spluttery fountain when I heard a hiss.

'Falco!' It was Sosia. 'Come into the garden; come and talk!'

It would have been incorrect to gossip with the young lady of the house even if I had remained in her uncle's employ. I try not to upset senators by meddling with their wards in their own front halls where the servants see everything that goes on. If I spoke to Sosia at all – which I must do now, since her noble personage had spoken to me – any chat must be quick. And we should stay in the hall.

I scuffed the marble floor tiles with my heel.

'Oh Didius Falco, please!'

From sheer spite I followed her.

She led me to an internal courtyard I had not seen before. Glaring white stonework fought the cold black-green of clipped cypress trees. There were cooing doves and a bigger fountain which worked. A peacock screeched behind one of the lichen-covered urns, which were planted with stately white lilies. It was a cool, pretty, quiet place, but I refused to sink into the shade under the pergola and be soothed. Sosia sat; I faced her, on my feet, with my arms folded. In some ways this was just as well; however much I was tempted to slide an arm around her, I had denied myself the chance.

She was wearing a red dress hemmed with damson braid. It emphasized the paleness of her skin beneath the artificial colours she applied. Leaning towards me with a pinched and troubled face, she was for a moment a wan little creature. She seemed apologetic on behalf of her family, though as she tried to win me over she became more earnest than I had ever seen her. Somebody at sometime had taught her how to stand her ground.

'I overheard. Falco, you can't let Vespasian be murdered; he's going to be a good Emperor!'

'I doubt it,' I said.

'He's not cruel; he's not mad. He leads a simple life. He works hard. He's old, but he has a gifted son – ' This came out

54

with spirit; she believed it, though I knew such a theory could not originate with her. I was surprised to find the Emperor could claim such support, for he lacked all the traditional advantages. None of Vespasian's family had ever held high office. I did not blame him for that; neither had any of mine.

'Who stuffed you with this horsehair?' I raged.

'Helena.'

Helena. The cousin she had mentioned. The senator's daughter, the one some poor sap of a husband with a great deal of luck had managed to divorce.

'I see . . . So what's she like, this Helena of yours?'

'She's wonderful!' Sosia exclaimed at once, but then she decided with equal certainty, 'You wouldn't like her much.'

'Why's that?' I laughed.

She shrugged. I had never met her cousin, yet my instinct had been to resent the woman ever since Sosia first tried to use her name as a disguise when she would not trust me. In fact my only real grudge against Helena was that I could see she wielded considerable influence over Sosia Camillina. I preferred to influence Sosia myself. I reckoned Sosia was wrong anyway. I normally liked women. But if this Helena felt protective towards her younger relative, as I gathered she did, the chances were that *she* would not like *me*.

'I write to her,' Sosia explained, as if she read my thoughts.

I said nothing. I was leaving. There was no longer anything to say. I stood, half aware of the clean scents of summer flowers and the lazy warmth beating off the stones.

'I tell Helena everything.'

I stared at her more kindly, smitten with unease. It is an odd fact, you feel more ashamed when you have nothing to answer for than when you are disguising some brazen act of scandal.

Since I was still silent, Sosia continued to talk. It was her one annoying habit; she never could sit quiet.

'You're really going away? I won't see you again? There's something I want to say. Marcus Didius Falco, I've been wondering for days how to – '

She had used my formal name. No one ever did that. Her respectful tone was more than I could bear. I had stumbled into a real emergency. My anger fled.

'Don't!' I exclaimed urgently. 'Sosia, believe me, when you need to spend days composing your script, the reason is it's best to say nothing at all!'

She hesitated.

'You don't know – '

55

I was a spare-time poet; there were many things I would never know, but I recognized this. 'Oh Sosia – I know!'

For one fantastic moment I flashed into a dream where I took Sosia Camillina into my life. I flashed back. Only a fool tries to step across the barriers of rank in that way. A man may buy himself into the middle class, or have the gold ring donated to him for services to the Emperor (especially if the services are of a dubious kind), but so long as her father and her uncle knew what they were about – and her uncle must, he was a millionaire – then even with that queer problem of having no mother to name, Sosia Camillina would be disposed of in some way to enhance her own position and their family bank account. Our two lives could never converge. At heart she understood, for despite her brave attempt she stared at her toes in their knotted gold sandals, biting her lip but accepting what I said.

'If I need you – ' she began in a subdued tone.

I replied briskly, for my own sake. 'You won't. In your sweet, sheltered life you have no need of anyone like me. And Sosia Camillina, I really don't need you!'

I left quickly so I should not see her face.

I walked home. Rome, my city, which had been until then a neverfailing solace, lay before me like a woman, secretive and beautiful, demanding and rewarding, eternally seductive. For the first time in my life, I refused to be seduced.

XVII

I did see Sosia Camillina again. She asked me to meet her. Of course I went. I went as soon as I could.

By then summer was nuzzling autumn's neck. The days seemed equally long and hot, but towards dusk the air began to cool more quickly. I went out to the Campagna for a grape gathering holiday, but my heart was never in it and I came home.

I had not been able to shift the silver pigs from my mind. This puzzle had gripped my interest; no amount of raging at the way I had been teased along by Decimus Camillus could alter that. Whenever I saw him, Petronius Longus asked after my progress. He knew how I felt, but was too enthralled for tact. I started to avoid him, which depressed me even more. In addition, the whole world was watching our new emperor Vespasian. There was no possibility of gossiping at the barber's or the baths, the racetrack or the theatre, without an awkward twinge because I could not forget what I knew.

For six weeks or longer I lay low. I bungled divorce cases, failed to serve writs, forgot the dates of court appearances, tore ligaments at the gym, insulted my family, dodged my landlord, drank too much, ate too little, gave up women for good. If I went to the theatre I lost the thread of the plot.

Then one day Lenia cornered me.

'Falco! Your girlfriend's been.'

Out of habit I demanded *which*? I still liked to imply I was harassed by half-naked Tripolitanian acrobats every afternoon. Lenia knew perfectly well I had given up women; she missed the clip of their little sandals and the giggles on the stairs when I brought them in. She also missed the shrieks of indignation when my mother swept them out with the dust next day.

'Little miss dainty with the pedigree and bangles. I let her pee in the bleach vat, then she wrote a note upstairs . . .'

I took the stairs in a rush. I reached the apartment all asplutter with a hacking throat. My mother had been: a pile of mended tunics, a picture of a chariot drawn on a slate by my niece, a mullet in a covered dish. I flung these aside as I searched.

The note was in my bedroom. An odd pang caught me, to imagine Sosia there. She had pegged her message on my pile of poetry under the jet bracelet that I knew. I wondered if she noticed that 'Aglaia, Radiant Goddess', was really about her. All the girls in my odes are called Aglaia, a poet needs to protect himself.

Sosia had left me a wooden tablet, unlaced from one of those four-page pocketbooks and then inscribed deeply with a stylus in a round hand that had never done serious writing:

Didius Falco, I know a place where they may keep the silver pigs. If I show you, you can claim your bonus. Will you meet me at the Golden Milestone in two hours? If you are too busy, I will go for you and see . . .

I pounded back downstairs in a blind panic.
'Lenia! Lenia, what time was she here – '
They were waiting for me calmly, at the foot of the last flight. *Smaractus!*

Below me, shadows moved, their bare feet noiseless on the stone steps: my landlord's gladiators, after my unpaid rent.

I have an arrangement with the cloakmaker who lives on the second floor that in an emergency I can run through his room, fling myself over the balcony onto the fire-fighting porch, then drop into the street. I had passed the cloakmaker's door. I half turned back. The door opened. Someone who was not the cloakmaker came out.

They were straight from Smaractus' insanitary gym and in full fighting rig. Below me, the type called myrmillons, glistening with oil above their body-belts, their right arms padded and ringed with metal from collarbone to fist, their solid high-crested helmets shaped like curling, sneering fish. Above me, when I whirled round, two light, laughing men in tunics only, but each with a fiendish net coiled on his arm – his fishermen.

I whipped back.
'Didius Falco! What's the rush?'
I recognized the one who spoke. I recognized his build. He crouched slightly, in fighting stance, faceless behind his helmet grille. I must have exclaimed.

'Oh no! Not now, oh gods, not *now* –'

'Now, Falco!'

'You can't, oh you can't – '

'Oh we can! Let's show the man . . .' Then both fishers flung their nets down over my head.

I knew, as I struggled hopelessly in two ten foot circles of biting cords, that it was going to be much worse than being arrested by the aedile's bullyboys. If Smaractus was just making his point, they would tenderize me like an octopus slammed on the foreshore rocks. If he had found himself a new tenant for upstairs, I was finished. It was going to be as bad as anything could be. My only comfort was that I would know very little about it once I managed to pass out, and that perhaps I would never wake up.

There were probably five of them, but it seemed more. The fishers could not be seen with their spiked tridents in the open streets, but the myrmillons had brought their wooden practice swords. As I flailed in the nets, they beat me systematically until I faded in a smother of disjointed sounds.

I was coming to. New tenants must be thin on the ground. Perhaps they had heard what life in a Smaractus apartment is like. The office was mine still; I was waking up.

Not in my room; somewhere else.

I felt desperately tired. Pain lapped around me as thick as spilt nectar, then I swirled in a torrent of sensation and fierce noise back up from the whirlpool.

'He's coming round! Say something, Falco!' Lenia ordered.

My brain uttered words. I heard no sound; my cotton ball mouth never moved.

I felt sorry for this Falco if he hurt as much as me. I had left the world for perhaps thirty seconds, perhaps a hundred years. Wherever I had been was better than here, and I wanted to go back.

'Marcus!' Not Lenia any more. 'Don't try to talk, son.' Lenia had sent for my mother. Good heavens.

Slowly the red blur behind my eyelids solidified. Slowly I and that other poor man they called Falco fused together.

'This is – ' Who said that? Me or Falco? Him I think.

My mother's voice, acid with relief, spoke: 'This is why people keep up with their rent!'

Lenia loomed over me, her neck haggard as a giant lizard. 'Lie still!' she said. I sat up.

My mother had helped. Anything to lie down again, but her

arm at my back held me upright like a puppeteer's softwood stick.

My mother raised my head, holding me under the chin with the firm, neutral grip of a lifelong nurse. She treats me like a hopeless case. She speaks to me as if I were a delinquent child. The loss of my great-hearted brother burns between us like wormwood in the throat, a perpetual reproach. I don't even know what she reproaches me for. I suspect she doesn't know herself.

She seemed to believe in me now. Mother said, in a voice that forced sense deep into the mash that had once been my brain, 'Marcus! I am worried about the little girl. We read her note. I sent Petronius to find her, but you ought to go – '

I reached the Forum in a litter, shouldered through the crowds like some gross eunuch with more money than taste. We jostled to the Golden Milestone, from which all the roads in the Empire take their distance. I thought of her, waiting to meet me at the heart of the world. No sign of her now. One of Petro's troopers gave me a message to meet his captain in Nap Lane. The man held back, still expecting someone else. I set off on foot.

Hunting for the right back alley I found some sewermen, ferreting round a manhole as sewermen like to do. They were working with more energy than usual. Concrete was being shovelled underground frantically, with not a wine gourd of refreshment in sight.

I addressed them with a formality of tone I reserve for specialists: 'Sorry to interrupt. Have you possibly had a moment to spot Petronius Longus, the captain of the Aventine watch?'

The foreman gave me the benefit of his philosophy of life: 'Listen centurion, when the Great Drain starts gulping the Sacred Way into the shit after five hundred years, the navvies shoring up the culvert have better things to do than take a census of passers-by!'

'Thanks for your trouble,' I replied politely. For once it worked.

'Back of the pepper warehouses,' he admitted gruffly. 'Whole crowd of silly devils stirring up the dust.' I was already half way there, calling my thanks.

There was no rush.

Nap Lane lay on the south side of the Forum near the spice markets. It was typical of the steep, twisty side routes that dive off our major streets, only just wide enough for a waggon to force through, clogged with dry mud, littered with broken spars of wood and waste. Shutters leaned off their hinges overhead where the buildings jutted over the street, hiding the sky. There was a musty smell of night-time occupation by degenerates. A cat yowled viciously as I went past. It was the sort of hole where you worry if you see someone coming – and worry if you don't. It seemed a sorry end for the stately caravans that swung the treasures of Arabia, India and China halfway across the world for sale in Rome.

The warehouse I wanted looked abandoned; there was lush vegetation clogging the ruts in its gateway and a wrecked waggon lurching on one axle outside. I found them in an open yard, Petronius Longus and nearly a dozen men. Even before I turned in at the gate, the voices of saddened professionals warned me what to expect. I had heard that subdued note so many times before.

Petro strode towards me. 'Marcus!'

I lost any hope or doubt.

He reached me, he grasped both my hands. His eyes flickered over my bruises, too preoccupied to take them in. He would never be hardened. While other men sit in oyster bars being cynical over nothing, Petronius Longus merely gives his slow, tolerant smile. Turning back at some movement, he put an arm round my shoulders, completely unable to tell me what had happened. It didn't matter. I already knew.

They had found her inside the warehouse. I arrived at the moment when they were carrying her out, so that was when I saw her for the last time. Her white dress hung like a hank of wool over a grim trooper's arm while her head lolled backwards in a way that was unmistakable: Sosia Camillina was dead.

XVIII

Darkness, flares, the patrol waiting for the magistrate. They coped with strangled prostitutes and fishwives battered with staves, but this touched the senate – no worse to solve, but menacing paperwork.

Petronius groaned in despair. 'We wasted hours searching. Squeezed the throats of a trail of pimps who had watched her. Found the lane, battered five different watchmen before we identified the place. Too late. Nothing I could do. Just nothing I could do . . . *This damned city!*'

He loved Rome.

They laid her down in the yard.

It is usually easy to maintain some detachment at this point. I rarely know the victim; I don't meet the victim until after the crime. That order of events is what I recommend.

I covered my face.

I was aware of Petronius Longus dragging back his men. We had been colleagues for a long time. We fought life from the same side. He granted me as much leeway as he could.

I stood, a yard from her. Petronius came to my shoulder. He muttered. Crouching, his big hand softly closed her eyes. He stood by me again. We were both looking down at her. He was looking at Sosia to avoid looking at me. I was looking at Sosia because there was nothing else on this earth that I ever wanted to look at again.

Her sweet face was still bright with the flimflammery a young woman of her station paints on. Beneath, her skin tones were stone-white as alabaster. It was her; yet it would never be her. There was no light and no laughter, only a motionless, eggshell-white case. It was a corpse, yet I could not deal with it as a corpse.

'She cannot have realized,' Petro murmured. He cleared his throat. 'That was all. No nasty work.'

Rape. He meant rape, torture, indignity, indecency.

She was dead and this poor fool was trying to tell me she had not been terrorized! I wanted to rage at him that nothing else mattered. He was trying to tell me it was quick. I could see that! One short, hard, violent upward blow had killed Sosia Camillina before she guessed what the man would do. There was very little blood; she had died of shock.

'Was she dead when you arrived?' I asked 'Did she say anything?'

Routine questions, Marcus. Cling to your routine.

Pointless even to ask. Petronius shrugged helplessly, then moved away.

So I stood there, and was as nearly alone with Sosia as I would ever be again. I wanted to hold her in my arms, but there were too many people. After a while I just dropped down on my heels and stayed with her while Petro kept his squaddies at rest. I could not speak to her, not even in my head. I no longer really looked at her, lest the sluggish wake of her spilt blood should defeat me.

I sat there, living through what must have happened. It was the nearest I could come to helping her. It was the only way I could comfort her for dying so alone.

I know who it was. He must realize that. One day, however carefully he protects himself, the man will answer to me.

She found him there, writing (that was evident). Writing what? Not a tally of the silver bars, for she was wrong, there were no bars, though we turned the deserted warehouse over for days. But he was writing, because lampblack from the wet ink stained her white dress around the wound. Perhaps she knew him. When she found him, he realized she needed to be silenced, so he stood up and rapidly stabbed her, a rising blow through the heart, once, *with his pen.*

Petronius was right. Sosia Camillina could not have expected that.

I rose. I managed neither to stumble nor break down.

'Her father . . .'

'I'll tell them,' stated Petronius drably. A task he so hated. 'Go home. I'll tell the family. Marcus, just go home!'

I decided after all to let him tell them.

I could feel his eyes watching me as I walked away. He wanted to help. He knew there was nothing anyone could do.

XIX

I went to the funeral. In my line of work, this is traditional. Petronius came with me.

According to custom, they conducted the ceremony out of doors. They came in procession from her father's house, bringing Sosia Camillina in an open bier with garlands in her hair. The cremation took place outside the city near the family mausoleum on the Appian Way. They dispensed with professional mourners. Young men who were friends of the family carried her funeral bed.

There was a blustery wind. They brought her through Rome in daylight, with flute music and lamentation, disrupting the city streets. At the pyre, built of untrimmed wood like an altar and with dark leaves woven round the sides, one of the young bearers stumbled. I stepped forward to help, without looking. The bier was so light it nearly flew from our hands as we swung it up.

Her father's oration was short, almost perfunctory. That seemed right. So too had been her life. What Publius Camillus said that day was simple, and simply the truth.

'This was my only daughter, Sosia Camillina. She was fair, reverent and dutiful, snatched from the world before she could know the love of a husband or child. Receive her young soul gently, O ye gods . . .' He seized one of the torches and, with formally averted gaze, he lit the pyre.

'Sosia Camillina, Hail and Farewell!'

Surrounded by flowers, small trinkets, sweet oils, she left us. People wept. I was one of them. Scented flames crackled up. I glimpsed her once through the smoke. She was gone.

Petronius and I had endured the respectful ritual scores of times. We never liked it. I raged under my breath, as we stood to one side. 'This is obscene. Remind me again what in Hades I'm doing here!'

He answered in his low voice, lecturing me to steady me, 'Official sympathy. Plus a forlorn hope that the maniac we are looking for may turn up too. Fascinated by his crime, flaunting his mad mask at the mausoleum . . .'

Keeping on my funeral face, I scoffed, 'Exposing himself to curious scrutiny in the one place where he knows uncomfortable law agents are standing about, just longing for a chance to gallop after any uninvited guest who has a funny look about the eyes – '

Petro dropped a hand on my arm. 'Then again, you know, we may spot a mood in the family that doesn't fit.'

'We can rule out the family,' I declared.

Petronius raised an eyebrow. He had left this delicate issue to the praetor – let a magistrate of their own rank plant his nice clean shoe in the manure. I think he assumed I was too brokenhearted to consider it. But I had.

'Women not strong enough, children not tall enough. Decimus Verus has fifty members of the government – whose word I don't rate a bean – and the old slave from the Black Sea who cleans his boots – who is good enough for me – to swear he was at the senate, while Publius Meto was discussing merchant ships with his brother's daughter's divorced husband – which incidentally, Petro, has ruled out the ex-husband too, before we even bothered to rule him in.' I had checked. I knew the whereabouts of relations the senator and his brother had forgotten they ever owned.

The only thing I had *not* done was to meet Helena Justina's ex-husband. Never even troubled to ask his name. I excused him for two reasons. The useful Black Sea boot-slave had told me where he was. And anyway, Helena's husband had got himself divorced. I had seen enough of other people's marriages to believe that the parties concerned were usually best off when they put an end to their formal union. If Helena's husband agreed with me, he was obviously a reasonable sort of man.

Do not imagine my stalwart old tent mate stayed idle. Petronius had planted himself on the local praetor's staff. He made himself indispensable to the aedile on the case (happily not Pertinax here: we were in Sector Eight, the Roman Forum District now). Petro himself led a search through every store and hovel in Nap Lane. It turned out the warehouse where Sosia was found belonged to an ancient ex-consul called Caprenius Marcellus, who was dying of some slow malady on a country estate fifty miles south of Rome. The praetor would have accepted that dying was an alibi, but Petronius still travelled the distance and back to make sure. It could not be Caprenius Marcellus. He was in too much pain even to see Petro standing beside his bed.

The warehouse was empty when we found it, but we were certain it had been used. There were recent waggon ruts in the yard. Anyone who knew the owner was ill could have secretly moved in. Yet apparently they moved out afterwards.

There were no incidents at the funeral. We recognized no villains. Petronius and I were the people who felt out of place.

By now the close family were waiting to gather the ashes; it was time for other mourners to depart. Before we left, I forced myself to approach Sosia Camillina's bereaved papa.

'Publius Camillus Meto.'

It was the first time I had seen him since that day with Pertinax. He was a man you forget: the smooth oval face that carried so little expression, the remote gaze with a hint of justified contempt. This was almost the only occasion, too, when I saw him with his brother. Publius seemed older with that bald head, but today it was covered while he officiated here and, as he turned to avoid me, I noticed a handsome, decisive cast to his profile which my man Decimus lacked. When he moved off he left a faint haze of myrrh, and he wore a gold intaglio ring with a substantial emerald, slight touches of bachelor vanity which I had missed before. Noticing these things, which were so unimportant, added to my awkwardness.

'Sir, I expect this is the last thing you want to hear from me – ' I could see from his expression that I was right ' – Sir, I promise you – as I promise her – I will find out who killed your child. Whatever it costs and however long it takes.'

He stared at me as though he had forgotten how to speak. Julia Justa, his brother's wife, briefly touched my arm. She flashed an irritated glance at me, but I stood my ground. Publius was a man whose grief caught him smiling gently, but the gentleness only hid a hardness I had never seen before.

'You have done quite enough for my daughter!' he exclaimed. 'Take yourself off! Leave us all alone!' His clipped voice rose nearly to a shout.

It jarred. Well, the star of the morning had dimmed for us both and here was I, battering him. He knew no one else to blame; the man blamed me.

Yet that was not the reason. It jarred because Publius Camillus Meto looked like someone whom grief steers into rigid self-

66

control; like a man who would break, but not yet; break, but not in public; not today, not here. He had previously been so persuasive – this loss had shaken him.

I mourned his vibrant child as honestly as he. For her sake I ached for him. For her sake I addressed him with an open heart.

'Sir, we share – '

'We share nothing, Falco!' He strode away.

I watched the senator's pale wife, who had taken it on herself to guide her husband's brother through this appalling day, lead him towards the pyre. Servants were scooping up the smaller children. Family slaves huddled together. Important men, about to leave, clasped the senator's hand and followed his brother with sombre eyes.

I knew I could make contact with the senator. With his younger brother Publius I was grasping air, but Decimus and I could always talk. I waited.

The two brothers had shared Sosia's life; they were sharing her departure. Decimus was presiding now. Publius would only stare at those threads of bone on the pyre. While Sosia's father stood apart, alone, it was her uncle who prepared to pour the wine to douse the embers. On this cue, mourners were moving off. Decimus paused in his task, waiting for privacy.

In the manner of a man at a funeral going through the polite motions of permitting strangers to present condolences, Decimus walked over to Petronius Longus – decent officialdom. Three paces from us, the senator spoke in a heavy voice. His weariness clove to mine.

'Watch captain, thank you for coming. Didius Falco! Tell me if you are willing to go on with the case?' No fuss. No reference to me severing our contract. No escape.

I answered with real bitterness.

'I'll go on! The magistrate's team have run into the ground. There was nothing in the warehouses. Nobody saw the man, nothing to identify his pen. But the silver pigs will lead us to him in the end.'

'What will you do?' the senator asked, frowning.

I sensed Petronius shift his weight. We had not discussed it. Until that moment I had been unsure. She was gone now. My mind cleared. There was an obvious course. And there was nothing for me in Rome. No place, no pleasure, no peace.

'Sir, Rome's too big. But our thread starts in one small community in a province under strict army control. Hiding knots out there must be much more difficult. We have been fools. I should have gone before.'

67

Petro, who had hated the place so dismally, could no longer keep quiet. 'Oh Marcus! Dear gods – '

'Britain,' I confirmed.

Britain in winter. It was already October; I would be lucky to get there before the sea passages closed. Britain in winter. I had been there, so I knew how bad it was. The fine mist that tangles sticky as fish glue in your hair; the cold that leaps straight into your shoulders and knees; the sea fogs and hill blizzards; the dreadful dark months when dawn and evening seem hardly separate.

It did not matter. None of that mattered to me. The more uncivilized the better. Nothing mattered any more.

PART II

BRITAIN
Winter, AD 70–71

XX

If you ever want to go there, I advise you not to bother.

If you simply cannot avoid it, you will find the province of Britain out beyond civilization in the realms of the North Wind. If your mapskin has grown ragged at the edges you will have lost it, in which case so much the better is all I can say. Getting away from Britain must be the reason why old Boreas keeps blowing his fat cheeks out, tearing off south.

My cover ran that Camillus Verus had despatched me to bring home his daughter Helena Justina from the visit to her aunt. Actually he appeared to be more fond of his youngest sister, the British aunt. When we spoke, he had murmured, 'Falco, escort my daughter if she agrees, but I leave you to decide the details with Helena herself.'

From the way he said it, I deduced the young woman had a mind of her own. He sounded so uncertain I asked him bluntly, 'Will she disregard your advice? Is your daughter a difficult customer?'

'She has had an unhappy marriage!' her father exclaimed defensively.

'I'm sorry to hear it, sir.' I was too wrapped up in my own grief for Sosia to want to involve myself in other people's problems, but perhaps personal misery made me more compassionate.

'The divorce was for the best,' he said briefly, making it plain that his noble daughter's private life was not for discussion with the likes of me.

I had made a mistake; he *was* fond of Helena, but looked honestly afraid of her – though even in those days, before I achieved it myself, I thought fathering a girl might make any man crack. From the moment the leering midwives place that crinkled red scrap between your hands and demand that you pronounce a name for it, a lifetime of panic drops on you like a blight . . .

I had coped with headstrong females before. I assumed that

71

a few firm words from me would bring this Helena under control.

I went to Britain overland. Although I hated myself, I could never send anyone the whole distance by sea, between the Pillars of Hercules and out into the wild Atlantic round Lusitania and Tarraconensian Spain. Crossing direct from Gaul is bad enough.

Everything had been done to smooth my outward journey: abundant cash and a special pass. I threw away the money on cloak pins and nutmeg custard. The pass carried a signature so like the Emperor's it caused sleepy dogs in border posts to sit up publicly and beg. My main worry was losing my apartment, but it turned out that during this high-flown mission I could charge a retainer. The senator's smart Greek accountant would organize things with Smaractus – a confrontation I was sorry to miss.

My mother sniffily informed me that if she had known I was going back, she would have kept the tray I brought her as a present from Britain the first time I was there. This item had been carved of a soapy grey shale from the mid-south coast. Apparently the stuff needs constant oiling. I never knew that, so I never told her and the object had disintegrated. Ma thought I ought to find the peddler and demand my money back.

Petronius lent me a pair of socks from his old British gear. He never throws anything away. I had chucked mine down a well in Gaul. If I had known about this unhappy trip, I might have jumped down after them.

On the way there was a lot of time for thought.

But thinking took me no further. Plenty of people could want to depose Vespasian. Changing Emperors had been fashionable for the past two years. After Nero's numbing concerts finally lost their appeal for the tone-deaf toffs in the orchestra stalls, he stabbed himself and we suffered a free-for-all. First Galba, a doddering old autocrat from Spain. Next Otho, who had been Nero's ponce and so judged himself Nero's legitimate heir. After him, Vitellius, a bullying glutton who drank himself into and out of the job with a certain ironclad style, and then had a recipe for mushy peas named after him in return.

All that in twelve months. It was getting to seem that anyone with half an education and a winning smile could persuade the Empire that purple was just his colour. Then, with Rome vandalized and battered, up cropped this canny old general

Vespasian, who possessed one great advantage in that no one knew much about him for better or worse, and a priceless confederate in his son Titus, who gripped the chance of political glory like a terrier shaking a rat . . .

My man Decimus Camillus Verus believed anyone opposing Vespasian must wait until Titus came home from Judaea. Vespasian himself had been quelling a Jewish rebellion when he scrambled into power. He returned to Rome as Emperor, leaving Titus to complete that popular job with his usual panache. Edging out Vespasian would merely allow his brilliant elder son to inherit the Empire early. His younger son Domitian was a lightweight, but Vespasian and Titus must be swept off their perch together or any conspiracy against them was destined to fail. This meant I had just as long to solve the mystery as it took Titus to capture Jerusalem – though from what Festus had told me before he threw away his life at Bethel, Titus would rattle through Jerusalem in two shakes of a centaur's tail. (Titus had commanded the Fifteenth Legion, in which my brother served.)

So there we were. Anyone with the rank and the clout who fancied his own chance as Emperor could be trying to batter the new dynasty out of its olive tree. There were six hundred men in the senate. It could be any one of them.

I did not believe it was Camillus Verus. Was that because I knew him? As my client, the poor duffer seemed more human than the rest (though I had been caught like that before). Even if he was sound, that left five hundred and ninety nine.

It was someone who knew Britain. Or knew someone else who did. A quarter of a century had passed since Rome invaded the province (and incidentally first made Vespasian's name). Since then countless brave souls had tramped north for their tour of duty, many of them men with shiny reputations who might be feeling ambitious now. Titus himself had been typical. I remembered him there, the young military tribune who commanded the reinforcements brought over from the Rhine to reconstruct the province after the Revolt. Britain provided a social fitness test. No one liked the place, but no good Roman family nowadays was without a son or a nephew who had done his chilly stint in the bogs at the back of the world. I could be looking for any one of them.

It could be someone who had served in northern Gaul.

It could be someone in the British Channel fleet.

It could be anybody who owned any kind of ship. One of the merchants who ferried British grain to the military bases on the

Rhine. An importer of hides or hunting dogs into Italy. An exporter of pottery and wine. Or, knowing merchants, a whole sticky consortium.

It could be the British provincial governor.

It could be his wife.

It could be the man I was travelling to meet, Gaius Flavius Hilaris, my senator's brother-in-law, who was the procurator in charge of finance now after choosing to live in Britain for the past twenty years – a choice that was so eccentric it implied Hilaris *must* be running away from something (unless he was completely off his head . . .).

By the time I reached the Britannic Ocean, I had thought through so many wild schemes I felt dizzy. I stood on the cliffs at the far rim of Gaul, watching the white horses scud over that churning water and felt worse. I set the problem to one side while I concentrated on trying not to be seasick as the boat I was taking attempted to put out across the Strait. Don't know why I bothered trying, I always am.

It took us five tries to clear the harbour at Gesoriacum, and by the time we made open water I only wanted to turn back.

XXI

I was aiming west so my passport booked me east. After seven years in the army that came as no surprise.

I had planned a gentle trip, with a few days on my own in Londinium to acclimatize myself. The harbourmaster at Gesoriacum must have signalled across to the depot at Dubris the minute he spotted me. Londinium knew I was coming before I left Gaul. On the quay at Rutupiae a special envoy was tapping his fur-stuffed boot, ready to whisk me out of trouble the minute I fell off the boat.

The procurator's envoy was a decurion who had jumped at special duties in the pompous way such heroes always do. He introduced himself, but he was a lard-faced, lank-haired, unfriendly beggar whose name I eagerly forgot. His legion was the Twentieth Valeria, dull worthies who had covered themselves with glory defeating Queen Boudicca in the Revolt. Now their HQ faced the mountains at Viroconium, ahead of the frontier, and the only useful detail I managed to squeeze out of him was that despite the efforts of succeeding governors, the frontier still lay in the same place: the old diagonal boundary road from Isca to Lindum, beyond which most of the island still lay outside Roman control. I remembered that the silver mines were the wrong side of the line.

Nothing in Britain had substantially changed. Civilization simply topped the province like a film of wax on an apothecary's ointment pot – easy enough to press your finger through. Vespasian was sending lawyers and academics to turn the tribesmen into democrats you could safely ask to dinner. The lawyers and academics would need to be good. Rutupiae bore all the marks of an Imperial entry port, but once we rode out down the supply road south of the River Tamesis, it was the old scene of smoky round huts clustered in poky square fields, surly cattle drifting under ominous skies, and a definite sense

75

that you could travel for days over the downs and through the forests before you found an altar to any god whose name you recognized.

When I last saw Londonium it was a field of ash with an acrid smell, where the skulls of massacred commercial settlers were tumbling over one another like pebbles in a clogged and reddened stream. Now it was a new administrative capital. We rode in from the south. We found a spanking bridge, clean-cut wharves, warehouses and workshops, taverns and baths: not a stick more than ten years old. I caught smells both familiar and exotic, and heard six languages in the first ten minutes. We passed a bare, black site earmarked for the governor's palace; and another great space later where the Forum would be. Government buildings reared everywhere, one of which – a busy finance complex with courtyard verandahs and sixty offices – housed the procurator and his family.

The procurator's private suite had depressing British style: closed-in courtyards, cramped rooms, dark hall, dim corridors with an airless smell. White-faced, white-legged people existed here among sufficient Arretine dinnerware and Phoenician glass to make life bearable. There were wall paintings in ox blood and ochre, with borders of storks and vineleaves executed by a plasterer who might twenty years ago have seen a stork and a bunch of grapes. I arrived halfway through October and already there was a buffeting blast from the underfloor heating as soon as I walked through the door.

Flavius Hilaris strode out from his study to greet me himself.

'Didius Falco? Welcome to Britain! How was your trip? You made good time! Come in and talk while I have your baggage taken up.'

He was a winsome, vigorous man I had to admire since he had stuck it in government service for nearly thirty years. He had crisp brown hair cut to outline a neat head, and lean firm hands with straight-cut, clean fingernails. He wore a broad gold ring, the badge of the middle rank. As a republican I despised the rank, but from the start I thought the man himself was excellent. His mistake was that he did a thorough job and saw the funny side. People liked him, but to conventional judges these were not the signs of a 'good mind'.

The room which the public works officials had designated his private study was in fact used by Hilaris as an extra public office. As well as his own reading couch, shapeless with use, he kept a table with benches where meetings could be held. There were plenty of sconces, all blazing, for it was late. His secretaries had left him on his own, immersed in figurework and thought.

He poured me wine. Kind gesture, I thought, putting me at ease. Then with a shock I realized, maybe putting me off guard!

Our interview was conducted with exhausting thoroughness. Compared with this Hilaris, my client Camillus Verus was just a squashy plum. I had already deleted the procurator from my suspects list (too obvious), but he made a point of discussing the Emperor, to demonstrate where his sympathies lay.

'No better man for the Empire – but this is new for Rome! Vespasian's father was a middle rank finance officer, yet now Vespasian's Emperor. *My* father was a finance officer – and so am I!'

I warmed to him. 'Not quite, sir. You are the leading civilian in a prestigious new province, with an Emperor who looks on you as a friend! No one but the governor carries more weight in Britain than you. Your father's highest position was as a third-grade tax collector, in a one-ox town in Dalmatia –' The only reason I knew this was because I had delved into his background before I came out. He realized that. He smiled. So did I.

'And *your* father was an auctioneer –' he threw back at me. My father disappeared so long ago, not many people are aware of that.

'Possibly still is!' I admitted morosely.

He made no comment. A polite man, though one who had made sure before I came out to his province that he knew all about me:

'As for you, Falco, two years' army service, then five more as what the legions would call a scout – the type of army agent native tribesmen hang as a spy –'

'If they catch you!'

'Which they never did . . . So you were invalided out, recovered briskly – perhaps so briskly it smacks of sharp practice – then you took up your present work. My sources say you have a dozy reputation, though past clients speak well of you. Some of the women,' he observed, looking down with a prim mouth, 'have an odd look when they do!'

I let that pass.

Then he confronted me with what we had been skirting round since the interview began: 'You and I,' smiled the British financial procurator, 'served in the same legion, Didius Falco.'

Well, *I* knew that. He must have realized.

Twenty years apart. Same legion, same province. He served when the glorious Second Augusta were the crack troops in the British invasion force. Vespasian was his commander – that was how they met. I served in the Second at Isca, at the time when Paulinus the British governor decided to invade Mona – Druids' Island – to clear out that rats' nest of troublemakers once and for all. Paulinus left us at Isca, guarding his back, but was accompanied by our commandant among his advisory corps. We were stuck therefore with an incompetent Camp Prefect named Poenius Postumus, who called Queen Boudicca's Revolt 'just a local tiff'. When the governor's frantic orders arrived informing this halfwit that the Iceni had swept a bloody swathe all through the south, instead of haring off to join the beleaguered field army, either from terror or further misjudgement Postumus refused to march out. *I* served in our legion when its glorious name stank.

'Not your fault!' remarked my new colleague gently, reading my mind.

I said nothing.

After the rebels were annihilated and the truth came out, our peabrained Camp Prefect fell on his sword. We made sure of that. But first he had forced us to abandon twenty thousand comrades in open country with no supplies and nowhere to retreat, facing two hundred thousand screaming Celts. Eighty thousand civilians had been massacred while we polished our studs in barracks. We might have lost all four British legions. We might have lost the governor. We might have lost the province.

If a Roman province had fallen, in a native rebellion, led by a mere woman, the whole Empire might have blown away. It could have been the end of Rome. That was the kind of 'local tiff' the British rebellion was.

Afterwards we witnessed what the barbarians had done. We saw Camulodunum, where the huddled townsfolk had melted in each other's arms during a four day inferno at the Temple of Claudius. We choked in the black dust of Verulamium and Londinium. We cut down the crucified settlers at their lonely country villas; we flung earth on the burned skeletons of their strangled slaves. We stared in shock and horror at mutilated women hanging like crimson rags from the trees in the pagan groves. I was twenty years old.

That was why, when I could, I left the army. It took five years to arrange, but I had never had second thoughts. I worked for myself. Never again would I entrust myself to orders from a man of such criminal ineptitude. Never again would I be part of the establishment that foists such fools into positions of command.

Flavius Hilaris was still watching me in my reverie.

'None of us will ever quite recover,' he acknowledged, sounding pretty hoarse himself. His face had shadowed too. While the governor Paulinus was frightening mountain tribesmen, this man had been prospecting for copper and gold. Now his job was finance. Below the governor he sat on the second highest administrative notch. But ten years ago, at the time of the Revolt, Gaius Flavius Hilaris had occupied a more junior post; he was the procurator in charge of the British mines.

It *could* be him! My weary brain kept telling me that this clever man with the clear-eyed smile could be the villain I had come to find. He understood the mines, and he could fudge the paperwork. No one in the Empire was so beautifully placed.

'You must be exhausted!' he exclaimed softly. I felt drained. 'You missed dinner. I'll send sustenance to your room, but do use our bathhouse first. After you eat I want to introduce you to my wife . . .'

These were my first dealings with the diplomatic middle class. Until then they had escaped me, for the simple reason that they led lives so lacking in deceit that they attracted nobody else's unkind attention and never needed to employ me for themselves. I had come expecting to be treated like a servant. Instead I found myself lodged incognito in the procurator's private suite, being offered a welcome more suited to a family guest.

Fortunately I had packed one set of decent clothes.

XXII

My billet was disturbingly cosy. I had a spacious room with a bed groaning under colourful quilts. Oil lamps flickered. Warmth filtered through the wall flues. There were seats with low square footstools, cushions, floor rugs, writing materials for my private use, late apples in a glossy ceramic bowl.

A dapper slave escorted me to the bath suite, another scraped me down, then back to find a pudgy boy struggling to unload a tray of silverware covering cold game and glazed ham. I packed in the victuals while I could. The boy waited to serve me; he seemed impressed. I winked at him – then looked away in case he got the wrong idea.

As a compliment to my host I combed my hair. Then I rooted out my best tunic, a limp off-white article which according to my clothes dealer had only been worn by one other person before me. (My mother says always ask what they died of, but so long as there are no visible bloodstains, I don't. What dealer is going to confess that your predecessor had a flaky skin disease?)

Opening my baggage roll, I sucked thoughtfully at the remnants of ham that had trapped themselves between my teeth. It had been skilfully done, but during our talk in the study my props had been searched.

I found Hilaris reclining, minus his belt, in a warm family room. He was reading for pleasure, so had emerged from the study to sit with his wife. I identified her as the slender, rather ordinary woman in a crimson dress, slightly uneasy within her elegant attire. A baby slept on her own arm, while a little girl of two or three was sprawling over the knees of a younger woman in much darker clothing, who was by an oversight not immediately introduced.

Flavius Hilaris sprang up eagerly.

'Didius Falco – Aelia Camilla, my wife.' The one in crimson.

I had no great hopes. He was a dedicated long-term diplomat: he would have married a good, plain woman who could serve sweetmeats to a governor from the proper shape of dish, or be polite to a tribal king for three hours at a time, then remove the royal paw from her knee without giving offence.

I was right. Aelia Camilla, the senator's sister, was a good, plain woman. She could do all that. But she had vividly eloquent eyes. It would be a brave king – or governor – who took liberties with her.

Though her husband did. As soon as he had jumped up to bring me in, he abandoned his own couch and relaxed beside her instead, dropping a hand onto her thigh as if it were quite natural for a man to fondle his wife. Neither looked embarrassed. It would never happen in Rome. I felt amazed.

Decimus Camillus had spoken of his sister with affection. She was younger than him, an afterthought in their family, still somewhere short of forty, a shy, private woman excelling in her public role. She smiled at me, a special smile, which she used so well it seemed real.

'So you are Sosia Camillina's friend!'

'Not a very good one,' I confessed. Then I drowned my sorrows in those sympathetic eyes.

Good, plain women meant nothing to me, yet I took to Sosia's aunt at once. This was the sweet-natured lady a boy dreams of when he decides he has been lost at birth by his real mother and is being brought up by scolding strangers in a foreign land . . . Oh I was fantasizing merrily. But I was whirling through a personal nightmare and had just racked up fourteen hundred miles.

Friend Gaius motioned me to a couch, but they had a brazier for extra cheer so I perched on a small stool near that, holding out my hands to the charcoal glow. In a different situation I would have stayed silent about my discovery upstairs, but I prefer to hit clients with frankness, then hear them squeal.

'I gather somebody picked over my belongings. Can't have been pleasant. Thousand miles of unwashed undertunics – '

'It won't happen twice!' Hilaris said, smiling. 'Just cautious,' he added. It was not an apology. Nor was I disturbed. A professional risk, which we acknowledged to one another with polite nods on both sides.

A violent voice broke in so abruptly I jumped.

'You have a bracelet that belonged to my cousin!'

I half turned: the stiff young woman with the little girl. Eyes like burnt caramel in a bitter almond face. Golden hoop earrings, each hung with a fine carnelian bead. Suddenly I understood; this was my senator's daughter, this was Helena.

She was sitting in a half-round basket weave chair, the child happily squirming on and off her lap. (I knew she had no children of her own, so the little girl must belong here.) No one would call the young woman plain, but in appeal she raised no competition for her aunt. She had her father's domineering eyebrows, but her air of tight-lipped distaste reminded me of his brother Publius.

'You should return it, Falco!'

Females with loud voices and bad manners were never my type. 'Thanks, but I'll keep it.'

'I gave it to her!'

'She gave it to me.'

I could see why the senator was so attached to his kind-eyed sister, if this was the spiteful virago he had spawned himself.

As the tension flashed between us, Aelia Camilla interrupted, a note of reproof in her light voice. 'It seems to me we shall all need to be adult in our loyalties! Didius Falco, you were fond of my poor niece?' She was the classic type of Roman matron; Aelia Camilla did not permit angry scenes.

After thirty years of deflecting my mother, questions about women slide by me.

'I'm so sorry!' Aelia Camilla reproached herself. 'That was unforgivable.'

These open, intelligent people were shaking my confidence. I managed to reply, 'Madam, anyone who knew your niece would have been fond of her.'

She smiled sadly. We both realized my mundane compliment was not what she had meant.

Aelia Camilla glanced at her husband, who took over the conversation again.

'I received a formal brief, of course, on why you were coming to Britain, though I should like to hear your own account of your motives,' he put to me with his acceptable bluntness. 'Do you blame yourself?'

'I blame the man who killed her, sir,' I stated. I saw his thinning eyebrows lift. 'But until he is identified, I take responsibility.'

The woman I had quarrelled with extracted herself from the child then swiftly left the room. She was tall. Watching her, I remembered bleakly how once I had liked women who were tall.

Since it pays to be hypocritical, I spoke up with gravelly respect. 'Have I just had the honour of offending the noble daughter of my client?'

Aelia Camilla was looking anxious over the way the young girl had stormed out. Hilaris gave his finger to the baby, which clasped hold of it while still asleep, kicking out haphazardly with one foot. Evidently he took a wry view of tantrums. Rather than grin too broadly, he concentrated on reattaching his baby's tiny felt boot as he spoke. 'Falco, my apologies! That is Helena Justina, my wife's niece. I ought to have introduced you – I believe there is a suggestion you should escort our Helena home?'

I held his eye long enough to share the joke, then replied without commitment that I believed there was.

XXIII

I felt gloomy enough, without a confrontation with this angry witch Helena Justina. She would have a long trek home, across barbarian territory, so I understood why the senator was so keen to provide her with some sort of professional escort – although after the disaster of my involvement with Sosia Camillina, it seemed ludicrous that he had selected me. I wanted to be helpful to him, but now I had seen her, the prospect of close contact with his bad-tempered offspring started to loom depressingly. Once, winning her over might have been a challenge. Now I was in too much pain from Sosia's death to raise the energy. Only the fact that I liked Decimus Camillus Verus gave me patience to deal with this situation at all.

The night we met, Helena Justina's finer qualities – if she had any – were lost on me. For reasons I could not begin to imagine, she held me in contempt. I could tolerate rudeness, but she even seemed insubordinate to her uncle and aunt.

She was not gone long. I suspected she could not bear to miss the chance of finding more to despise in me. When she barged back I ignored her. With hardened types it is the best way.

All the same, I was curious. Just because you give up women does not mean you give up looking. She had a brutal nature but a bonny figure, and I quite liked the way she twisted up her hair. I noticed the little Flavian girl ran back to her at once; not everyone can charm a child like that. So here she was: my lost soul's famous cousin.

Their fathers were brothers but they were not at all alike. Helena Justina was by then twenty-something, yet she appeared completely self-possessed. She burned with a strong, calm flame beside which the immature Sosia would have seemed positively foolish. She was everything that Sosia had promised to be and could never now become. I hated her for that, and she knew I hated her. She bitterly resented me.

84

When I end up at strange houses I try to fit in. Although exhausted, I sat tight. After a while, Aelia Camilla excused herself and left the room, taking both the baby and her little girl. I saw my host follow his wife with his eyes, then soon he went out too. Helena Justina and I stayed there alone.

To say our eyes met would imply too much. What happened was that I looked at her, because when a man is left alone with a woman in a quiet room it is the natural thing for him to do. She stared back at me. I had no idea why she was doing that.

I refused to speak; the senator's termagant daughter taunted me. 'Didius Falco! Isn't this journey a pointless exercise?'

Still on my stool, I leaned my elbows on my knees and waited for her to explain. My obstinate interrogator ignored my curiosity.

'It may be,' I said finally. I stared at the floor. Then added, as the confrontation continued in silence, 'Look, ladyship, I shall not ask whatever is the matter with you because frankly I don't care. Unpleasant females are a hazard of my work. I have come to a place I hate on a dangerous errand because it is the only throw your father or I can attempt – '

'That would be a good speech if it came from an honest man!'

'Then it's a good speech.'

'Lies, Falco!'

'You'll have to elaborate. You think me useless. I can't help that; I am doing my best.'

'I should like to know,' sneered the senator's daughter in her unlovely way, 'whether you are dragging out your contract for mere profit, or whether this is deliberate sabotage. Are you a traitor, Falco, or only wasting time?'

Either I was dense, or she was crazy.

'Just explain, will you?' I instructed her.

'Sosia Camillina saw one of the men who abducted her go into a house she knew. She wrote and told me – though not whose house it was. She said she had told you.'

'No!' I said.

'Yes.'

'No!' I was horrified. 'She may have *intended* to tell me – '

'No, she said she had.'

We both stopped talking.

Something must have gone wrong. Sosia was skittish and excitable, but despite her inexperience she was bright as Scythian gold. She would not overlook anything so important; she was too proud of her discoveries, too eager for me to know.

My mind raced. She could have written another note, but if so where was it? Two unused tablets of her pocket-book were with her when she was found, she had left another one in my room, and we had no reason to suppose the fourth had been used for anything more serious than a shopping list at home.

Something had gone wrong.

'No. Lady, you will have to take my word.'

'Why should I take your word?' Helena Justina scoffed.

'Because I only lie when there is something to gain.'

Her face cracked into pain. 'Did you lie to her? Oh my poor cousin!' I shot her a look that stopped her for a moment, though it was like trying to calm a runaway ox by holding out a handful of hay. 'She was only sixteen!' exclaimed the senator's daughter, as if that said everything.

Well, it told me what she imagined I had done, and why she held me in such formidable contempt.

With an exasperated explosion, Helena Justina sprang to her feet. She seemed to enjoy rushing out of rooms. She swept past with a curt goodnight. It surprised me to receive even that.

I stayed on my stool for a while, listening warily to this unfamiliar house. Though I tried not to think about Sosia, simply because I was so tired I could not bear it, I felt burdened with troubles, desperately lonely, and a very long way from home.

I had been right: nothing in Britain had substantially changed.

XXIV

Flavius Hilaris explained his plan next day.

Unsettled in a strange house, I had heaved awake as soon as people began to stir. I put on four layers of tunics and edged cautiously downstairs. A slave with a raw cough pointed out the dining room, where a murmur of serious voices stopped immediately I appeared. Aelia Camilla greeted me with her flooding smile.

'Here he is! You emerge early for a man who arrived so late!' She was on her feet ready to go about her household tasks, but first set a breakfast plate for me herself. The informality in this official house was tipping me off balance.

Hilaris himself, with his napkin under his chin, passed me a bread basket. The crab-faced young woman Helena was there. I half expected her to withdraw demurely with her aunt, but she stayed, glowering, with her hands locked round a beaker. Hardly a demure flower.

'Having been stationed here,' her uncle began at once, being the single-minded type who burrowed into business as soon as he trapped an audience, 'I expect you've kept abreast of recent events.'

I adopted the pious expression of a man who keeps abreast of events.

Fortunately, the procurator was accustomed to starting meetings with a local résumé. He could hardly approach his dinner table without calling for an up-to-date pricelist of in season vegetables. He brought me abreast himself:

'Precious metals were the main reason for investing in Britain, as you know. We have ironworks in the Southeast forests, organized by the navy in their ragtaggle way.' Ever at heart an army man, I grinned. 'There is gold in the far western mountains, and some lead in the central Peak District, though its silver yield is low – the prize mines are in the southwest. The Second Augusta once ran them direct, but we ended that in the process of encouraging self-government by the tribes. We keep fortresses at all the mines to give us an overview, but lease out their day-to-day management to local contractors.' I was trying not to wriggle with mirth at the procurator's evident enjoyment of his work. No wonder the establishment never took him seriously! 'In the Mendips, an entrepreneur called Claudius Triferus holds the franchise now, creams off his percentage, then ships the balance to the Treasury. A British native. I shall have him apprehended once I know how the ingots are lifted and shipped.'

I finished eating, so to aid digestion sat up cross-legged on my couch. Flavius Hilaris did the same. He had the pinched look of a man with stones, who from anxiety or embarrassment never found time to let his doctor examine him.

'Your job will be to investigate the theft, Falco. I want to plant you in the mines, establish you among the work force – '

'I had my eye on a management post!'

He let out a disparaging laugh. 'All filled up with senators' dim nephews out here for the boar hunting – sorry, Helena!'

As a senator's daughter she might well have objected, yet she forced a cranky smile. I meanwhile became a mite preoccupied.

My new job demanded stamina. Mines are worked by the grimmest types of criminal. Slave gangs labour there from sunrise to sunset, it's heavy work, and although the lead seams in the Mendips lie fairly near the surface, what those mines lack in physical danger they make up for in the utter desolation of the spot.

'Falco?' asked Flavius. 'Pondering your good luck?'

'Frankly, I'd prefer to sit in full formal dress without a sun umbrella, in some blazing hot amphitheatre where the gate-keepers ban winejars and the musicians are on strike, watching five hours of an inaudible Greek play! To whom,' I enquired fastidiously, 'do I owe this bracing winter holiday?'

Hilaris folded his napkin. 'I believe Helena Justina first had the idea.'

I had to smile.

'May the gods protect your ladyship! I trust you'll explain to my little grey-haired mother when my back's broken and they bury me in a bog? Do you answer to the Furies, madam, for wreaking this hard vengeance on me?'

She stared into her beaker and did not reply.

I caught her uncle's quizzical eye.

'Helena Justina answers to herself,' he said briefly.

It seemed to me that was her problem. To say so achieved

nothing, and I had no wish to criticize her father Decimus. No man can ever be entirely to blame for the women in his house. That was something I knew long before I possessed women in my own.

XXV

Flavius Hilaris made arrangements to have me taken west, which I thought decent of him until I grasped what his arrangements were. He sent me round by sea. He owned a town house in the middle of the south coast and an estate with a private summer villa even further west; for passing to and fro between his properties he had acquired a clinker-built Celtic ketch which he jovially called his yacht. This old and robust barnacled hulk was not exactly fit for dreaming in the August sun on Lake Volsinii. It probably seemed a good idea to him, but I made my own arrangements after that.

I was dropped off at Isca. Eighty Roman miles from the mines, but that was good: no point arriving straight off the procurator's boat, virtually with a standard-bearer proclaiming 'procurator's spy'. I knew Isca. It's my superstition that it helps to dive into a whirlpool from a rock where your feet feel at home.

There had been military regrouping since my time ten years before. Of the four original British legions, the Fourteenth Gemina were currently held in Europe pending Vespasian's decision on their future: they had been active in the civil war – on the wrong side. The Ninth Hispana were in mid-transfer north to Eboracum, the Twentieth Valeria had plunged out towards the western mountains, while my old unit the Second Augusta advanced to Glevum, astride the upper reaches of the great Sabrina Estuary. Their present task was pegging down the dark Siluran tribesmen, preparing for the next push west as soon as they felt confident.

Isca without the Second was a ghost town to me. It seemed odd to see our fort again, but odder still to find all the gates open and the granaries stripped, with higgledy-piggledy workshops cluttering the crossroads, and a native magistrate lording over the commander's house. Behind the fort, as I expected, once the lean-to cabins and shops thinned out there were the smallholdings of those veterans who retired while the Second

90

was still there. Hard luck to take your land grant in order to live near your mates, then watch them march out to a new fort a hundred miles away. Still, intermarriage with the natives would be holding some of them. In this disgusting province, I ruled out any idea that they stayed because they liked the climate or the scenery.

I was relying on the veterans. Relying on the fact they would be here beside the Second's fort – and the fact that the Second had gone. It seemed likely that if I came offering adventure now, I might find myself a crony with itchy feet.

Rufrius Vitalis was an ex-centurion who lived in a small stone-corridored house on a red-soiled farm huddled below the sullen threat of the moors. All his neighbours were grizzled specimens farming in similar style. I spotted him in the town, bumped into him on purpose, than claimed to know him better than I actually did. He was so desperate for news from Rome we were instant old pals.

He was a fit, sturdy, impatiently capable man with alert eyes and a grey-bristled chin in a leather face. He came from farming stock on the Campagna. Even in Britain he worked outdoors bare-armed; he was so full of energy he could ignore the cold. Before retirement he had put in thirty years – five more than he needed, but after the Revolt experienced men in Britain were offered extra time at privilege rates. It never ceases to amaze me what folk will do for double pay.

We spent some time in a wine shop, gossiping. When he took me home I was not surprised to find he lived with a native woman considerably younger than himself. Veterans usually do. Her name was Truforna. She was shapeless and colourless, just a floury dumpling with pale grey eyes, but I could see how in a hovel beyond the ocean a man might convince himself Truforna was both shapely and colourful. He ignored her; she moved about the little place watching him.

At his house Rufrius Vitalis and I talked some more. We used an unexcited tone, so Truforna would not be alarmed. He asked why I had come. I mentioned theft. I touched on the political slant, though without saying what; nor did he ask. Any ranker who gets made up to centurion before he retires has too much experience to be excited by politics. He wanted to know my strategy.

'Get in, investigate what happens, get out.' He looked at me in disbelief. 'That's not facetious. That's all I have.'

'Can't the procurator get you in?'

'What worries me is getting out!'

He looked at me again. We shared deep misgivings about the administrative class. He understood why I wanted my own scheme, someone I trusted to haul up my rope when I called.

'Need a partner, Falco?'

'Yes, but who can I ask?'

'Me?'

'What about your farm?'

He shrugged. That was up to him. He asked the real question: 'We get you in, we get you out. What happens afterwards?'

'Sunshine, I whip straight back to Rome!'

My hook was through his throat. We had talked about Rome until his heart strove against his ribs. He asked if there would be scope for anyone else to tag along, so I offered to sign him up as Helena Justina's baggage master. Our eyes, with veiled lids, covered Truforna.

'What about her?' I murmured delicately.

'She won't have to know,' Vitalis declared, with too much confidence. I thought: *O centurion!* Still, that too was up to him.

He knew the district. I let him work out the plan.

A week later we arrived at the Vebiodunum silver mines, Vitalis astride a pony in the leather and furs of a bounty hunter, me running behind in the rags of a slave. He told the contractor's foreman he was working through the limestone gorges, rounding up runaways from the caves. He extracted the names of the owners they had eluded, then handed back his wretched contraband for reward. I had refused to say where I belonged, so after three weeks of feeding me Vitalis was losing patience and wanted to restore my memory with a spell of hard labour in the mines.

Rufrius Vitalis outrageously embroidered on the story we agreed, not least – once I was safely shackled – by hitting me so hard he split open my cheek, then hurling me in some toothless villager's pile of pig manure. My sullen look on delivery was as genuine as my smell. At Vebiodunum, Vitalis claimed there must be a good chance I had murdered my master if I would not admit who I was. This extra certificate of good character was a luxury I could have managed without.

'I call him Chirpy,' he said, 'because he isn't. Don't let him escape. I'll be back when I can, to see if he wants a little chat.'

The foreman always called me Chirpy. I never was.

XXVI

From the neighbouring countryside the upland is deceptive. The limestone ridge where the lead mines lie looks no more hostile than any of the low hills characteristic of southern Britain. Only when you approach this ridge directly from the south or west do stark crags suddenly rise in your face, quite unlike the gentle swell of the downs elsewhere. On the southern side are the Gorges – ancient caves and unpredictable waters which plunge underground or rise in a ferocious spate during sudden rain. On the kinder northern edge, small hamlets cling to the steep slopes, joined by precarious tracks that jerk up and over the contours among patches of pasture land.

From the east, the terrain hardly seems to rise at all. The route to the mines is unmarked; anyone with official business comes provided with a guide. For casual visitors the settlement is deliberately difficult to find.

Riding in from the frontier side, woodland and farmland give way imperceptibly. Almost without warning, you lose sight of the countryside below, and the road crosses a cold, featureless plateau. It leads only to the mines; there is nothing else there. Travelling its bare length is a lonely experience. Thoughout this region there is a tendency to greyness, as if the wide Sabrina Estuary makes its surging presence constantly felt, even inland. This high-flung narrow road strikes purposefully across the limestone outcrop for ten miles, and with every mile the emptiness of the landscape and the tugging of the wind attack the spirit with melancholy. Even in high summer the long upland is stormed by desolate winds, and even then there is no blaze of sunshine, only remote high-piled clouds endlessly shadowing the deserted scene.

I worked in the lead mines for three months. After the Revolt, it was the worst time of my life.

I manoeuvred my way through all the sections of the mine.

From the open seams and pits where ore was clawed physically from the ground, back indoors to the clay stacks for the first smelt – the hottest work in the world – then promotion to the cupellation hearths, where bellowsmen strained to blast the silver, separating it at white heat from the refined lumps. There I worked the bellows first, afterwards as picker, gathering the silver from the cooled hearth at the day's end. For a slave, picking was the prize job. With luck and scalded fingers you could scratch up a drip or two for yourself. That put a light back in your brain: *escape!*

Every day there was a body search, but we found our own foul ways round that.

Occasionally now I wake, bolt upright in my bed, in a drowning sweat. My wife says I never make a sound. A slave learns: lock in every thought.

It would be easy to say it was only Sosia's death that held me on my track. Easy but foolish. I never considered her. To recall such brightness in this murderous hole would bring increased agony. What forced me on as I inched through my search was sheer self-discipline.

Anyway, you forget.

There is no time for leisured recollection in a slave's day. We enjoyed no hope for the future, no memory of the past. We woke at dawn; that is, while it was still dark. We snarled blearily over bowls of gruel ladled out by a filthy woman who never seemed to sleep. We marched in silence through the shuttered settlement while our white breath wreathed around us like our own ghosts. They chained us in links with neck rings. One or two lucky ones pulled caps down over their filthy heads. I never had a cap; I never have any luck. In that hour when the cold light seems half-excited and half-ominous, when the dew soaks your feet and every sound carries through the still air for miles, we stumbled to the current workings. They unchained us; we began. We dug all day, with one break during which we sat empty-eyed, each withdrawn into his own dead soul. When it was too dark to see, we stood head down like exhausted animals to be rechained. We marched back. We were fed. We dropped into sleep. We awoke in the dark the next day. We did it all again.

I say 'we'. These were criminals, prisoners of war (mostly Britons and Gauls), runaway slaves (again mainly Celts of different kinds, but with others – Sardinians, Africans, Spaniards, Lycians). From the first, there was no need for me to act. The life we led made me one of them. I believed I was a slave.

94

I was bruised, muscles torn, hair matted, fingers cracked, cut, blistered, blackened, engrimed with my own and others' filth. I itched. I itched in parts of my body where it was a challenge making fingers reach to scratch. I rarely spoke. If I spoke I swore. My headful of dreams had been drained off like an abcess by the punishment of my present life. A poem would have filled me with staring scorn, like the senseless lilt of a foreign tongue.

I could swear in seven languages: I was proud of that.

It was while I was a picker that I stumbled into glimmerings of organized theft. In fact once I started to identify the signs, I soon found corruption ran so rife throughout the system that it was difficult to distinguish the petty fiddles every individual put his hand to, from the major fraud that could only have been set up by the management itself. Everyone knew about that. No one talked. No one talked, because at every stage each man involved took his small cut. Once he had, he stood guilty of a capital offence. (There were two punishments: execution or slavery in the mines. Anyone who had lived at Vebiodunum and seen our conditions knew execution was the preferable fate.)

At the end of December, as a Saturnalian treat, Rufrius Vitalis turned up looking prosperous with a hide whip pushed through a huge brown belt, to see if I had discovered enough to let me be pulled out. When he saw my dull-eyed state his honest face grew grim.

He extracted me from the furnace, then drove me some distance down the track, cracking at me with his whip for show. We crouched out of doors in a bank of wet bracken where we were unlikely to be overheard.

'Falco! It looks as if you need to get out quick!'

'Can't go. Not yet.'

By this time I had slid into a sullen mood. I no longer believed in release. I felt my life for ever would be scrambling round the cupellation hearth in nothing but a loincloth with my shaved hair frizzling on my mucky head and my hands red raw. My only challenge was how many silver scratchings I could steal for myself. My mental and physical strength were both so depleted I had almost lost interest in the reason I was there. Almost, but not quite.

'Falco, are you cracked? Going on with this is suicide – '

'That doesn't matter. If I pull out too early I won't want to live with myself in any case. Vitalis, I have to finish it – ' He was starting to grumble, but I interrupted urgently. 'I'm glad to see you. I need to smuggle out information in case I never get a chance to make a full report myself.'

'Who's this for?'

'The financial procurator.'

'Flavius Hilaris?'

'You know him?'

'I know of him. They say he's all right. Look, laddie, there's not much time. It will look suspicious if I hang about. I'll find him. Just tell me what I have to say.'

'He should be at his villa near Durnovaria.' Gaius had promised to locate himself there, within reach if I managed to send messages. 'Tell him this, Vitalis. There's flagrant corruption all through the mine. First, when the rough ingots leave the smelt for cupellation, they are counted out by a weasel who can't actually count. He scratches marks on a tally stick; sometimes he "forgets" to make his nick. So what the contractor Triferus declares to the Treasury as his overall production is fraudulent from the start.'

'Hah!' Vitalis let out this exclamation like a man who assumes he has heard almost everything, but who is not surprised to learn of some new dodge.

'Next, every day a few of the rough ingots are held back from the cupellation hearth. It's surprising how many, though I guess the number has crept up gradually over many years. This has the effect that the silver yield per ingot appears less than it really ought to be. I gather the declining yield was explained to Rome during Nero's time as *geological variations in the ore being mined*. Things were notoriously slack then, so in case Vespasian has anybody looking at the figures it's customary nowadays to slip in extra ingots some weeks, and claim the mineralogist has discovered a better seam.'

'Delicate touch!'

'Oh yes, we're dealing with experts here. Will you be able to remember all this hogwash?'

'Have to try. Falco, trust me. Go on.'

'Right. Now, regarding the ingots of pure silver which are produced at the cupellation hearth. Some get lost. This is *natural wastage*.' Rufrius Vitalis scoffed admiringly again. 'Then, when the lead bars that have had their silver extracted go back for a second smelt – '

'What's that for?'

'To remove any other impurities before carting them out for sale – *Mars Ultor*, Vitalis, don't let's knot ourselves up in technicalities, this is complex enough as it is! Hilaris will know what the procedures are – ' He shushed me to calm me down; I was sweating with the effort of ensuring I told him everything. Frowning, I pressed on. 'After the second smelt more ingots disappear – though since their value is by then so much reduced, this last wrinkle in the system is considered to lack finesse! Apparently it's permitted to the overseers, as a privilege that keeps them sweet.'

I fell silent. I was so unused to talking that presenting these details in an ordered form had tired me out. I could see Vitalis watching me closely, though after his first attempt he made no more suggestions for restoring me to civilization prematurely. My choice of comrade had been an intelligent one; I could see he understood the implications of what I had said.

'How do they get away with it, Falco?'

'It's a completely enclosed community; no outsiders are allowed.'

'But they have a civilian settlement – '

'Where every baker, barber and blacksmith comes under licence, specifically to supply the mines! They're all human; pretty well on arrival they are all suborned.'

'So what do those young dreamers at the fort think they're playing at?'

There was a small fortress overlooking the settlement, an outpost of the Second Augusta which was supposed to supervise the mines. I smiled at Vitalis for his assumption that immediately after he himself retired, all military discipline went to the dogs.

'That's the centurion in you talking! No one can blame them. All operations are subject to inspection, of course – '

'Both officers and men should be regularly changed – '

'They are. And I've seen details coming down from the fort to peer around. I imagine they are hampered by the fact ingots look identical: how can they tell whether what they are shown even contains silver or not?'

'How can *anyone* tell?'

'Ah! The ingots that are stolen before cupellation are specially stamped: 'T CL TRIF' four times.'

'Falco, you've seen it?'

'I've seen them here – and tell the procurator Flavius, I've seen one like that in Rome!'

It was still lying in Lenia's bleaching vat.

Rome! I lived there once . . .

Our snatched conversation was about to be disturbed. My present life had taught me to smell trouble on the wind like a forest deer. I touched Vitalis on the arm to warn him, and our faces closed guardedly.

'Io, Vitalis! Has that punk admitted anything?'

It was Cornix.

This Cornix was an obscene bully of a foreman, a real specialist in administering tortures to slaves. A slab-shouldered sadist with a face marbled like a side of beef by his depraved life. He had picked on me mercilessly from the moment I arrived, but owned just enough working ooze in his chickpea brain to be wary in case one day I went back to some previous life and talked.

Vitalis shrugged. 'Nothing. Tight as a virgin's apron string. Shall I leave him a bit longer? Is he any use to you?'

'Never was,' Cornix lied.

Quite untrue. They had worn me to a runt by now, but I had been well fed and sturdy when I first arrived. I scowled at the ground while Vitalis and Cornix pretended to negotiate.

'Take a thorough squint at him,' Rufrius Vitalis urged the foreman scornfully. I stood there looking pitiful. 'Another few weeks of fog and frost up here and he'll be pleading to go home. But I won't get much back for him in his present state – can't you fatten the bastard up a bit? I'd be willing to go halves on any reward . . .'

On this welcome hint, Cornix promptly agreed he would have me transferred to lighter work. When Vitalis left, with a curt nod to me as his only possible goodbye, I had ended my stint as a picker, and was about to be made up to a driver instead.

'Your lucky day, Chirpy!' Cornix leered unpleasantly. 'Let's go and celebrate!'

Avoiding the privilege of being selected as Cornix's partner in sexual dalliance had so far occupied a lot of my ingenuity.

I told the brute I had a headache, and was violently kicked for my pains.

XXVII

Driving seemed quite straightforward. We used mules rather than oxen, because of the hills. A cartload comprised four ingots. They were a dead weight and transporting them was fiendishly slow.

I was tucked in behind the leader at the front of the train. The excuse was that a new boy didn't know the way. Really, until you proved yourself a trusty it was a precaution against escape.

No one would ever be a trusty who worked as a slave in the mines. Still, I had learned by then to look as much like a trusty as anybody else.

There was one final check to stop anyone thieving the Empire's loot. On leaving the mines we drove past the fort, where the soldiers counted every ingot and drew up a manifest. This manifest remained with the silver all the way to Rome. There was one good road out of Vebiodunum, the road back to the frontier. Every cart capable of carrying bars had to pass along that road, for the crossways were too narrow and too rough to bear the weight. That meant every single ingot that ever left the mines was registered on an official manifest.

Our destination was the military port at Abona. To reach the great Estuary, we first turned our backs on it, drove ten miles east to the frontier highway, followed it northwards to the sacred springs of Sul, then west again along another spur round the third side of a square – say thirty Roman miles in all. Heavy barges drew up the Estuary for the ingots, which they hauled round the Two Promontaries and then, under guard from the British Fleet, right along the Channel to cross Europe overland. Most of the silver went south through Germany, where the dense military presence guaranteed its route.

I knew Abona already.

Nothing had changed. The place where Petronius Longus and I once spent two drizzling years in a customs post. It was still there, still manned by teenage soldiers with the dye brilliant in their brand-new cloaks, striding about like lords, ignoring the sad slaves who brought in the Empire's treasure. These lads all had pinched faces and runny noses, but unlike our private weasels in the mines all of them could count. They checked off our manifest, counting the ingots carefully into their pound; when the barges arrived, they counted them back out. Heaven help the contractor Triferus if ever anything failed to match.

It always matched. But it would. After we first drove the waggons out along the road from Veb, we always stopped for the drivers to relieve themselves at an upland village just before the main frontier. We stopped at this village whether anybody needed to or not.

The manifest was altered while we were there.

Now the end lay in sight for me.

After three trips, I worked my way far enough down the regular line of waggons to be able to see what happened once we left that bundle of wattle shacks where a corrupt clerk doctored the paperwork. As the main line turned north on the frontier, the last couple of carts silently peeled away south. For the thieves to use the military road might appear foolish, though it was a good fast highway giving access to every beachhead on the southern coast. Regular transports which passed openly week after week would be waved through cheerily by any troops they met. But moving the Second Augusta away up to Glevum said clearly enough that this section of road was no longer actively patrolled.

I was back on form now. I had a clear goal: winning sufficient trust to be put to driving one of those carts that slipped off south. I was desperate to discover where they went. If we found their embarkation port we could pinpoint the ship that carried the stolen pigs to Rome; the ship – and its owner, who must be in the conspiracy.

I was old enough to recognize the risk that my nerve might fail. After three months of hard labour and cruelty on the worst diet in the Empire, I was in poor physical and mental shape. Still, a new challenge works wonders. My concentration revived. I kept my nerve under grim control.

What I overlooked was the Didius Falco luck.

It was at the end of January that I won my chance. Half the workers were confined to the slave sheds, shamming sick, some so effectively they had given up and died. Those of us who kept on our feet felt rough, but it was worth the extra effort since there were more rations available if you did. Eating the stuff was hideous, but it helped fight off the cold.

There had been a light snowfall, with much incertainty whether the week's transports should be sent out. The weather cleared so it seemed as though the really bitter grip of winter had yet to descend. A last-minute consignment was despatched with a scratch crew. Even the waggon master was a substitute. I ended up in the last cart but one. Nothing was said, but I knew what it meant.

We paraded at the fort. A desultory decurion with swollen, marsh fever eyes came out and stamped our manifest. We set off.

It was so cold they had issued us rough felt cloaks with pointed hoods; we even had mittens so our numb hands could keep hold of the reins. On the uplands the wind swooped at us from a low, sodden sky, tearing our clothes, and so bitter we screwed our eyes into slits and bared our teeth, squealing with misery. The dark line of carts crept along that lonely road, at one point plunging into a dip where the mules skidded through slush and we had to dismount to lead them, heaving back up a sheer slope into the wild scream of the wind. Then we wound across more grey landscape where the low round burial mounds of forgotten native kings loomed and were lost again in a fine, teasing mist.

When we halted to have the manifest forged we were all so badly chilled that for once overseers and slaves seemed one in their agony. The corrupt clerk had trouble: too dark indoors, too windy when he tried coming to the door of his shack. We stood about for what seemed ages, hunched up in the lee of the carts, wretchedly crouching in the slightest shelter from that wind. It had taken twice as long as normal to come this far, and the sky was developing a dismal yellow-grey that boded snow.

At last we were ready for the road again. Two miles to the turn-off at the frontier. The waggon master gave me a wink. The line lurched forward. Starting off with such a weight was always a struggle for the mules, and today with the road in such a bad state they resented it more than usual. Mine skidded in their iron shoes on the slush that was turning to ice almost as we looked. They plunged wildly; one of the cart's axles stuck – iced up. The jammed rear wheels slithered sideways, the axle cracked, a wheel gave way, a corner of the cart suddenly

101

dipped, the mules screamed and reared, I stood up – then next moment I pitched into the road, my load jiggered down a ditch, the wrecked cart sagged to one side, one mule had hurt itself so badly we had to cut its throat, and the other had broken its traces and galloped away.

For some reason, everyone else blamed me.

There was a long debate about my disrupted load.

Taking it to Abona meant amending the manifest again, apart from the problem of having to haul the extra ingots five to a cart. Besides, mine were four special bars: stolen pigs to be sold to strangers, stolen pigs that still contained their silver. *Not* for Abona! The other cart designated to go south could never carry eight. After much irrelevant argument of the type you get from men who are unused to solving problems at all, let alone standing outside on a dark day in the bitter cold, it was decided to leave my load here and smuggle it back to Vebiodunum on the return trip.

I volunteered to stay with the load.

After the rest left it grew horribly quiet. The few native huts were used by herdsmen in summer, deserted now. I had shelter, but as the weather hardened I realized that if it snowed badly my companions might be held up. I could be trapped here without food for a long while. Over the uplands came a veil of rain, so fine it neither settled nor fell, but clung to my face and clothes when I peered outside. For the first time in three months I found myself completely alone.

'Hello, Marcus!' I said, as if I was greeting a friend.

I stood and thought. This would have been the moment to escape, but the only reason I had been left there alone was that in the depths of winter the uplands were too isolated. Anyone who tried to run off would be found dead with the frozen cattle and drowned sheep in the spring. I might make it to the Gorges, but there was nothing there for me.

I still wanted to know how the ingots were shipped.

The rain stopped. It grew colder. I decided to act. Bent double, I clutched the ingots one at a time and staggered as far as I could across the ditch and away from the road. I then scraped a hiding place in the sodden ground. That was when I noticed only one of the bars carried the four stamps we used to denote that its silver still remained. Triferus was cheating the conspirators: they were trying to bribe the Praetorians with pipe lead! I sat back on my heels. If we told the Praetorians that, the conspirators would find themselves in trouble and Vespasian would be safe.

I buried all four bars. I marked the spot with a cairn of stones. Then I set out to walk back to the mines.

It was eight miles. Plenty of time to convince myself I was a fool. To keep my feet marching I had a long talk with Festus, my brother. Not that it helped; Festus thought I was a fool too.

Talking to a dead hero sounds strange, yet Festus was the type of magic character whose conversation made you feel light-headed even when he was alive. Out here, under a bloated sky, a frozen dot trudging over a dark plateau back into painful slavery of my own free will, talking to Festus smacked of greater reality than my own wild world.

Half a day later, on the final stretch, I plunged off the road taking a short cut across a bend. Roman roads go straight unless there is a reason. There was a reason for the great curve here: avoiding the gullies and pits of a worked out mine. As I stumbled through chest-high spears of dead bracken, the ground disappeared. My feet slipped on the fine frosted turf, I shot forwards on my back, crashing down into one of the pits. One heel caught awkwardly as I slid. Nothing hurt at first. When I started to climb out, lancing pain told me at once; I had broken a bone in my leg. Festus told me that it could only happen to me.

I lay on my back staring at the frozen sky and told my heroic brother a few home truths.

It began to snow. Dense silence settled. If I lay here, I would die. If I died here I might have atoned for what happened to Sosia, but apart from the report I had smuggled out to Hilaris – if Rufrius Vitalis ever found him and managed to make it intelligible – I had achieved nothing else. To die without telling my story would make nonsense of all I had endured.

Snow, cruelly tranquil, continued to fall. I had walked myself warm, but I could feel the heat leaving my body even as I lay. I spoke; no one answered me now.

Better to make the effort, even if the effort fails. I contrived a splint, as well as I could. I found an old stake, and tied it on with the goathair string I had been using as a belt. It was a poor job, but kept me upright, just.

I began to lurch on. Back to Veb. I would be useless at Veb, but I had nowhere else to go.

Someone – a woman I knew – asked me once, afterwards, why I did not claim sanctuary with the soldiers at the fortress.

103

There were two reasons – three. One: I still hoped to find out where the stolen pigs were sent. Two: a crazy, skeletal slave coming off the moor and whining that he was the finance secretary's personal representative on business affecting the Emperor could only expect a thrashing. Three: not all informers are perfect. I never thought of it.

I was numb. Exhausted. Windblown inside and out. My brain was wrenched about with disappointment and pain. I homed in on the mines. Limping into the current diggings, I stumbled before the foreman Cornix. When I told him I had left four stolen ingots unattended he let out a roar and seized one of the pit props we sometimes used to support an overhang. I opened my mouth to say I had buried the pigs safely. Then, before I could speak, through the snow gluing my eyelashes I dimly saw Cornix swinging the post towards me. It caught me in the midriff, cracking several ribs. My leg gave way, the splint collapsed, and I fainted as I fell.

When they flung me in a cell I came round just enough to hear Cornix exclaim, 'Let him rot!'

'What if the bounty hunter calls?'

'Nobody wants this sniveller back.' Cornix let out his rasping laugh. 'If anyone asks, say he's dead – *he will be soon!*'

That was when I really knew, I was never going home.

XXVIII

My hearing seemed unusually sharp. Understandable. Only noises from outside were keeping me sane; only my dregs of sanity kept me alive.

I could not move. No one came to speak to me. I could see nothing except the different shades of greyness that distinguished day from night on the pitted stones of my cell's damp walls. There were no windows. Some days the door cracked open for them to push in a thick-lipped bowl of greasy food. I marginally preferred the days when they forgot.

I did not know how long I had been here. Probably not even a week. A week to a man who has been left for dead feels a long time.

From the shuffling of their footsteps as the chained slaves were marched about, I had learned to distinguish whether it was raining or merely drifting with the eternal winter mist. Rumbling waggons were the common traffic, though sometimes I caught the jaunty clip of a pony's hooves and knew an officer from the fort had ridden past in his scarlet cloak. With the wind right, I could make out the distant chipping of axes and the thonk of wooden hods at the seams. The smelting furnace was a perpetual roar, varied only by the fervent wheeze of bellows on the cupellation hearths.

Sometimes now I remember what happened next, and smile.

One day a pony, drawing some sort of dainty cart amid a tangle of businesslike riders, passed the works then pulled up smartly nearby. A military voice named the procurator Flavius. Someone grumbled. Then another voice – sharp as the scream of an adze on wood: ' . . . the one you call Chirpy.'

Now I was in a bad way. Delirium, if not death itself, was snuggling up to me: it sounded like the senator's daughter. At first I could not even remember her name. Then I dragged it back to mind from another world: Helena.

'Now which was that . . . Dead, I believe – '

'Then I'll have to inspect the body! If he's buried, dig him up.'

Oh lady, let my servants fetch the silver wine set out for you!

The door creaked ajar on its one hinge in the unexpected dazzle of a flare.

'Oh yes! That's him – our precious runaway!'

I was almost too hoarse to swear at her, but I managed it.

Cornix the foreman stood just behind her shoulder, pitifully subdued.

After one distasteful glance around my cell she quipped tartly, 'What's this he has? Bedrest and special nursing?'

I felt sorry for Cornix. Her attitude was intolerable. Besides, she had a military escort; there was nothing he could do.

He hauled me from my thin pallet of stinking ferns to stretch me at her feet in the mud outside. I closed my eyes against the glazed light of huge wan clouds. I carried with me a young woman's sturdy shape in swathes of dark blue material, the crinkled woollen fringe on her dress, a frowning white face beneath twists of soft straight hair.

For a moment I nearly collapsed.

'Marcus!' rapped Helena Justina, in the patronizing tone she would naturally use to a disgraced slave.

My face lay in a puddle only inches from her feet.

Smart shoes. Slate-grey leather, punched with spirals of tiny holes. Much better ankles than she deserved.

'This is a fine scene! Uncle Gaius had such faith in you. Look at you now!' What did she expect? A runaway rarely packs clean tunics and his personal toilet sponge . . . I clung to reality in the chalky smudge of that familiar hostile face. 'Oh really Marcus! What have you achieved? A broken leg, fractured ribs, chilblains, ringworm, and filth!' She considered the dirt uneasily. She had me put through the baths they provided for officials before I disgraced her aunt's good pony trap. A soldier who must have known who I really was tied my leg to a new splint, too shamefaced to do it properly.

By the time Helena allowed me to ease into the cart, I had been thoroughly sluiced down and my rags exchanged for somebody's third-best tunic, which had a smell I found uncomfortable, though it was several times better than how I had stunk before. Cornix had slunk away for one of his afternoon bouts of torture and fornication in the sheds. I was shuddering;

her ladyship flung a travel rug over me with an angry hiss. I still felt damp. I had managed a rough and ready scrub, but bathing under the eyes of a soldier and Cornix was not a time for drying carefully between your toes.

My scalp itched madly with the shock of being clean. All my skin felt alive. The lightest breath of breeze bruised my face.

Helena Justina produced a cloak, which I vaguely recalled had been mine in another existence. Decent dark green garment with a stout metal toggle: I must have been a lad of taste and style. Somehow I clambered into the pony cart.

'Nice rig!' I told Helena, struggling to sound more like myself. Then since she was a woman, I offered like a good boy, 'Want me to drive?'

'No,' she said. Some people might have said 'No, thanks'. Still, I could barely stick upright on the seat as it was.

She organized herself before she deigned to speak again. 'If you had charge of a vehicle would you let me drive yours?'

'No,' I agreed.

'You wouldn't trust a woman; well, I won't trust a man.'

'Fair enough,' I said. Quite right; most men are wicked on wheels.

The pony set off jauntily and we soon left the settlement behind. Helena Justina, as you might expect, surged away in front; her small but stalwart mounted escort jingled meekly in the rear.

'Tell me if I go too fast and frighten you,' she challenged me, gazing straight ahead.

'You drive too fast – but you don't frighten me!' She had turned down a byway. 'This isn't right – take the road east over the uplands, lady, will you?'

'No. We have soldiers; there's no need to stay on the frontier. We need to go north. You have your friend Vitalis to thank for being rescued today. Last time he saw you he told Uncle Gaius you ought to be withdrawn whether you had completed your work or not. I volunteered to fetch you – better camouflage. Besides, I felt guilty about your grey-haired mother . . .' Since I could not remember discussing my mother, I let her rattle on. 'Uncle Gaius has that man Triferus under arrest at Glevum – '

Unused to explanations, my brain balked at so many facts. 'I see. North, eh?'

Conversation seemed a pointless effort. Let someone else take charge. This cart was a pretty toy; too fragile to bear four ingots' weight. We might at a pinch have organized something with the soldiers' ponies – but I was too exhausted to care. Still, I must have shifted restlessly. She slowed the cart.

'What have you been up to on the moor? Falco! Tell me the truth.'

'I hid four stolen ingots under a cairn.'

'Evidence?' she demanded.

'If you like.'

She must have drawn her own conclusions, for she whipped up the poor pony until it flew along. Her eyes flashed.

'You mean, a nice little pension for you!'

We left them behind. For all I know my four ingots are still there.

Helena Justina continued to drive fast. Her husband probably divorced her to save his skin. However, I was never really frightened. She handled the pony cart well. She had the proper combination of patience and courage. The horse trusted her entirely; after a few miles so did I. It was fifty miles to Glevum, so that was just as well.

We stopped a couple of times. She let me slide out. The first time I was sick, though it had nothing to do with her driving. She left me to rest, while she spoke in a low voice to one of the soldiers, then before we set off again she brought me some sweetened wine from a flask. Her steadying grip stayed on my shoulder. At the strange touch of a woman's hand I began to sweat.

'We can stop down the road at a *mansio* if you want.' She was matter-of-fact, though watching me closely.

I shook my head without speaking. I wanted to go on. I preferred to die in a military fort where they would bury me with a headstone over my urn, rather than in a roadhouse where I would be pitched into a trench with a ton of broken winejars and their run-over tabby cat. It struck me there might be a reason why Helena Justina whipped along at such a cracking pace: she did not want to be stuck in the wilderness with my corpse. I thanked Jove for her ruthless good sense. I did not want my corpse to be stuck with her in any case.

She read my mind, or more likely my sick face.

'Don't worry, Falco, I'll bury you properly!'

XXIX

I thought I was back at the mines.

No. Another world. I had left the mines, though they will never quite leave me.

I was lying on a high, hard bed in a small square room at a legionary hospital. Unhurried footsteps sometimes paced the long corridor round the courtyard at the back of their administration block. I recognized the evil reek of antiseptic turpentine. I felt the reassuring pressure of neat, firm bandaging. I was warm. I was clean. I was resting in tranquillity in a quiet, caring place.

Yet I was terrified.

What had woken me was a trumpet on the ramparts, sounding the night watch. A fort, I could cope with a fort. I heard the spiteful squawk of sea gulls. Must be Glevum. Glevum stood on the Estuary. She had done it then. For hours now I had been asleep in the Second Augusta's big new headquarters base. The Second. I belonged to them; I was home.

I wanted to cry.

'Thinks he's back on army service,' said the dryly amused voice of the procurator Flavius.

I never saw him. I was a felled log surging through warm barley soup, though my legs and arms could hardly thrash against the bumbling grains; they had filled me with poppyjuice to kill the pain.

'Marcus, rest now, I've had your report from Vitalis; I've been able to act on it already. Well done!'

Gaius, my friend; *my friend, who sent me there* . . .

I struggled abruptly; someone else gripped my arm. 'Hush! It's over; you're quite safe.'

Helena, his niece, my enemy. *My enemy, who came and fetched me back* . . .

'Lie still, Falco; don't make such a fuss . . .'

The dependable vindictiveness of Helena's voice swung with me through delirium. To a freed slave, tyranny can be oddly comforting.

XXX

Awake again.

Their opium had ebbed away. When I moved pain shot back. A red tunic, brooched on one shoulder with the medical snake and staff, loomed over me, then sheered off again when I stared him in the eye. I recognized the complete absence of bedside manner: must be the chief orderly. Pupils stretched their necks behind him like awestruck ducklings jostling their mother duck.

'Tell me the truth, Hippocrates!' I jested. They never tell you the truth.

He tickled me up and down my ribs like a moneychanger on an abacus. I yelped, though not because his hands were cold.

'Still in discomfort – that will last several months. He can expect a great deal of pain. No real problems if he avoids getting pneumonia . . .' He sounded disappointed at the thought that I might. 'Emaciated specimen; he's vulnerable to gangrene in this leg.' My heart sank. 'Best amputate, whilst he has some strength.' I glared at him with a heartbreak that brightened him up. 'We can give him something!' he consoled his listeners. Did you know, the main part of a surgeon's training is how to ignore the screams?

'Why not wait and see what develops!' I managed to croak.

'Your young woman asked me that – ' Now he sounded quite respectful; probably impressed to discover someone even more bad mannered than him.

'She's not mine! Don't insult me,' I growled viciously, letting myself get annoyed over the girl as a way of fighting off what he had said. But it had to be faced. 'Do what you have to then – *take the leg!*'

I went back to sleep.

He woke me up again.

'Flavius Hilaris wants to interview you urgently. Is that all right?'

111

'You're the doctor.'
'What do you want me to do?'
'Leave me alone.'
I went back to sleep again.

They never leave you alone.
'Marcus – ' Flavius Hilaris. He wanted me to tell him again everything about the mine that I had already passed on through Rufrius Vitalis. He was too polite to say he was taking formal evidence now in case I died under surgery – but I understood.

I told him all I knew. Anything to make him go away.

As far as the plot went, Gaius told me that Triferus the contractor was refusing to talk. It was deep winter now, snow in the hills. No chance of trailing the waggons that turned south – no waggons moving, probably for many weeks. Gaius would lock Triferus in a cell and abandon him; try again when I could help. I would be carried to the Sacred Springs to convalesce – if I lived.

He sat for a long time at my bedside, grasping my wrist; he seemed upset. He said he had told Rome they should pay me double rates, I smiled. After thirty years of service he should have known better than to try. I remembered thinking a long time ago, *it could be him!* I smiled again.

I drifted back to sleep.

The surgeon was called Simplex. When they introduce themselves by name, you know the intended treatment is at best a drastic gamble and at worst very painful indeed.

Simplex had spent fourteen years in the army. He could calm a sixteen-year-old soldier with an arrow shot into his head. He could seal blisters, dose dysentery, bathe eyes, even deliver babies from the wives the legionaries were not supposed to have. He was bored with all that. I was his favourite patient now. Among his set of spatulas, scalpels, probes, shears, and forceps, he owned a shiny great mallet big enough to bash in fencing stakes. Its use in surgery was for amputations, driving home his chisel through soldiers' joints. He had the chisel and the saw too: a complete toolbag, all laid out on a table by my bed.

They drugged me, but not enough. Flavius Hilaris wished me luck, then slipped out of the room. I don't blame him. If I hadn't been strapped down to the bed with four six-foot set-faced cavalrymen grappling my shoulders and feet, I would have shot straight out after him myself.

112

Through the drugs I saw Simplex approach. I had changed my mind. Now I knew him for a knife-happy maniac. I tried to speak; no sound emerged. I tried to shout.

Someone else cried out: a woman's voice.

'*Stop it at once!*' Helena Justina. I had no idea when she came in. I had not realized she was there. 'There's no gangrene!' stormed the senator's daughter. She seemed to lose her temper wherever she was. 'I would expect an army surgeon to know – gangrene has its own distinctive smell. Didius Falco's feet may be cheesy, but they're not that bad!' Wonderful woman; an informer in trouble could always count on her. 'He has chilblains. In Britain that's nothing to wonder at – all he needs for those is a hot turnip mash! Pull his leg as straight as you can, then leave him alone; *the poor man has suffered enough!*'

I passed out with relief.

They tried twice to pull my leg straight. The first time I ground the pad of cloth between my teeth in shocked silence while hot tears raced down either side of my neck. The second time I was expecting it; the second time I screamed.

Someone sobbed.

I gurgled, but before I suffocated, a hand – presumably attached to one of the heavy-squad holding me down – removed the pad from my mouth. I was drenched in perspiration. Someone took the trouble to wipe my face.

At the same time a shaft of piquant perfume pierced my senses, marvellous as that Regal Balsam concocted for the kings of Parthia from the essences of twenty-five individual fine oils. (I had never been there, but any spare-time poet knows about the long-haired rulers of Parthia; they are always good for enlivening a limp ode.)

It was not Regal Balsam, but still a wonderful smell. I remember thinking cheerfully, some of these fifteen-stone horse guards are not all that they appear . . .

XXXI

At Aquae Sulis I spent five weeks under the care of the procurator's personal physician. Hot springs gushed out of the rock at a shrine where puzzled Celts still came to dedicate coinage to Sul, gazing tolerantly at the brisk new plaque which announced that Roman Minerva was assuming management. There was that furtive atmosphere of commerce disguised as religion which always hangs around shrines. Rome had replaced some basic native equipment with a proper lead-lined reservoir, yet I could not believe that anything could ever be made of this place. Oh there were plans, but there are always plans. We sat in the reservoir, which was full of sand thrown up by the spring, drank flat, tepid water laden with foul-tasting minerals, and watched red-nosed building surveyors clambering about the cliffs, trying to convince themselves there was scope for a vibrant leisure spa.

We played a lot of draughts. I hate draughts. I *loathe* draughts played against an Egyptian physician who always wins. However, there was not much else to do in a spa that was still on the drawing board, in Britain, at the end of a snowy March. I might have chased after women, but I had given women up. In my present state, even if I caught one it would be hard work doing anything a woman would appreciate.

The hot springs helped, but while I lay in them I stared into space with a dark look. The bones might heal, but never my slave's soul. The procurator's physician said drinking the water had given him piles. I answered I was sorry to hear that, but he may have noticed that I sounded insincere.

Sometimes I brooded about Sosia; it did nothing to help.

Back to Glevum. Hilaris and I tackled Triferus together. Action did me good, and we made a strong team. Gaius sat on his official chair of office, a folding do with yellowed ivory legs

114

that he told me was ruin for the back. I roamed about in a menacing way.

Triferus was a loud British wideboy, all twisty electrum necklets and narrow, pointed shoes. He wore the toga such middlemen had been encouraged to adopt, but the soldiers who dragged him in peeled that off him at a nod from us. We parked him on a stool so if he turned his head in either direction he was eyeball to muscled thigh with chain-mailed auxiliaries – two morose Spanish horsemen, who ignored his shifty jokes. (Only their officers spoke Latin; we had chosen the guards for that reason.)

Apart from the torques beneath that puffy British face, he could have been any barrow boy in any city in the world. He used the forenames Tiberius Claudius – possibly a freed slave named for the old Emperor, but more likely some minor tribal dignitary, honoured as an ally at some past date. I doubted he could produce a diploma to support his citizenship.

'We know how you operate: just cough up the names!' I barked at him.

'All right, Falco,' murmured Gaius, like a senior man being hopelessly overruled from Rome. 'This is Britain, we do things differently here. Triferus, whether I can help is up to you. This man is an Imperial agent – '

Triferus tried bluff. 'Weights and measures? Safety regulations? What's your problem, officer?' He had a high voice with an irritating nasal lilt. He belonged to the Coritani, a self-sufficient tribe on the midland plain.

I tested the point of a dagger between my thumbs. I glanced at Gaius; he nodded.

'There's nothing you can tell me about the lead mines,' I began. 'Triferus, I've been in there to explore the whole shambles for myself.' His face shone with sweat; I had caught him off guard. 'Your system stinks, from the shafts to the furnaces. Even the bakers in the village are using silver shavings for small change – '

'Trouble with the dockets is it?' he whined with an innocent wink. 'Treasury interference? Procedures to clear?'

I flung my nugget of silver onto a tripod table where it spun in front of Triferus on a level with his nose. I slammed my hand onto it. Even Gaius looked surprised.

'Three weeks on the cupellation bellows and that was my haul! Make a dainty finger ring for some lucky skirt in Rome.'

Triferus abruptly came the brave boy: 'Shove it up your arse!'

115

I beamed at him pleasantly: *'Oh I've done that!'*
Gaius blenched.

I strode up to Triferus, grabbing at one of his skinny torques
so it pressed against his jugular just enough to make a dent.

'A smart slave can buy his passage to Gaul, if he survives
your murderous foreman. Cornix diddles his tax-free bonus;
the chain gangs have their sad little dodges; *you* organize a
private racket of your own. How did these traitors from Rome
lean on you – threaten exposure unless you cut them in?'

'Look, you clerks have to face facts!' For one last desperate
moment Triferus continued to pretend. 'Mining is a special
case. It's not like selling beer and oysters to the troops – '

'Don't waste time on him, sir!' I snarled at the procurator.
'Let me take him back to Rome. We have decent equipment
there; he'll squeal. After that, the Vatican Circus – lion-feed!'
Releasing the torque as if the owner disgusted me too much to
bother, I turned to Gaius with an irritable shout. 'Ask him about
the stamps! The ingots he steals himself are banged four times
if they still contain silver – that's one bar in four. The rest have
been bled, but this enterprising bastard sells them as intact.
How long before our political hopefuls spot his double-cross? I
wouldn't like to wear the boots of a man who bribes the
Praetorians with counterfeit dosh!'

'Triferus, can't you see they know!' For the first time the
financial procurator spoke in a voice stripped of all pretence.
'British ingots have been found loose in Rome. Unless we arrest
the plotters before they get to you, you can kiss goodbye to
much more than your tender for the lead franchise in the
Malvern Peaks. Vespasian's in for the duration, whatever you
have been told. Save yourself, man, turn in whatever evidence
you can to the state – it's your only way to survive!'

Triferus took on a complexion like unpainted wall plaster.

He asked to speak to Gaius alone. He gave him two names.

Gaius wrote a letter to the Emperor, which I was to carry,
though he refused to tell me what the two names were. I
thought he was playing the pointless bureaucrat, though afterwards I understood why.

Gaius and I travelled coastwards to Durnovaria to his favourite villa, for me to ask his honourable niece Helena whether she
was ready to travel home and if so, would she wish to be
escorted through Europe by such as me. Gaius drove me down.

116

We tripped a hundred miles at a pace so sedate I longed to wrench the reins out of his hand.

I have to admit I hankered for Helena Justina's nippier driving style.

XXXII

Gaius came with me to his villa because he wanted to prune his vines. They were miserable specimens. He had lived in Britain so long he had forgotten what a vine was really like.

The procurator's villa was a rich farm in a small river valley with views of low green hills. The soft climate seemed well-suited to a man with a pain in his ribs. The house was full of books and toys. His wife and children had retreated to Londinium after the Saturnalian holiday, but I could imagine what life was like in summer when they were here. It was a house where I could have languished for a long time, the sort I wanted one day for myself.

Gaius amused himself pottering into Durnovaria to officiate as local magistrate. His objectionable niece was at the villa, but she kept to herself. Had I liked Helena Justina better I might have thought her shy; as I didn't, I called her unsociable instead. Since she had not returned to the comforts of Londinium with Aelia Camilla, she presumably intended going back to Rome now, but plans for her journey remained happily vague.

I was enjoying myself in this hospitable house. By day I read, wrote letters, or limped around the farm. The staff were friendly and being pampered felt quite acceptable. Every evening I talked cheerfully with my host. Even in Britain this was an ideal Roman life. I did not want to find the energy to leave.

One day, when it was raining too dismally for Gaius to drive off and impose fines on Celtic cattle thieves, he approached me. 'Rufrius Vitalis asked me to have a word with you. I gather you had arranged to fix him up with a passage to Rome, acting as Helena's baggage master?'

'Let me guess – he doesn't want to go?'

'Well, it's partly my fault,' Gaius grinned. 'I was impressed with him. I've offered him a contract in the lead mine, clearing up the procedural abuses as my official auditor.'

118

'Good choice. He'll do well for you. Besides which,' I chortled, 'I reckon he and a certain dumpling called Truforna cannot bear to part!'

The procurator smiled in his prim way, avoiding details of other people's personal lives. Then he pointed out that if Vitalis was absenting himself, someone else would have to shepherd Helena . . .

'Has she spoken to you, Falco?'

'We don't speak. She thinks I'm a rat.'

He looked pained. 'Oh I'm sure that's not right. Helena Justina appreciates all you have done. She was deeply shocked by your condition when she picked you up at the mines – '

'Oh I can live with it!' I was lying on a couch, making good use of a bowl of winter pears which the villa steward had carefully selected for me from the farm store. I took the opportunity to probe. 'Your niece seems, let's be polite about it, rather overwrought.' Flavius Hilaris gave me a stern glance. I added in a reasonable tone, 'I'm not trying to gossip. If I do escort her, it will help if I know what the problem is.'

'That's fair.' My new friend Gaius was also a reasonable man. 'Well! When she came out to stay with us after her divorce, she seemed subdued and confused. I suspect she still is – only she hides it better now.'

'Can you tell me what went wrong?'

'Only hearsay. As far as I know, the couple were never close. Her uncle, my wife's brother Publius, had known the young man; it was Publius who proposed the match to her father. At the time Helena described her future husband to my wife in a letter as *a senator of standing, without indecent habits.*'

'Pretty cool!'

'Quite. Aelia Camilla did not approve of it.'

'Still, safer than starting starry-eyed.'

'Perhaps. Anyway, Helena never expected a passionate meeting of minds, but eventually she found that for her a high position and good manners were not enough. She did confide in me recently. She would rather he had picked his nose and goosed the kitchen girls – then at least talked to her!'

We both laughed at this, though sympathetically. If I had liked women with a sense of humour, a wench who could say that might have appealed to me.

'Have I got it wrong then, Gaius, did *he* divorce *her*?'

'No. Once she found they were incompatible, Helena Justina wrote the notice of divorce herself.'

'Ah! She does not believe in pretence!'

'No. But she's sensitive – so you've seen the results!'

By now it was obvious the procurator's conscience was prickling him for speaking so freely. So, I let the subject drop.

The next time Gaius was going into town I tagged along. I took the opportunity to acquire twenty assorted pewter beakers, local products made from an alloy of tin and lead.

'Souvenirs for my nephews and nieces! Plus a few "silver" porridge spoons for the new members of the family my sisters are bound to present to me proudly when I get home.'

'The Gauls should hear you coming!' Gaius scoffed. (My twenty beakers were rattling well.)

It was still difficult to think sensibly of going home.

This being Britain, much of the time we were at Durnovaria Helena Justina had had a ferocious cold. While she stayed in her room with her head buried in a jug of steaming pine oil it was easy to forget she was there. When she emerged, and dashed off somewhere in a pony cart, I became curious. She was out all day. She could hardly have gone shopping – I knew from my own attempts there was nothing much to buy. When my friend the steward brought me some leeks in wine sauce to tempt my appetite (which was heartily improved, and I come from a market-gardening family so I love leeks), I asked where their young lady had gone. He didn't know, but chaffed me about my well-known reluctance to travel with her.

'She can't be as fearsome as all that!' he remonstrated.

'The honourable Helena Justina,' I stated callously, spooning away at the leeks like a true market gardener's grandson, 'would make Medusa's snakes look as harmless as a pot of fishing worms!'

At that moment, Helena Justina whipped into the room.

She ignored me. That was normal. She looked deeply upset. That was not. I was certain she had heard.

The steward absconded rapidly, which was all I could expect. On my invalid couch, I sank into a nest of tasselled cushions. I waited for the tidal wave to break.

Helena had taken a ladylike chair. Her feet perched on a footstool, her hands lay in her lap. She was wearing a dull grey dress and an expensively tasteful necklace of tubular agate beads in a mixture of red and brown. For a moment she seemed lost in some grave, introspective mood. I noticed something: when she was not crackling at me, the senator's daughter could transform her face. To anyone else she might have appeared a calm, competent, thoughtful young woman, whose good birth

120

made her go pink doing business with men, yet perfectly approachable.

She roused herself.

'Feeling better, Falco?' she demanded derisively. I lay on my couch and looked pale. 'What are you writing?' Changing the subject with a cool look, she caught me off guard.

'Nothing.'

'Don't be so childish; I know you write poetry!'

With an exaggerated gesture I laid open my wax tablet. She jumped out of her chair and marched across to look. The tablet was blank. I did not write poetry any more. I felt no obligation to tell her why.

Disconcerted myself, I waded in: 'Your uncle tells me you'll be leaving Britain soon?'

'No choice,' she clipped tersely. 'Uncle Gaius is insisting I take the Imperial post with you.'

'Take the post by all means,' I remarked.

'Are you saying you won't act for me?'

I smiled slightly. 'Lady, you have not asked.'

Helena bit her lip.

'Is this because of the mines?'

The face I was wearing belonged in a chain gang but I said, 'No. Helena Justina, I am open to offers – but don't assume you can dictate which I accept.'

'Didius Falco, I assume nothing about you; not any more!' We were sparring, but without our usual relish; her concentration seemed to be painfully distracted. 'Given your choice – and acceptable pay – will you consent to escort me home?'

I had intended to refuse. Helena Justina looked at me steadily, acknowledging that. She had clear, sensible, persuasive eyes in an intriguing shade of brown . . . I heard myself saying, 'Given the choice, of course.'

'Oh Falco! Tell me your rates.'

'Your father is paying me.'

'Let him. I'll pay you myself – then if I want to end your contract I will.'

Every contract should have an escape clause. I told her my rates.

She was evidently still angry.

'Is anything the matter, ladyship?'

'I've been down to the coast,' she told me, frowning. 'Trying to organize our crossing to Gaul.'

121

'I would have done that!'

'Well, it's done.' I watched her hesitate. She needed some-body to share some trouble; there was only me. 'Done, but not without annoyance. I found a boat. But Falco, there was a ship at the shale yards that I hoped would have taken us – the captain refused. The ship belongs to my ex-husband,' she forced out. I said nothing. She went on brooding. 'Petty!' she remarked. 'Petty, unnecessary, bad-mannered, and vile!'

The hysterical edge in her tone had disturbed me. Still, I make it my rule, never to interfere between married couples – even when they are not married any more.

When we went to the coast, Flavius Hilaris embraced me on the quayside like a friend.

Of all the men I met on this business I liked him the most. I never told him that. (I know he realized.) But I did tell him, no one but me could have found a case where only the civil servants were straight. We both laughed, as we grimaced with regret.

'Look after our young woman,' Gaius commanded me, hug-ging Helena goodbye. Then to her, 'And you look after him!'

I suppose he meant, if I was seasick. Which I was, though needless to say I looked after myself.

XXXIII

We had a long sea crossing, in a boat wallowing under a load of blue-grey British marble, to Gesoriacum in Gaul. Then overland to Durocortorum, where we turned off through Belgium into Germany and down the military corridor on the Rhine.

Use of the Imperial courier service is a dismal privilege. The special messengers on horseback cover fifty miles a day. We classed ourselves as a less urgent despatch and took an official carriage: four wheels on stout axles, high seats, change of mules every dozen miles, and after the double distance food and lodging – all charged to the locals thanks to our pass. We were bitterly cold all the way.

We reached a professional understanding; we had to. It was too far to keep quarrelling. I was competent, she could see that; she could behave when she chose. Whenever we stopped she stayed within sight, and if she hardly ever talked to me, neither did she invite trouble from thieves, lechers, or tiresome inn landlords who tried to talk to her. Village idiots and beggars at bridges took one look at the set of her jaw, then slunk away.

All the couriers and drivers thought I slept with her, but I expected that. By her taut expression when she spoke to them I could tell she knew what they thought. She and I avoided the subject. Being viewed as the lover of Helena Justina was something I found difficult to pass off as a joke.

At the big military base of Argentoratum on the Rhine we met Helena's younger brother, who was stationed there. I got on well with him: those of us with ferocious sisters usually find common ground. Young Camillus organized a dinner that was the one bright spot on our appalling trip. Afterwards he took me aside and enquired anxiously whether anyone had thought to pay me for escorting her ladyship. I did admit I was already booking her twice. When he stopped laughing we rolled out to tour the nightlife of the town. He told me in confidence that his sister had had to endure a tragic life. I didn't laugh; he was a lad, he had a kind heart, and anyway the idiot was drunk.

She looked fond of her brother. That was fair enough. What tickled me was his affection for her.

At Lugdunum, where we picked up a boat down the Rhodanus, I narrowly escaped falling in. We had almost missed the boat altogether: it had already pulled in its gangplank and cast off, but the crew hooked the vessel to the river bank for us to leap across if we chose. I lobbed our baggage over the rail, then since none of the rivermen showed any sign of helping, parked myself with one foot on the deck and one on land to act as a human handrope while her ladyship pulled herself aboard.

Helena was not a girl to betray doubts. I held out both my hands. While the boat bobbed almost out of reach, she grasped hold bravely and I passed her across. The boatmen lifted up their grappling hooks at once. I was left dangling. As the gap widened I braced myself for the shock of the icy Rhodanus until her ladyship glanced back, saw what was happening, then gripped my arm. For a second I hung spread-eagled; then she tightened her grip, I kicked off from land, and clapped down on the boat deck like a crab.

I was highly embarrassed. Most people would have exchanged a grin. But Helena Justina turned away without a word.

Fourteen hundred miles: long, bruising days, then nights in identical foreign resthouses full of what she rightly thought were quite appalling men. She never complained. Bad weather, spring tides, the couriers a contemptuous bunch, *me*: not a moan out of her. By Massilia I was mildly impressed.

I was also concerned. She looked tired; her voice sounded colourless. The inn was crammed and by now I knew how much she would hate the crush. I went to her room to collect her at dinnertime in case she felt nervous. She hung back, reluctant, pretending she was not hungry, but my cheery visage managed to lure her out.

'You all right?'

'Yes. Falco, don't fuss.'

'Look a bit poorly.'

'I'm all right.' One of those days. She was human after all.

I tucked a shawl round her; I'd cosset a prickly porcupine if it was paying me twice.

'Thank you.'

124

'All part of the service,' I said, and took her to dine.

I was glad that she came. I did not want to eat alone. It was my birthday. No one knew. I was thirty years old.

We stayed at Massilia at an inn near the port. It was no worse and no better than the rest of Massilia; it was terrible. Too many strangers do a town no good. I was stiff from the road, and worried about my aching ribs. I felt a constant prickle as if we were being watched. I hated the food.

The acoustics in the dining hall were appalling. It was deafening. At one point I was called away by our ship's captain who wanted to make arrangements for embarkation. Quite straightforward: pay in advance, no frills, dawn start, bring your own baggage, find your own way to the docks or miss the boat. *Thanks. What a wonderful town!*

When I rejoined Helena she was driving off the innkeeper's lurcher who had his muzzle in my bowl. It being southern Gaul, where they know how to make strangers suffer, we were eating fish stew – grainy stuff dyed red and full of broken bits of shell. I put my bowl on the floor for the dog. Few punishments match a birthday in Massilia, starving, and with a girl who regards you as if you had a niffy smell.

I persuaded Helena to sit out in the garden. That meant I went too, which was why I bothered to ask: I wanted some air. It was dusk. We could hear distant sounds of the port, there was running water and a fishpond with plopping frogs. No one else was about. Although it was cold, we sat on a stone bench. We were both tired, both allowing ourselves to relax slightly now Rome was only another sailing trip away.

'This is more peaceful! Feeling better now?'

'Don't fidget me,' she complained, so I reproached her with my birthday.

'Bad luck,' was all she said.

'Well, Marcus!' I mused. 'Celebrating your feast day five hundred miles from home: gritty fish stew, filthy Gallic wine, a pain in your side, a callous client . . .' As I rambled on amiably, Helena Justina finally smiled at me.

'Stop grumbling. It's your own fault. If I'd known it was your birthday I'd have bought you a tipsy cake. How old now?'

'Thirty. Downhill to the dark boat across the Styx. Probably be sick over the side in Charon's ferry too . . . So how old are you?' This was daring, but she sounded almost sorry to have missed the tipsy cake.

'Oh . . . Twenty-three.'

I laughed. 'Time yet to rope in a new husband . . .' Then I ventured in a casual voice, 'My ladies usually like to tell me about their divorces.'

'It's your feast day,' Helena Justina snorted.

'So treat me . . . Where did you go wrong?'

'Fornication at the horse barracks!'

'Liar!' I didn't like her, but that had to be untrue. She was strict as a brick. That was probably the reason why I thought I didn't like her. 'His fault then. What did he do? Too mean with the opal earrings or too free with the Syrian flute girls?'

She just said, 'No.'

'Beat you?' I risked. By now I was insatiably curious.

'No. If you really need to know,' Helena declared, with an effort, 'he was not sufficiently interested in anything about me to bother. We were married for four years. We had no children. Neither of us was unfaithful – ' She paused. Probably knew, you can never be sure. 'I enjoyed running my own household but what was it for? So I divorced him.'

She was a secretive person; I felt sorry I asked. Usually around this point they cry; not her.

'Want to talk about it? Did you quarrel?'

'Once.'

'What about?'

'Oh . . . Politics.'

It was the last thing I expected, yet utterly typical. I burst out laughing. 'Look, I'm sorry! But you can't stop there – do tell!'

I was glimpsing now what all the matter was. Helena Justina was brave enough not only to have brought her restlessness upon herself, but also to see how badly her present sense of despair affected her soul. Quite possibly the better life she was striving for did not even exist.

I wanted to reach out to squeeze her hand, but she was not that sort of woman. Perhaps that was how her husband had felt about her too.

She decided to tell me. I waited to be startled, for nothing she ever said was conventional. She began to speak, in a cautious tone; I listened gravely. Helena explained what had led to her divorce.

And as she told me, my mind returned in stunned disbelief to the silver pigs.

XXXIV

'In the Year of the Four Emperors,' Helena began, 'my family
– father, Uncle Gaius, *me* – supported Vespasian. Uncle Gaius
had known him for years. We all admired the man. My husband
had no strong views. He was a trader – Arabian spices, ivory,
Indian porphyry, pearls. One day, some people at our house
were talking about Vespasian's second son, Domitian. It was
when he tried to involve himself in the German revolt, just
before Vespasian came home. They convinced themselves this
callow youth would make an ideal Emperor – attractive enough
to be popular, yet easy for them to manipulate. I was furious!
When they left, I tackled my husband – ' She hesitated. I
squinted at her sideways, deciding it was best not to interrupt.
In the twilight her eyes had become the colour of old honey –
the last dark scrape that lurks just out of reach of your finger
in the bottom corners of the pot so you cannot bear to throw it
away.

'Oh, Didius Falco, what can I say? This quarrel was not the
end of our marriage, but it made me see the distance between
us. He would not admit me to his confidence; I could not
support him as I should. Worst of all, he would never even
listen to my point of view!' A wild Cretan bull would not have
made me declare the man feared she was right.

'On spices and porphyry he must have been well set up,' I
suggested. 'You could have led a quiet life, no interference – '

'So I could!' she agreed angrily. Some women would have
thought themselves fortunate, taken a lover, taken several,
complained to their mothers while they spent their husbands'
cash. Reluctantly, I admired her single-mindedness.

'Why did he marry you?'

'Public life – a wife was compulsory. And choosing me tied
him to Uncle Publius.'

'Did your father approve of him?'

'You know families. The undertow of pressure, built up

over years. My father has a habit of doing what his brother wants. Anyway, my husband looked a perfectly normal man: overdeveloped sense of self-interest, undernourished sense of fun – '

Not a lot a man could say! To calm her I asked a practical question: 'I thought senators were not allowed to engage in trade?'

'That was why he went into partnership with Uncle Publius. He provided the investment, all the documents were in my uncle's name.'

'So your man was rich?'

'His father was. Though they suffered in the Year of the Four Emperors – '

'What happened then?'

'Is this an interrogation, Falco?' Quite suddenly she laughed. It was the first time I heard that twist of private amusement, an unexpectedly appealing note that made me inadvertently giggle in return. 'Oh well! When Vespasian announced his claim and blockaded the corn supplies at Alexandria to put pressure on the senate to support him, there were difficulties trading east. My husband and my uncle tried to explore new European markets – Uncle Publius even visited Britain to investigate tribal exports from the Celts! Uncle Gaius was not altogether pleased,' Helena added.

'Why not?'

'They don't get on.'

'Why not?'

'Different types.'

'What does Aelia Camilla think? Did she side with her husband or her brother Publius?'

'Oh, she has a very soft spot for Uncle Publius – for the same reasons he irritates Uncle Gaius.'

Her ladyship was still amused. She had the kind of laugh I wanted to hear again. I nudged at it: 'What's so funny? What reasons?'

'I won't say. Well, don't mock . . . Years ago when they lived in Bithynia, when my aunt was a child, Uncle Publius taught her to drive his racing chariot!' I could not imagine it. Aelia Camilla had appeared so dignified. 'You know Uncle Gaius – the nicest kind of man, often adventurous, but he can be rather staid.' I had guessed. 'Uncle Gaius complains that Aunt Aelia *drives too fast*! I'm afraid she taught me,' Helena confessed.

I leaned back my head and sombrely tutted at the sky. 'My good friend your uncle is quite right!'

'Didius Falco, don't be ungrateful. You were so desperately ill I had to hurry – you were perfectly safe!'

Out of character, she raised her arm and pretended to box me round the ears. I blocked the movement, casually catching her wrist. Then I stopped.

I turned Helena Justina's hand palm upwards and wrinkled my nose, breathing in the perfume I had noticed. She had a firm wrist, bare of jewellery tonight. Her hands were cold, like mine, but the scent hummed – something like cinnamon but much more deeply resonant. Made me think of Parthian kings.

'Now there's an exotic attar!'

'Malabathron,' she told me, wriggling, but not much. 'From India. An immensely expensive relic of my husband – '

'Generous!'

'Waste of money. The fool never noticed it.'

'Perhaps,' I teased, 'he had a cold he couldn't shift.'

'For four years?'

We were both laughing. I would have to let her go. No opportunity appearing, I bent my head and enjoyed another sniff.

'*Malabathron!* Lovely. My favourite! Does it come from the gods?'

'No, it comes from a tree.' I could feel her growing anxious, but she was too proud to tell me to let go.

'Four years, so you were a bride at what – nineteen?'

'Eighteen. Quite old. Like my husband's cold – difficult to shift!'

'Oh I doubt that!' I commented gallantly.

When they favour me with their stories, I always give them my advice. 'You should laugh at him more.'

'Perhaps I should laugh at myself.'

Only a maniac would have tried to kiss her hand. I replaced it like a gentleman in Helena Justina's lap.

'Thank you,' I said quietly, in a changed voice.

'What's that for?'

'Something you once did.'

We sat quietly. I leaned back, stretching my leg and folding one hand over my sorely aching ribs. I wondered what she was like, before the rich fool with the snuffle made Helena so venomous to other people and so wretched with herself.

While I was wondering, the evening star materialized among

high rags of racing cloud. The noises from the inn behind us had become more subdued as the clientele told dirty stories in twelve languages during the lull between simple gluttony and drinking themselves sick. Carp in the pond broke surface with a greater urgency. It was a good time for thinking, here at the end of a long journey with nothing to do but wait for our boat. Here in a garden. Here, speaking to a sensible woman with whom a man who took a little trouble could so easily exchange thoughts.

'*Mars Ultor*, I came so close . . . I just wish I had managed to find how those ingots are shipped out!'

Fretting aloud. Hardly expecting answers.

'Falco,' Helena began carefully. 'You know I went to the coast. The day I came back angry – '

I chuckled. 'A day, like any other day!'

'Listen! There was something I never told you. They were loading shale. Lopsided pantry goods – beakers, bowls, candlesticks, smirking sea lion table legs. It's hideous stuff. Goodness knows who would ever buy it. It needs to be oiled or it crumbles away . . .'

I squirmed guiltily, remembering the tray I had given to my mother. 'Oh lady! Something like that could be their cover. Did you think to ask – '

'Of course. Falco, the man with this gimcrack export market is – Atius Pertinax.'

Pertinax! His was the last name I expected to encounter here. Pertinax, trading in poor quality kitchenware! Atius Pertinax: that pointy-nosed aedile who had me arrested when he was looking for Sosia, then beat me up and broke my furniture! I spat out a short word used by slaves in lead mines which I hoped Helena would not understand.

'There's no need to be disgusting,' she replied in a still voice.

'There's every need, lady! Do you know that twitchy tick?'

Helena Justina the senator's daughter, who constantly caused me such astonishment, recited in a voice which became uncharacteristically subdued, 'Didius Falco, you're not very bright. Yes I know him. Of course I know him; I was married to the man.'

Too much travelling finally overwhelmed me. I felt squashed and sick.

XXXV

'Now you think it's me.'

'What?'

You spend months stalking a problem that constantly escapes. Then cover more ground in half a second than your brain can comprehend.

This was why Decimus had spoken of Pertinax in such a reluctant tone: Pertinax was his misery of a son-in-law. *Atius Pertinax!* Now I knew. I knew how the silver pigs were carried to Italy, by whom, and how concealed: under a cargo so dull the customs force at Ostia – who operate the luxury tax and have perfect artistic taste – glanced once inside the hold, groaned at the ghastly shale, then never stooped to search his boat. Poor Helena had innocently tried to arrange our passage on a ship weighed down to the gunnels with silver pigs!

More. At the start of all this Atius Pertinax, as aedile in the Capena Gate Sector, would have been the snoop in the praetor's office who heard where his praetor's friend Decimus had hidden the lost ingot in the Forum – probably *he* arranged to have Sosia Camillina snatched from home. After I spoiled that, he nosed out that she was with me, told her father, then used Publius as an excuse to arrest me for stalking in too close. All this in high panic, because the ingot lost in the street might have pointed to him.

Helena was his wife.

'Your first thought,' she insisted, 'will be that this implicates me.'

She was not his wife now.

'You're too straight.' My second thought – always the best.

She goaded me on.

'Now can your dull brain tease it out? The two names Triferus gave to Uncle Gaius must be my husband Pertinax, and Domitian, Vespasian's son.'

131

'Yes,' I said. I felt about as useless as she always implied. It must be because Pertinax had been her husband that Gaius had refused to tell us whose names they were.

There was a long pause. Somewhat stiffly I asked, 'Tell me, lady, how long ago did you work this out?'

For a moment she remained silent. 'When the captain of my husband's ship refused to carry us. Gnaeus and I had parted kindly. It was such a spiteful act.' So she still called him Gnaeus!

'The captain of your ex-husband's ship must have felt quite dismayed when you asked! How close,' I demanded as another aspect struck me, 'is your ex-husband to your Uncle Publius?'

'Uncle Publius cannot know about this.'

'Sure?'

'Not possibly!'

'Any views on Vespasian?'

'Uncle Publius supports him of course. He's a businessman; he wants stability. Vespasian stands for a well-run state: high taxation – also high profits in trade.'

'Your uncle provides wonderful camouflage for Pertinax in more than one way.'

'Oh Juno, my poor uncle!'

'Is he? Tell me, what line did Publius take in the discussion about Domitian Caesar that made you quarrel with Pertinax?'

'None. He wasn't there. He only came to our house for family events. Stop hounding my uncle!'

'I have to.'

'Falco! Why? For heaven's sake, Falco, he's Sosia's papa!'

'That's why. It would be too easy for me to ignore him – '

'Didius Falco, your one certainty must be that none of her relations – her father least of all – can be part of anything that let that child be harmed!'

'What about your own father?'

'Oh really, Falco!'

'Pertinax was his son-in-law; a close tie.'

'My father seriously disliked him after I was divorced.' It fitted what I had seen. Decimus had been clearly annoyed when I mentioned Pertinax.

I asked her who *was* party to the Domitian conversation. She listed some names that meant nothing to me.

'You know anything about an alley called Nap Lane?' I sprang the question at her; she looked at me, wide-eyed, as I pressed on. 'Sosia Camillina died in a warehouse there. Belongs to an old patrician stick, fading from the world on his country estate – a man called Caprenius Marcellus – '

'I know him slightly,' Helena interrupted in a steady voice. 'I have been in his warehouse; Sosia came with me. A dried out, painfully dying old stick who had no son. He adopted an heir. Common enough. A presentable young man with no hopes of his own, who was pleased to be welcomed by Marcellus into his noble house, honour his resplendent ancestors, promise to bury him with devoted respect – and in return supervise the substantial Marcellus estates. The Censor's office would have told you if you bothered to ask. My husband's – my ex-husband's – full legal name is Gnaeus Atius Pertinax Caprenius Marcellus.'

'Believe me,' I commented blackly, 'your ex-husband has several other filthy names!'

It seemed most comfortable not to talk for a while.

'Falco, I suppose you searched the warehouse?'

'You may suppose we did.'

'Empty?'

'By the time we searched.'

More frogs plopped. Some of them croaked. Some fish plopped. I threw a stone into the little pond and *that* plopped. Clearing my throat, I croaked.

'It seems to me,' the senator's daughter dictated, sounding like her British aunt, 'boors in a praetor's office and brats at the Palace cannot organize world events.'

'Oh no, a real manager runs this monkey troupe!'

'I don't believe,' she said, in a much smaller voice, 'Atius Pertinax is capable of murder.'

'If you say so.'

'I do say so! Be cynical if you must. Perhaps people never really *know* anybody else. Yet we must try. In your work you must trust your own judgement – '

'I trust yours,' I admitted simply, since the compliment was true.

'Yet you don't trust me!'

My ribs were causing me severe distress, and my leg hurt.

'I do need your opinion,' I said. 'I do value it. For her sake – Sosia's sake – there can be no luxuries in this case. No loyalty, no trust – then with any luck, no errors.'

133

I limped to my feet, distancing myself as I spoke that name. It was a long time since I had thought of Sosia so directly; the memory was still unbearable. If I was going to think about Sosia Camillina, I wanted to be alone.

I walked over to the fishpond, huddled in my cloak. Helena remained on the bench. She must have spoken to no more than a grey shape, whose cloak flapped occasionally in the night wind rising off the sea. I heard her call out quietly.

'Before I face my people it would be helpful to know how my cousin died.'

Gaius, who must have broken the news to her, would suppress details if he could. Since I respected her, I told her the bare facts.

'Where were you?' Helena asked in a low voice.

'Unconscious in a laundry.'

'Was that connected?'

'No.'

'Were you her lover?' she managed to force out. Silence. 'Answer me! *I'm paying you, Falco!*'

Only because I knew her stubbornness, did I eventually answer. 'No.'

'Did you want to be?'

I remained silent long enough for that to be an answer in itself.

'You had the chance! I know you did . . . Why not then?'

'Class,' I stated. 'Age. Experience.' After a moment I added, 'Stupidity!'

Then she asked me about morals. It seemed to me my morality was self-evident. It was none of her business, but in the end I told her a man should not abuse the eagerness of a young girl who has seen what she wants, and owns the instincts to obtain it, but lacks courage to cope with the inevitable grief afterwards.

'Had she lived, someone else would have brought Sosia disillusion. I did not want it to be me.'

The night wind was rising, tugging at my cloak. My heart felt very grey. I needed to stop this.

'I'm going in.' I had no intention of leaving my client alone in the dark; by now if there was any justice she knew that. Raucous revelry intruded from the *mansio*. She was uneasy in public places, and Massilia during drinking time is no place for a lady. No place for anyone; I was starting to feel unhappy out here in the open myself.

I waited, not impatiently.

'Better see you up.'

I took her to the door of her room, as I had always done before. Probably she never knew how many offensive types I warned away during our trip. One night in a place where locks had yet to be invented and the clientele were particularly vile, I had slept across her threshold with my knife. Since I never told her, she had no chance to be grateful. I preferred it that way. It was my job. This, even though she was too awkward to have spelled out the contract, was what the precious little lady was paying me for.

She grieved more closely for Sosia then I realized. When, in the shadowed corridor, I turned to say goodnight and finally looked at her, I could see that although in the garden I heard nothing, she had wept.

While I stood, helpless at this unlikely spectacle, she remarked in her usual way, 'Thank you, Falco.'

I assumed my own normal face, a shade too humble to be true. Helena Justina ignored that, as she always did. Just before she turned away she murmured, 'Happy birthday!'

Then because it was my birthday she kissed me on the cheek.

XXXVI

She must have felt me flinch.

'I'm sorry!' she exclaimed. She should have stormed off. We could have left it there. I really would not have minded; her gesture had been civilized enough.

The damned woman did not know what to do.

'I am so sorry – '

'Never apologize!' I heard my own voice grate. Since Sosia died, I had shrunk into myself. I could not deal with women any more. 'Nothing new, lady! Rich piece of brisket looking for thick gravy – gladiators get this all the time! If that was what I wanted you'd have known long before now!'

She ought to have turned into her room at once. She just stood there looking anxious.

'Oh for heavens sake!' I cried irritably. 'Stop looking at me like that!' Her great tired eyes were lakes of misery.

For two hours I had been speculating how it would feel to kiss her. So I did. Completely exasperated, I stepped up to the doorway then gripped her with my elbows, while my two hands spread either side of her bone-white face. It was over quite quickly, so lacking in enjoyment it must have been the emptiest gesture of my life.

She wrenched away. She was shaking with cold from the garden. Her whole face was cold, and her eyelashes still wet from when she wept. I had kissed her; yet I still did not know what it was really like.

I have known men who will tell you rough handling is what such women want. They are fools. She was distraught. To be perfectly honest, I was distraught myself.

Helena might have dealt with the situation but I allowed her no time. It was me who stormed off.

I did go back. What do you take me for?

I walked down that dark corridor as discreetly as a servant

136

with some message he had forgotten to deliver before. I tapped at her door – my special knock: three quick successive little knuckle raps. We had never made a formal arrangment, it just developed as my sign. Normally she came at once to let me in.

I knocked again. I tried the latch, knowing it would not budge (I had shown her myself how to wedge a latch when she was staying at an inn.) I leaned my forehead against the wood and spoke her full name quietly. She would not reply.

By now I grasped that she had supposed we had at last reached some kind of understanding. She had offered me a truce, which I in my stupidity could not even recognize, let alone accept. She was as generous as I was crass. I would have liked a chance to tell her I was sorry. She would not, or could not, give me the chance.

The time came when to wait there any longer would subject her to scandal. She had hired me to protect her from that. The only thing I could do for her was to walk away.

XXXVII

In the morning I dressed, packed, then banged her ladyship's door as I went by. She did not appear until I was sitting on the step outside the *mansio* buffing my boots with goose-grease. She stood slightly behind me. I strapped on my boots slowly to avoid looking up. I had never been so embarrassed in my life.

Helena Justina stated crisply, 'We shall both be happier if we end our contract now.'

'Lady, I'll finish what I began.'

'I won't pay you,' she said.

'Consider your contract ended!' said I.

I would not allow myself to abandon her. I seized her luggage whether she liked it or not and strode ahead. A sailor handed her quite decently onto the boat; no one bothered about me. She marched off and stood in the prow by herself. I lounged on deck with my feet on her baggage.

She was seasick. I was not. I walked up to her.

'Can I help?'

'Go away.'

I went away. That seemed to help.

All the way from Gaul to Italy those were the only words we said. At Ostia, in the morning crush, she stood next to me while we waited to disembark. Neither of us spoke. I let her be buffeted once or twice by other passengers, then I moved her in front of me and took the buffeting myself. She stared straight ahead. So did I.

I walked down the gangway first and commandeered a chair; she brushed past and climbed in by herself. I flung my baggage on the opposite seat, then travelled in a separate chair with hers.

We were entering Rome in the late afternoon. Spring now, and traffic increasing on the roads. We stopped for a hold-up

138

at the Ostia Gate, so I paid a boy to run ahead and warn her family she was on her way. I walked forward, craning at the hold-up that was jamming the Gate. Helena Justina put her head out of the window of her chair as I went by. I stopped.

I went on looking up the road. After a moment she asked quietly, 'Can you see what it is?'

I leaned my elbow more sociably in the window of her chair. 'Delivery carts,' I replied, still gazing ahead. 'Waiting to enter at curfew. Looks like a waggon of wine barrels has shed a sticky load.' I turned my head and looked her in the face. 'Plus some sort of official rumpus with soldiers and banners: some mighty personage and an escort to match, entering the city with a flourish . . .'

She held my gaze. I was never good at mending quarrels; I could feel the tendons setting in my neck.

'Didius Falco, do you know my father and Uncle Gaius have a bet?' Helena offered with a wan smile. 'Uncle Gaius reckons *I* will dismiss you in a huff; father says that *you* will leave me first.'

'Couple of villains,' I remarked, carefully.

'We could prove them wrong, Falco.'

My face twitched. 'Waste of their stakes.'

She thought I meant it; abruptly she looked away.

I had a hard pain in the pit of my stomach which I diagnosed as guilt. I touched her cheek with one finger as if she had been Marcia, my little niece. She closed her eyes, presumably in distaste. The traffic began to move again. Then Helena whispered to me dismally, 'I don't want to go home!'

My heart ached for her.

I understood how she felt. She left as a bride, grew up as a wife, ran her own establishment – probably ran it well. Now she had no place. She shrank from remarriage; her brother in Germany had told me that. She must return to her father. Rome permitted women to live no other way. She would be trapped, in a girl's useless life, a life she had outgrown. Visiting Britain had been her brief escape. Now she was back.

I recognized real panic. She would never have made the confession otherwise, not to me.

Feeling responsible, I said, 'You still look seasick. I like to deliver my commissions in a healthy condition. Come and get a glow. I'll take you on the Embankment and show you Rome!'

How do I invent such harebrained schemes? In the east of the city, miles from where her father lived, you can climb the high earthworks of the original city wall. Once past the squeaking booths of the puppeteers, the men with trained marmosets and the self-employed loomworkers plying for hire, the ancient Servian ramparts form a breezy promenade. To reach it we had to forge right into the city centre, across the main Forum, then out to the Esquiline Hill. Most people turn north towards the Colline Gate; at least I had the sense to walk her in the opposite direction and come down half way home on the Sacred Way.

Heaven knows what the bearers thought. Well, knowing the things that bearers regularly see, I can guess what they thought.

We climbed up, then strolled side by side. In early April, just before dinner, we were virtually alone. It was all there. Nothing like it in the world. Six-storey apartment blocks thrust upwards from the narrow streets, confronting palaces and private homes with brotherly disregard for social niceties. Mushroom-beige light flaked the roofs of the temples or shimmered in the fountain sprays. Even in April the air felt warm after the British wetness and cold. As we walked along peacefully, Helena and I counted off the Seven Hills together. While we came west along the Esquiline ridge, we had an evening wind in our faces. It bore tantalizing traces of rich meat dumplings gurgling in dark gravies in five hundred dubious cookshops, oysters simmering with coriander in white wine sauce, pork braising with fennel, peppercorns and pine nuts in the busy kitchen of some private mansion immediately below. Up to our high spot rose a distant murmur of the permanent hubbub below: touts and orators, crashing loads, donkeys and doorbells, the crunch of a marching Guards detachment, the swarming cries of humanity more densely packed than anywhere in the Empire or the known world beyond.

I stopped. I turned my face towards the Capitol, smiling, with Helena so close that her long mantle clapped against my side. I experienced a sense of approaching climax. Somewhere in this metropolis lurked the men I sought. It remained only to find proof that would satisfy the Emperor, then discover the whereabouts of the stolen silver pigs. I was half way to the answer; the end lay here – and my confidence was up. Finally, while I absorbed the familiar scene of home, knowing that at least in Britain I had done all a man could, the desolation which had gripped me in its vice since Sosia died finally relaxed.

Turning back to Helena Justina, I found her watching me. She had her own misery under control now. There was nothing really wrong with her: she was a girl who had made herself unhappy for a time. Plenty of people do that. Some people do it all their lives; some people seem to enjoy unhappiness. Not Helena. She was too straightforward and too honest with herself. Left alone, she had a deeply tranquil face and a gentle soul. I felt sure she would recover her patience with herself. Not with me perhaps, but if she hated me I could hardly quibble, since when I met her I had hated myself.

'I shall miss you,' she mocked.

'Like a blister when the pain stops!'

'Yes.'

We laughed.

'Some of my ladies ask to see me again!' I teased her suggestively.

'Why?' Helena flung back in her fierce way, bright-eyed. 'Do you cheat them so obviously when you send in your bill?'

She had lost a few pounds lately but she still had a bonny figure and I still quite liked the way she did her hair. So I grinned, 'Only if I want to see them!'

And she scoffed back, 'I shall warn my accountant to jump hard on mistakes!'

Her father and her uncle had lost their bet. It would never last, but at that moment we were friends.

She looked nicely dishevelled and pink; I could safely hand her over to her relations looking like that. They would think the worst of me, but that was better than the truth.

There are two reasons for taking a girl on the Embankment. One is to breathe fresh air. We had done that. I thought about the other reason, then thought better of it. Our long journey was over. I took her home.

PART III

ROME
Spring, AD 71

XXXVIII

A reception party was waiting for us in her father's street.

We had arrived without incident in the Capena Gate Sector, jiggled down a few side streets then lurched towards the senator's house. The chairs stopped. We were both climbing out. Helena gasped. I turned: four or five slave market rejects were rushing us. Each had a pointed hat pulled down more securely over his face than his smallpox scars required, and one hand buried under his cloak as if whatever was hidden there would not be a satchel of bread rolls and country cheese.

'Hercules, lady! Bang the bell until someone comes!'

Helena flew to her father's door as I rapidly unhooked a sedan chair's carrying rod.

I glanced around. Passers-by were melting off the pavements into goldsmiths and flower shops, open for the evening trade with lanterns on their porticos. The area was far too select to expect help. The strollers were vanishing like bursting bubbles on the Tiber in flood.

The rejects were brisk, but not as brisk as me. Under the cloaks they were carrying thornwood cudgels, but after three months in a lead mine I had more pent-up aggression than they may have realized. I could do a lot of damage whirling an eight-foot pole.

Eventually Camillus burst out with his slaves in response to her ladyship's spirited bell jangling. The rejects abruptly scattered. They left a trail of blood and one man dead. He had lunged at Helena. I hauled her sideways, pulling out the knife I stash down my boot, then stamped his shin like a soldier and stabbed upwards as he came. It would never have stopped anyone who had an army training, but plainly he had not; I finished him.

It is illegal to carry a weapon in Rome. Still, I was defending a senator's daughter; no prosecution lawyer could make a magistrate convict. Besides, I hadn't endured her for fourteen

145

hundred miles to give her up on the home doorstep and throw away my double fee.

Camillus Verus, sword in hand, breathed heavily and surveyed the lively scene. Chaos welled round us, seeping down the street. Dusk made everything seem more ominous.

'Lost them! Out of touch, but I nicked one – '

'Not bad, sir. I'll introduce you at my fencing gym!'

'Falco, you look a bit sick.'

'Overwhelmed by the warmth of our welcome . . .'

Killing people has a bad effect on me.

Both the senator and his wife, who came flittering out among her flock of slab-faced maids, were waiting to embrace their noble child. Once I grabbed her I had forgotten to let go. (A good rule with women, though difficult to follow up in a crowd.) It was probably the first time her honourable parents saw Helena Justina white-faced and silent, crushed to the palpitating chest of a badly shaved, mad-eyed ruffian waving a bloody knife. I released her with a hasty gesture into the arms of her papa.

He was so shocked at having nearly lost her that for a moment he lost all powers of speech.

I sat quaking on the edge of a great flowertub, while Helena Justina was passed about. Since no one liked to scold me for their fright, everyone scolded her. She seemed too stunned to object. I watched, so used to my role as her protector that I felt awkward hanging back here.

'Well done, Falco!' Her father strode across and hauled me to my feet. Then he asked, in the voice of a man who had money riding on my reply, 'Everything go well on your trip?'

'Oh, the quietness of the journey matched the thin pay!'

Helena shot me a tricky look. I gazed at the evening sky like a man who was simply very tired.

Decimus sent a message to the magistrate about the man I had killed, and in sharp order the body was tidied off his frontage at public expense. I heard no more about the incident.

No doubt what these villains wanted: when they all suddenly ran, our baggage skipped off with them.

I organized a search party and the Camillus slaves soon trundled back with our stuff, which they found abandoned only two streets away. I set a candelabrum on the cool tiled floor of the senator's hall. I was on my knees, spreading open

146

each pack for a systematic check; Helena crouched alongside, helping me. While I searched we spoke to each other in the low voices of people who had travelled together for weeks. Her mother looked uneasy, though we were too busy to deal with that. Everyone we met on the journey had livened up their own dull days by imagining some scandal; both of us were used to ignoring it. Even so, I sensed Julia Justa now viewed me as an embarrassment. I had to smile to myself: my proud young lady's elegant mother harried her as much as mine did me.

'These are hardly disturbed; there's very little gone,' I told Helena Justina, consulting her like my partner in the case.

'My uncle's letter – '

'Not fatal. Pointless in fact – he can write again.'

Something else. Something that had belonged to me.

At the moment when I realized, Helena must have seen my face. I knew from her look my own expression had become positively grey.

'Oh Falco – '

I touched her wrist. 'Lass, it doesn't matter.'

'But it does!'

I simply shook my head.

They had taken the jet bracelet, the one Helena gave to Sosia and Sosia gave to me.

XXXIX

The senator decided to go to the Palace that night. He would report all we knew, not least how we suspected that Domitian was involved. For me, nothing to do until further instructions; I could manage that.

They offered me dinner and a night in a feather bed, but I went home. For various reasons I wanted time on my own.

The laundry was closed so I left the adventure of greeting Lenia until next day. Six flights of stairs are an indecent obstacle to a travel-weary man. Trudging upwards, I decided to move house. When I reached my apartment, I grew stubborn and decided to stay.

Nothing had changed. There was an outer room in which a dog might just turn round if he was a thin dog with his tail between his legs. A wonky table, a slanty bench, shelf of pots, bank of bricks, gridiron, winejars (filthy), rubbish basket (overflowing) . . .

But my table was standing in the wrong place. The cooking bricks were blackened with soot. Some soulless bastard was starving a sparrow in a cage: someone else was living in my house.

I smelt him first. The air throbbed with the dusky reek of used woollen tunics, unwashed for a month. There was a cheesy scarlet dinner-robe I failed to recognize, and a pair of slippers whose whiff rushed to greet me from the far side of the room. Despite Decimus paying full whack to Smaractus, my disreputable landlord had let a hot-wine waiter with every kind of body odour invade my office as a subtenant while I was away.

He was out. At that moment, it was lucky for him.

I turfed his stuff onto the balcony, kicked his slippers across the landing outside the front door, fed his sparrow, then re-arranged the squalor to suit me. I ate the anchovy eggs he had left in my favourite bowl; they tasted three days old. When he

148

turned up he had greasy hair, bad teeth and a tendency to fart when he was frightened, which soon occurred whenever I glanced his way. That was quite often; he was the type you keep your eye on all the time.

I informed this wretch that whatever he was paying Smaractus, he ought to be paying me so either he could sleep outside with the stars until he found another room – or I would throw him straight out now. He chose the balcony.

'You've eaten my eggs!'

'Bad luck,' I said, scowling. He was not to know I was scowling because that expression had reminded me of someone else.

I won't say I missed her. Filthy-tempered women who reckon their lives are tragedies are two a penny where I live. What I missed was the warm sense of earning money just by keeping her company. I missed taking responsibility for another human being. I even missed the pulse of excitement wondering whatever the daft girl would do to irritate me next.

News still travelled fast in the Aventine. Petronius Longus banged in a good hour before I expected him; his familiar solid presence and that familiar modest grin. He had grown a beard. It looked terrible. I told him; he said nothing, but I knew next time I saw him he would have shaved.

The hot-wine waiter had discovered and drunk my cellar (though he denied it, since lying is what hot-wine waiters do best). Luckily Petro had lugged up an amphora of his favourite Campagnan. He perched on a bench, leaning back against the wall with his long legs stretched to the table and his booted heels up on its edge, balancing his cup on his stomach comfortably. It seemed a long time since I had last seen Petronius making himself at home. Taking one look at my gaunt face and frame, he merely asked, 'Rough?'

Nursing my ribcage, I summed up the past four months for him: '*Rough!*'

He was perfectly prepared to endure the whole story, but knew what I needed at that moment was a long stiff drink alongside a quiet friend. His brown eyes gleamed. 'And how was the lady client?'

Petronius has always been fascinated by the flocks of ardent women he visualizes besieging me. Usually I oblige him with salacious details even if I have to make them up. He could tell I was exhausted when all I managed was, 'Nothing to brag about. Just an ordinary girl.'

149

Give you any trouble?' he queried longingly.

I forced a sad smile. 'Oh, I soon sorted her out.'

He didn't believe me; I didn't believe myself.

We drank all his red Campagnan, without water, then I think I fell asleep.

XL

Helena Justina visited my office the next day. It was extremely embarrassing because I had a young lady in a short ruby tunic sprawled across my lap with her legs in the air; this chancy miss was sharing my breakfast and being rather silly about it too. The miss was pretty, the scene intimate, and Helena the last person I expected to see.

Helena Justina looked neat and cool in floating white, and I felt distinctly awkward that that light-robed stately creature had struggled up six flights to my grim hole before I had had a shave.

'I would have run down – '

'Not at all. I was longing to see you enthroned in your kingdom!' She surveyed me fastidiously, sniffing at the sordid air. 'The place looks clean. Does somebody look after you? I expected gloomy great swags of spiders' web and evidence of rats.'

Somebody – my mama – had bustled round earlier, so the spiders had temporarily hopped it under the rafters with the pigeons. I tried not to think about the rats.

I shifted my giggly armful sideways onto the bench.

'Go and wait on the balcony.'

'That man's there! He *stinks!*'

The waiter; he would have to go. I sighed. Her ladyship gave me a maddening smile.

'M Didius Falco: half-asleep and cradling a winecup. Bit early, Falco, even for you?'

'Hot milk,' I croaked.

It sounded as if I was lying, so Helena leaned over the table to see: it was hot milk.

The senator's daughter, amid her usual impolite aura of perfumed condescension, sat on the chair I keep for clients and stared at my squirming companion. I gave in.

'This is Marcia, my favourite little friend.' Marcia, my favourite friend, aged three, cuddled up possessively and glared over my arm in a gruff way that probably reminded Helena of me. I gripped the neck of her tunic, hoping to keep her under some kind of control.

Then to my horror the senator's daughter held out her arms to Marcia and heaved her over the table with the confidence of a person who has always been good with children until then. I thought of that clean, well-behaved little maiden I had seen on her lap in Londinium, and cursed inwardly. Marcia flopped like a sack in her arms looking thoughtful, gazed up at her, deliberately dribbled, then blew bubbles with the spit.

'Behave,' I instructed feebly. 'Wipe your face.'

Marcia wiped her face on the nearest material, which was the embroidered end of Helena Justina's long white scarf.

'Is she yours?' Helena asked me in a guarded tone.

It was my own affair if I let myself be used as a morning nursery school, so I just said, 'No.'

That was rude, even for me, so I condescended to add, 'My niece.' Marcia was the child my brother Festus never knew about.

'She's difficult because you spoil her,' Helena commented.

I told her somebody had to; she seemed satisfied with that.

Marcia began to examine Helena's earrings, which had blue glass beads hung on gold links. If she pulled the beads off she would eat them before I could reach across the table and grab them back. Fortunately they seemed well-soldered together and firmly hooked onto her ladyship's delicate ears. I myself would have gone for the ears, which lay close to her head and were pleading to be nibbled. Helena looked as if she guessed what I was thinking. Rather stiffly I enquired what I could do for her.

'Falco, my parents are dining tonight at the Palace; you're wanted there too.'

'Trough with Vespasian?' I was outraged. 'Certainly not; I'm a strict republican!'

'Oh Didius Falco, don't make such a fuss!' Helena snapped.

Marcia stopped blowing bubbles.

'Keep still!' I instructed as she suddenly rolled about, chortling with exaggerated glee; the child was as heavy and ungainly as a calf. 'Look, give her back; I can't talk to you while I'm worrying – '

152

Helena gripped her, sat her upright, dried her face again (identifying for herself the cloth I kept for this task) while competently straightening her earrings as she continued to do business with me. 'She's no trouble. There's no need to talk; Falco, you talk too much.'

'My papa's an auctioneer.'

'I can believe that! Just stop worrying.' I sealed my lips in a bitter line. For a moment she seemed to have finished, then she confessed, 'Falco, I've tried to see Pertinax.' I said nothing, since what I would have said was unfit for her respectable shell-like ears. The spectre of another girl in white, lying still at my feet, was strangling me. 'I went to the house. I suppose I wanted to confront him. He was not there – '

'Helena – ' I protested.

'I know; I should never have gone,' she muttered swiftly.

'Lady, *never* walk in alone on a man to inform him he's a criminal! He knows that. He's likely to prove it by coming at you with the first weapon to hand. Did you tell *anybody* where you were going?'

'He was my husband; I wasn't afraid – '

'You should have been!'

Quite suddenly her tone melted: 'And now you are afraid for me! Truly, I'm sorry.' A sick shiver ran round me under my belt. 'I wanted to take you – '

'I would have come.'

'Provided I asked you properly?' she teased.

'If I see you in that kind of trouble,' I said tersely, 'you won't have to ask.'

Her eyes widened, with a look of surprise and shock.

I drank my milk.

I was settling down again. Marcia lolled her tousled head against Helena's handsome bosom, watching us. I watched the child – well that was my excuse – as Helena cajoled me, 'Will you come tonight? It's a free dinner, Falco! One of your employers has rushed from abroad to meet you. You know you're too inquisitive to let that pass.'

'Employers plural!'

She said there were two – possibly three, though probably not. I tried suggesting two meant double rates but she retorted: 'Your rates are what my father agreed! Wear a toga; bring your dinner napkin. You might consider investing in a shave. And please, Falco, try not to embarrass me . . .'

'No need, lady – you embarrass yourself. Give me back my niece!' I snarled venomously; so at last she did.

When she had gone, Marcia and I walked onto the balcony hand in hand. We hauled out the hot-wine waiter, who had been snoring in a loincloth on a pallet, and waited in his foul fug until Helena Justina emerged into the street. We watched her climb aboard her chair, her head far below like a shining teakwood knob amidst a foam of snowy veils. She did not look up; I was sorry about that.

'That lady's lovely!' decided Marcia, who normally liked men. (I encouraged that condition, on the premise that if she liked men when she was three she would grow out of it and leave me a lot less to worry about by the time she was thirteen.)

'That lady has never been lovely to me!' I growled.

Marcia gave me a sideways look that was surprisingly mature. *'Oh Didius Falco, don't make such a fuss!'*

I went to visit Pertinax myself. Everything I had told Helena was true; it was a stupid thing to do. Luckily the bullying lout was still not at home.

XLI

As chance would have it, I met Petro the next day. He whistled, then held me gently at arms' length.

'Whew! Where are you off to, dazzler?'

In honour of dining with the lord of the civilized world, I was in my best tunic, buffed up in the laundry until all the old wine stains were almost invisible. I wore sandals (polished), a new belt (pungent), and my Great Uncle Scaro's obsidian signet ring. I had spent all afternoon at the baths and the barber's, not merely exchanging the news (though I had done that too, until my head spun). My hair was shorn so I felt as light-hearted as a lamb. Petronius inhaled the unusual wafts of bathing oil, shaving lotion, skin-relaxant and hair pomade amongst which I was making my fragrant way, then with one careful finger he lifted two pleats of my toga a quarter of an inch along my left shoulder, pretending to improve on the sartorial effect. This toga originally belonged to my brother, who like a good soldier reckoned to equip himself with everything of the best, whether he needed it or not. I was sweating under the weight of the wool, and my own embarrassment.

I said, lest my sceptical crony should deduce something incorrect, 'Just taking a rancid old vinegar pot to a party at the Palace.'

He looked shocked. 'Night assignments? Watch yourself, blossom! This could lead to trouble for a good-looking boy!'

I had no time to argue. I had spent so long at the barber's, I was already late.

The porter at the Camillus house refused to recognize me; I nearly had to thump him, ruining my good mood and neat attire. The senator and Julia Justa had already left. Fortunately Helena was waiting for me quietly in the hall, so she came out in response to the kerfuffle, already aboard her chair. She ran an eye over me through the window, but it was not until we

155

reached the Palatine that I had a proper chance to inspect her in return.

She gave me quite a shock.

I suppose money makes its point. As soon as I handed her out, wreathed in her ladylike mantle with a half-veil demurely tucked from ear to ear, I started to get that sense of unease when someone you know is so dressed up they seem to be a stranger. Unwrapped, I found her mother's miserable maids had really done their duty by the daughter of the house. Once they worked her over with the manicure prodders and eyebrow tweezers, curling tongs and earwax scoops, left her fermenting all afternoon in a mealy flour face mask, then finished her off with a delicate sponging of red ochre across the cheekbones and a fine gleam of antimony above the eyes, Helena Justina was bound to be presentable enough, even to me. In fact she looked burnished from the glint of the filigree tiara clipped around her elaborate hair to the beaded slippers sparkling through the flounce at the hem of her gown. She was bare-armed in sea-green silk. The effect was of a cool, tall, distinctly superior naiad.

I looked away. I looked back, clearing my throat.

I confessed somewhat hoarsely that I had never been out on the town with a naiad before. 'If you were on the beach at Baiae, there would be a strong danger some salty old sea god would throw you on your back to ravish you on a mattress of bladderwrack!'

She said she would punch him in the fins with his trident; I told her the attempt would still be worth his while.

We joined the slow throng that was wending its way to the dining room. This procession passed through Nero's grotesque corridors where gold fretted the pilasters, arches and ceilings in such quantity that it merged into one glaring wash of paint. Meticulous fauns and cherubs pirouetted under pergolas where roses ran riot without season, in detail so delicate that once the artists' scaffolding came down from the high walls the frescos could only be appreciated by wandering flies and moths. I felt glassy-eyed with luxury, like a man who had lost his vision staring at the sun.

'You've had your hair cut!' Helena Justina accused, muttering at me sideways as we went.

'Like it?'

'No,' she reported frankly. 'I liked you with your curls.'

Praise be to Jupiter, the girl was still herself. I glared in return at her modishly frazzled topknot.

156

'Well lady, since we're on the subject of curls, *I* liked *you* better without!'

Vespasian's banquets were extremely old-fashioned; the waitresses kept their clothes on and he never poisoned the food.

Vespasian was not a keen entertainer, though he gave regular banquets; he gave them to cheer up the people he invited and to keep caterers in funds. As a republican I refused to be impressed. Attending one of the Emperor's well-run dinners made me feel morose. I deny any recollection of what the menu was; I kept adding up how much it must have cost. Luckily Vespasian was seated too far away for me to tell him my views. He looked pretty silent. Knowing him, he too was totting up the damage to the privy purse.

Halfway through my refusing to enjoy myself, an usher tapped my shoulder. Helena Justina and I were slid out from the meal so skilfully I was still carrying a lobster claw and she had one cheek bulging with half-eaten squid-in-its-ink. A cloakroom slave whisked me into my toga, achieving in five seconds a dignified drape that back at home had taken me an hour; a shoe-boy had us respectably reshod; an escort led us to a lavish anteroom, two spear-carriers gave way to a bronzed inner door, a doorman opened it, the escort announced our names to a chamberlain, the chamberlain repeated them to his boy, the boy recited them again in a clear voice with only the fact that he got both slightly wrong spoiling an otherwise portentous effect. We passed inside. A slave who until then had been doing nothing in particular accepted what was left of my lobster claw.

A curtain dropped, muffling the outside noise. A young man – a man my own age, not over tall, with a jutting chin that was sprouting marble copies throughout Rome – bounded from a purple-draped chair. His body was hard as a brick; his energy made me groan. The gold braid acanthus leaves on the hem of his tunic rolled in padded waves an inch thick round a band four inches deep. He waved away the attendants and rushed forwards to greet us himself.

'Please come in! Didius Falco? I wanted to congratulate you on your efforts in the north.'

There was no need for Helena to touch my arm in warning. I knew who he was at once, and at once I understood who both my employers were. I was not, as I had assumed until then, working at the direction of some snobbish secretariat of oriental freedmen lurking in the lower echelons of Palace protocol.

It was Titus Caesar himself.

XLII

He had just spent five years in the desert, but by Jove he was fit. He was bursting with talent. You could see at once how he carried off commanding a legion at twenty-six, then mobilized half the Empire to win his father's throne.

Titus Flavius Vespasianus. The back of my throat, which had been tingling from a fiercely peppered sauce, rasped with dry ash. Two employers: Titus and Vespasian. Or two rather important victims, if we got it wrong.

This cheery young general was supposed to be locked in siege warfare at Jerusalem; he had evidently dealt with Jerusalem, and I quite believed that he swept up in his conquest the fabulous Judaean queen. Who could blame him? Whatever anyone thought of her background and morals (she had once married her uncle and was rumoured to sleep with her brother the king), Queen Berenice was the most beautiful woman in the world.

'Helena Justina!'

My teeth ground on a fragment of lobster shell. Having pocketed a queen for himself, he need not have encroached so keenly on my personal naiad. I could tell he had impressed her by the quiet way she asked him, 'You want to talk to Falco, sir; shall I withdraw?'

A pang of panic caught me when I thought that she might, but he waved us both rapidly into the room.

'No please; this concerns you too.'

We were in a chamber twenty-foot-high where painted figures from mythology leapt lightly about fantastic panels beneath arbours of intricate flowers. Every conceivable surface was lacquered with gold leaf. I blinked.

'Sorry about the dazzle,' Titus smiled. 'Nero's obscene idea of good taste. My poor father is in a quandary, as you can imagine, whether to put up with it or commit funds to building yet another new Palace on the site.'

I envied them the problem of whether to keep the Palace they already owned, or buy a new one.

Titus carried on gravely. 'Some of the rooms are so disgusting we have had to seal them up. With a complex that sprawls across three of the Seven Hills we are still hard put to find modest family accommodation, let alone a really functional public suite. Still, more urgent projects first – ' I had not come here to bandy taste in decor but he changed pace, indicating business, so I relaxed. 'My father has asked me to see you informally, because a public audience might be dangerous. Your news about the stolen ingots being stripped of their silver has been hinted to the Praetorians. They seemed interested to hear it, loyal as they are!' He was ironic without appearing cynical.

'It still leaves the conspirators at large – ' I replied.

'Let me bring you up to date. This morning we arrested Atius Pertinax Marcellus. The evidence was thin, but we must find out who else is involved. So . . .' He hesitated.

'The Mamertine Jail?' I asked. 'The political cells?'

Princes had died in them; the cells were notorious. Helena Justina drew a sharp breath. Titus told her, almost without apology, 'Not for long. He had a visitor – quite against the rules – don't yet know who. Half an hour later the prison guards found him strangled.'

'Oh no!'

He sprang this news of her husband's death quite casually; Helena Justina was visibly moved. So was I. I had promised myself the pleasure of dealing with Pertinax. It seemed typical that he chose the kind of associates who robbed me of the chance.

'Helena Justina, did you and Pertinax remain on good terms?'

'No terms at all.' Her answer was steady.

He stared at her thoughtfully: 'Are you mentioned in his will?'

'No. He was generous when we divided our property, then he made a new will.'

'You discussed that?'

'No. But my uncle was one of the witnesses.'

'Have you spoken to Atius Pertinax since your return from abroad?'

'No.'

'Then will you tell me,' Titus Caesar requested coolly, 'why you went to his house today?'

The Emperor's son was landing the kind of shocks I like to use myself. He had slid from pleasantries into inquisition in one seamless move. Helena answered him in her calm, positive way, though this turn of events plainly caught her unprepared.

'I had some idea, sir, knowing him, that I would face him with what we believed. His people told me he was not there – '

'No.' In the Mamertine; already dead. Titus looked slyly at me. 'So why did you go, Falco?'

'Stepping in, in case her man should turn uncouth.'

At that he smiled, then turned back to Helena; she had whisked towards me with a jerk of her head so the beaten gold disks on her antique earrings trembled in a slight shower of rustling sound. Ignoring her reproach, I prepared to intervene if Titus overstepped the mark.

'The Pertinax will has a codicil,' he announced. 'Written only yesterday, with new witnesses. It demands an explanation.'

'I know nothing about it,' Helena stated. Her face became tense.

'Is this necessary, Caesar?' I interrupted lightly. His jaw set but I persisted. 'Excuse me, sir. A woman summoned to the lawcourts expects a friend to speak for her.'

'I imagine Helena Justina can answer for herself!'

'Oh she can!' I gave him a swift grin. 'That's why you may prefer to deal with me!'

She sat in silence, as a woman should when she is being formally discussed by men. Her eyes remained on me. I liked that; though his Caesarship seemed none too keen.

'Your lady is not in court,' Titus remarked quietly, but I saw I had checked him. 'Falco, I thought you were working for us! Don't we pay you enough?' A man whose heart has been seduced by the world's most beautiful woman can be excused his romantic streak.

'Frankly, your rates are on the meagre side,' I told him without a flicker.

He smiled faintly. Everyone knew Vespasian was tight with cash.

'I'm afraid the new Emperor is famous for that! He needs four hundred million sesterces to restore the Empire to prosperity, and in his list of priorities you stand somewhere after rebuilding the Temple of Jupiter and draining the great lake in Nero's Golden House. He'll be relieved Helena Justina is ensuring you don't starve! So, Didius Falco, as her friend in court, let me tell you your client's ex-husband has left her a rather unusual bequest.'

160

'Any bequest from that leaking pustule is unusual in my book. What is it?' I demanded.

Titus sucked the back of his thumbnail, though it was perfectly manicured.

'The contents of a pepper warehouse in Nap Lane,' he said.

XLIII

I concealed my excitement, thinking fast.

'What do you think he had in mind, sir?'

'I have had men searching to find out.'

'Anything there?'

'Nothing for us. For the lady, a lavish pantry of spices and enough perfume to bathe like Cleopatra every day of her life.' He turned, with a changed tone. 'Helena Justina, has this upset you? Pertinax had no family except his adoptive father; perhaps he retained affection from when you were his wife.'

That did upset her. I sat still; it was not for me to tell her whether Pertinax felt affectionate – or whether she should want him to.

Titus went on worrying her, while her startled brain spun.

'A traitor's goods are forfeit – but recognizing your assistance, my father wishes your legacy to stand. In due course, this gift will be released to you – '

She was frowning. I would have liked to watch Helena demolish a Caesar, if only as a variation from demolishing me. Instead I advised sensibly, 'Helena Justina, you ought to tell Titus Caesar now about the people who came to your husband's house, the ones we discussed at Massilia.' Mentioning Massilia I tensed, trying not to think about the error I made at the inn. Helena received my encouragement as noncommittally as always.

Helena Justina repeated the story for Titus in her straightforward style. He demanded names; she stated her list. I remembered some of them this time, though they still meant nothing to me: Aufidius Crispus, Curtius Gordianus, Gordianus' brother Longinus, Faustus Ferentinus, Cornelius Gracilis . . .

Titus jumped for a notebook, making swift strokes with a stylus in rapid shorthand, omitting the bother – or danger – of calling in a secretary. He was famous for the speed of his own shorthand anyway.

While he studied the names I enquired, 'Is it indiscreet to ask whether your brother was coerced?'

He answered me coldly, and without expression: 'No material evidence implicates Domitian.' He had been a barrister; it was a barrister's reply. Suddenly he became restless. 'Do you know why I rushed home? Rumour!' he exploded. 'I had attended the consecration of the Apis Bull at Memphis. I was crowned with a diadem – it is part of the normal ritual – so Rome decides I am setting myself up as Emperor in the East!'

'The word at my barber's this afternoon,' I commented, 'was that even your father had doubts!'

'Then your barber should have seen us both when I rushed into the Palace yesterday crying *Father, here I am!* As for my brother, in the civil war he nearly lost his life on the Capitol while the Temple of Jupiter burned over his head. My uncle, who would have advised him, had just been murdered by supporters of Vitellius. At eighteen, with no political experience, Domitian discovered himself representing the Emperor in Rome. It was completely unexpected. He made choices that were foolish, as he realizes now. No one can ask me to condemn my brother, simply because he is so young!'

I caught Helena's eye; neither of us spoke.

Titus massaged his forehead.

'What's the word at your barber's about this tangle, Falco?'

'That your father hates disloyalty, but that he always listens to you. That while you were both at Alexandria, Vespasian lost his temper when he heard about your brother's intended foray into the German revolt against him, but you convinced him to be lenient with Domitian.' Since he did not deny it I added cheerily, 'You'll have spotted I choose my barber for his sharp information, sir!' Helena Justina glanced mournfully, I thought, at my lost curls; I tried not to look at her. 'So what now, Caesar?'

Titus sighed. 'My father has asked the Senate to award him a ceremonial Triumph. We shall celebrate the capture of Jerusalem in the grandest procession Rome has ever seen. If you have children, take them; they will view nothing like it in their lives again. It will be our gift to the city – and I dare say in return the future of the Flavian dynasty is assured.'

It was Helena who assessed the situation. 'Your father's two grown sons are one of his attractions as Emperor,' she remarked thoughtfully. 'The Flavians are offering Rome long-term stability, so you and Domitian *must* both ride in the parade. Everything must appear harmonious – '

Titus ducked that: 'By the end of this week my father's position will be established. Falco, the word at *my* barber's is, neither the Praetorians nor my brother will cooperate now in opposing my father. These people will wish to run to earth and let bygones be done. Now I hold this list of names I'm inclined to let them run –'

I gave him a long stare, then scoffed, 'So you go to your barber for his cutting!'

Titus Caesar had a vigorous bunch of locks, snipped to look smart below his gilded wreath, but long enough to keep the handsome curl. I hate good-looking men, especially when they keep glancing at the woman who came with me.

'What does that mean, Falco?' Titus asked, not amused.

'On the strength of his information, sir, your barber's a villain.'

'*Falco!*'

That was Helena, trying to save me from drowning again, but I careered on. 'He's wrong for two reasons, as the fact that people felt it necessary to silence Pertinax should convince you.' Titus quite mildly encouraged me to continue. 'Caesar, neither you nor I can let these traitors go. Even with Triferus cheating them, they hold a handy baulk of Imperial silver, which your father needs. Another reason, with due respect, is a bright, golden, *loyal*, sixteen-year-old girl called Sosia Camillina.'

Helena Justina was looking at me so steadily I felt odd. I stood my ground against them both.

Titus Caesar ran the fingers of both hands through his well-kept hair.

'You are perfectly right. My barber's a villain,' he said.

He gazed at me for a moment.

'People underestimate you, Falco.'

'People underrated Vespasian for sixty years!'

'Fools still do. Let me tell you his instructions.'

They had tried to bamboozle me. Titus still wanted to shuffle me off and allow the case against Domitian to die quietly, but I noticed he had a speech ready in case the attempt should fail. He leaned forward earnestly.

'Omit my brother's name from your enquiries. Find the silver – and the murderer of that innocent young girl. Most importantly, identify the man who planned all this.'

I suggested increasing my rates; he decided that for the same enquiry they would pay the same. Always a fool for logic, I accepted it.

'But I cannot omit Domitian – '

'You must,' Titus told me flatly.

Then the curtain behind us suddenly swung open. I began to twist round to investigate, when the person who had come in unannounced started whistling. With a shock, I recognized the tune.

It was a song about Vespasian; about Titus; about Berenice. Soldiers sang it with a slow, low, leery lurch at the end of the night. They sang it in bars and in brothels, with both envy and approval, but no soldier I had ever met would repeat it here. The words went:

> Oh the old man – *smiled!*
> Then the young man – *smiled!*
> So the Queen of all the *Jews*
> She really couldn't *lose*
> All she had to do was *choose*
> When the *old* man,
> And the *young* man – *smiled!*

Only one person would dare to whistle so outrageously in the presence of a Caesar: another Caesar. Vespasian was presiding over his banquet, so I knew who our rash visitor must be.

Domitian, Titus Caesar's younger brother: the imperial playboy who was implicated in our plot.

XLIV

'That must have been a contest, brother!'
'Not all of life is a contest,' Titus calmly said.

For Domitian, the courtesy title of Caesar seemed a fragile irony. He had the family curls, the creased Flavian chin, the bull neck, square body and stocky build. Somehow he failed to convince. He was ten years younger than Titus, which explained both his resentment and his brother's protective loyalty. He was twenty, his face still cherubic and soft.

'Sorry!' he exclaimed. My first impression was that he shared his brother's ability to disarm. My second impression was, he acted well. 'What's this – affairs of state?' I remembered how Domitian's role in the state had been terminated briskly by their imperial papa.

'Man called Didius Falco,' Titus told him, sounding the general. 'Relation of a decurion in my legion in Judaea.'

It finally struck me that I owed this commission to my own brother. Vespasian and Titus knew Festus, so they trusted me. Not for the first time in my life, I viewed big brother with mixed feelings. Not for the first time in this case, I felt hideously slow.

As if it had been prearranged, a servant issued me with a sack of coin I could hardly lift. Titus declared in a measured voice, 'That is my personal gift to your mother, Didius Falco, as commander of the Fifteenth Legion Apollinaris. A small compensation for the support she has lost. Didius Festus was irreplaceable to both of us.'

'You knew him?' I asked, not because I wanted to hear, but when I told my mother all this gilt-edged rubbish she would ask me.

'He was one of my soldiers; I tried to know them all.'

Domitian broke in, with a laugh that sounded genuine: 'We

166

are both lucky, Didius Falco, having brothers with such well-earned reputations!'

In that moment he enjoyed all the gifts of the Flavian house: grace, high intelligence, respect for the task in hand, sturdy wit, good sense. He could have been no less a statesman than his father or his brother; sometimes he managed it. Vespasian had shared his own talents with an even hand; the difference was, only one of his sons handled them with a truly sure grip.

Titus brought our interview to a close. 'Tell your mother to be proud, Falco.'

I managed to keep my peace.

As I turned, Domitian stepped aside.

'Who's the lady?' he asked me openly, when Helena Justina slipped to her feet in a sparkle of gold and a whisper of silk. His shameless eyes raked her, implying the wander of decadent hands.

Her discomfort made me so angry, I retaliated: *'The ex-wife of a dead aedile called Atius Pertinax.'*

And saw his flicker of anxiety at that name.

Titus had come down to us at the door, also putting his brother to the test: 'The aedile has left his lady a curious legacy. Now this fortune-hunter trails after her everywhere, keeping one eye on her interests at all turns . . .'

Domitian gave no further sign of nerves. He kissed Helena's hand, with the half-closed gaze of a very young man who imagines he is brilliant in bed. She stared at him stonily. Titus intervened, with a smoothness I envied, kissing her cheek like a relative as we reached the door. I let him. If she wanted, she was perfectly capable of stopping him herself.

I hoped she realized these two came from an old-fashioned Sabine family. Stripped of their purple, they were provincial and ordinary: close with their money, ruled by their women, and obsessed with work. They both had paunches already, and neither of them was as tall as me.

I had to leave Helena alone while I found someone to roust out her chair. The empty atrium seemed so vast I reeled, trying to take it in, but as soon as I returned I spotted her, a shaft of deep sea green sitting on a fountain edge. Overshadowed by the hundred-foot-high statue of Nero as the Sun God, she looked anxious and shy.

A man in a senator's wide purple stripes was addressing her;

the type who leans back with his gut heaving over his belt. Her replies were abrupt. Her glance settled on me gratefully as I skipped across.

'Where else should I look for a naiad but in front of a water-splash? There's a delay finding our chair but it will come – '

I planted myself alongside. Sir-in-the-stripes looked annoyed; I cheered up. She would not introduce us. After he took his leave I noticed her relax.

'Friend of yours?'

'No. Oddly enough, I'm a friend of his wife!'

'Well, just tip me a nod if you want me to disappear.'

'Oh thanks!' she stormed bleakly.

I sat down beside her on the fountain bowl, musing, 'Funny thing, divorce. Seems to hang a sign saying "vulnerable" round a woman's neck.'

We hit one of those rare moments when she allowed me to see her under private strain.

'Is this common? I was starting to feel I must be odd!' I saw her chair coming, so merely smiled in reply. 'Didius Falco, will you see me safe to the house?'

'Good gods, yes! This is Rome at night! Will your chair take me and my bag of gold?'

Dining out with the Caesars had given me extravagant ideas. Still she nodded, then coolly informed the bearers they were taking me as well.

We climbed aboard, both twisting diagonally to avoid bumping knees. The bearers set off, down the north side of the Palatine, going slowly because of the extra weight. It was not quite dark.

Helena Justina was looking so unhappy I had to say, 'Don't think about what happened to Pertinax.'

'No.'

'And don't try to convince yourself he was sorry when you divorced him – '

'No, Falco!' I leaned back in my corner of the chair, twisting my lip. In the near darkness she apologized. 'You're so passionate when you give advice! Did your hero brother have a wife?'

'A girl – and a child he never heard about.'

'Marcia!' she exclaimed. Her tone changed. 'I thought she must be yours.'

'I told you not!'

'Yes.'

'I *don't* lie to you!'

168

'No. I beg your pardon . . . Who looks after them now?'

'Me.'

I sounded terse and I was shifting about, but it had nothing to do with anything we had said. We had descended as far as the Forum before I was sure: furtive footsteps were keeping pace with us, too level and much too close.

'What's the matter, Falco?'

'We're being shadowed. All the way from the Palace – '

I banged on the roof, springing out as the chair stopped. Helena Justina slid after me almost before I offered my hand. I snatched up my mother's bag of gold, then I handed her ladyship straight off the open street and into the lighted doorway of the nearest dreadful dive, as if she were some bored socialite paying me to take her to see the low life of Rome at night.

In the lurid light of their entrance cubicle, she looked so highly strung I almost wondered if she wished she was.

XLV

There was a tiptilted head of Venus blowing her cheeks out beside a welcoming motto above the outside door, where a stupendous man extracted a stupendous entrance fee. It was a brothel. I couldn't help that. It took us off the streets; it was warm, dark, and no doubt confirmed her ladyship's abysmal opinion of me.

I would have to find the entrance money myself. Client or not, I could hardly ask the senator to excavate his bank box to pay for me taking his delicate daughter to a place as foul as this.

The proprietors here made a meagre living from the profits of fornication, and a small fortune from picking pockets and selling stolen clothes. There was one cavernous room, with hides hung on poles round the walls to form cubbyholes where fraud, theft or murder could take place in decent privacy. Other varieties of intercourse occurred in whatever patch of gloom the participants already occupied.

A torchlit floor show was in progress, enlivened by the clatter of fractured castanets. Three teenage girls with thin arms and amazing busts were cavorting together on a central mat wearing big fixed smiles and little leather thongs. Waiting on the sidelines they had a monkey; for what purpose, I refuse to speculate. At tables around the room dark figures with glassy faces drank overpriced liquor while they watched the show, from time to time exuding desultory cries.

A short stout hostess loomed at us in off-the-shoulder violet gauze, slashed from the waist to reveal a yard of varicose-veined leg. Her transparent attire made me long to see less of her not more, as she demanded with a remnant of tired allure, 'Bang on my tambourine, centurion?'

Before I could stop her, the senator's daughter rapped briskly, 'Don't cramp my style; his highness is with me!'

The woman revived at this exotic hint. (I revived slightly myself.)

'*Ooh!* It's two little gold pieces – or four if you bring your own girl!' The man outside had charged me more than that, but I suppose both he and the monkey wanted a cut.

'Corkage!' marvelled Helena; I was shocked. Women exchanging ribaldry are so coarse.

'Don't be so unladylike! Hades, we were followed. Fine pickle you've lured me into here – '

A phalanx of bulky shapes came sliding in through the entrance behind us with ominous intent. Protests from the doorman indicated they had not paid his fee; once they laid hands on us they were not intending to stay.

My companion muttered to her new friend, 'This clown's crossing his legs – is there a . . .'

'Out the back, dear – '

'Come on, Falco, I'll take you!'

She pulled me straight across the floor show. Hardly anyone noticed. Those that did, thought we were part of it – as for one ludicrous moment we were. A writhing young amazon with no sense of direction backed into Helena's arms; she passed her to me like an unwanted bread roll. I gave the girl a smacking kiss, regretted it (she tasted of sweat and garlic – only to be borne when you taste of the same), then I positioned her tidily on the nearest table where she disappeared under the lecherous clutch of a group of happy Corsicans who could not believe their luck. Rival foreign parties roared with jealousy. The table toppled over, pulling down a curtain to reveal some citizen's white backside rising like the Moon Goddess as he did his anxious duty by a maiden of the house; the poor rabbit froze in mid-thrust, then went into eclipse. A cheer went up. Helena giggled: '*Hail and Farewell!*'

By now outraged stokers and stevedores were swaying to their feet ready to spar with anyone, and not caring why. The monkey had been eating an apple while he waited until he was wanted. I clicked my fingers above his head, snatched his apple as he looked up, then drew back my arm like a javelin thrower to hurl the fruit at the gang who had followed us in. Baring his teeth, he leapt into their midst biting anyone whose face he could reach.

Helena Justina had found a low doorway; she ducked me out into the back alley before I could gasp. We never even had a drink.

Well, people don't go to a brothel for a drink.

The space between the buildings was half a yard at most. Dark balconies hung over our heads hiding the sky. There was a smell as strong as lion's piss and I banged my knee on an onion crate. Under my sandals I felt the soft slide of liquid mud which after a few steps welled up coldly between my naked toes.

As I limped bravely, the senator's daughter helped me to hurry with her sensible hand gripping my arm.

'Didius Falco, I didn't know you were shy!'

I glanced back over one shoulder, managing to mutter, 'I didn't know you were not!' Our steps jarred on the lava blocks of a properly paved street. 'Now that we've been to a brothel together, can I call you Helena?'

'No. The floor show looked amazing; I was sorry to miss that!'

'I thought we should leave; that mangy ape was giving you a funny look!'

'It was a chimpanzee,' Helena Justina retorted pedantically. 'And I thought he was rather taken with you!'

We slackened our pace but stumbled on until we came to a major street. Since we left the Palace the curfew had lifted and they were letting in the delivery carts. From all the gates of Rome ferocious vehicular activity converged on us; we covered our ears against the screeching of axles and cursing of carters. It was pitch dark, except where their lanterns bobbed. Suddenly there were shouts: we had been spotted. We were pursued by burly shapes. There was something about the way those shadows moved that convinced me they were soldiers. They came after us on unhurried feet, fanning down both sides of the highway, threading through the waggons like corks bobbing in a harbour, silently working their way through dark water into shore.

'More roughnecks! Better hitch a ride – '

'Oh Juno!' Helena wailed in despair. 'Falco, not a cart chase up and down the Seven Hills!'

The night came alive now. The streets clogged; queues; noise; spills and traffic jams. I put my foot on the back of a slow waggon, wriggled up then pulled Helena aboard. We cuddled a marble headstone for half a block, transferred to a manure cart, realized what it was, then stepped off hastily to share with some nets of cabbages instead.

I was trying to work south, where I knew the streets. The cabbage-carter stopped to exchange abuse with a competitor

172

who had scraped into his cart, so we scrambled down.

'Mind your feet!'

I nipped backwards from a passing wheel. 'Thanks. In here – ' We took advantage of a sideless dray. 'Try to look like an amphora of robust Latian wine – '

I collapsed in mild hysterics as her sober ladyship obediently imitated a winejar, with her hands on her hips like handles and a face like a cracked chalk bung.

Six ox carts later the shadows were still gaining. It was quicker to walk. We slithered down again; my party sandals landed in something warm a donkey had left behind. I was still carrying mother's sack of swag from Titus, and worrying about not being able to concentrate on protecting Helena. I had been frightened of losing her: no chance of that! While I was exclaiming, she seized my free hand ready to run. In the light from a tavern, her eyes flashed. I had let myself enjoy the delusion that Helena Justina was a staid piece. That was nonsense. She was determined not to be beaten, yet chortling at herself as she caught my startled look. Equally exhilarated, I laughed and ran faster myself.

The waggons had carried us out of the Forum, across the Via Aurelia and further south. We dashed round the Circus Maximus at the starting gate end and scuttled east until we were level with the central Obelisk. When we approached the Twelfth Sector I drew to a halt, bolting into the shelter of an alley, as we both struggled for breath. I backed her ladyship against a windowless wall, flung one arm across in front of her, and stared about, frantically listening. After a time I let my arm drop and lowered my bag of gold silently to the ground. There was nothing but the low throb of general noise beyond the buildings round about. Where we were seemed suddenly peaceful. We stood in a discrete pool of quietness: me, the senator's daughter, the silhouette of an owl on a roof-tree, and the smell of old beanskins from a nearby rubbish dump. It might have seemed quite romantic to anyone with a passion for broad beans.

'Lost them!' I whispered. 'Enjoying your trip out?'

She laughed, almost soundlessly in the back of her throat. 'Beats sitting by a fountain watching slavegirls sewing fringes onto frocks!'

I was about to do something – well say something, anyway,

173

– when into the space where my words would have gone, some other villain spoke.

'Now there's a fine Etruscan necklace, lady! Dangerous running about the streets like that. Better hand your glitter over to me!'

XLVI

Helena Justina rarely wore much jewellery, but all her best pieces were on her tonight. I sensed her anguish even in the dark.

Without moving, she asked me in a low voice, 'What shall I do?'

'Whatever he says, I think. He's not very big but he's armed.'

I had found a blacker shadow, two yards away on my right. Instinct told me about the blade. I scooped the lass across me to my left. The voice laughed scornfully: 'Freeing his sword arm – if he had a sword! Lady, let's have your loot!'

With a wrench of annoyance, Helena detached her scintillating earrings, a panther-headed bangle from each arm and the tiara from her hair. Holding all these, her fingers fumbled at her necklace catch.

'Let me.'

'Lot of practice?' scoffed the thief.

He was right; I had undone necklaces before. I could manage this. There were two loops of wire which I pushed together, then twisted apart; while it was on, the weight of the necklace held them in place. Her neck was soft, and warm from running. I know that because only a fool undoes a lady's necklace without tickling the lady's neck.

'Hercules knot!' I answered suavely, then let the light skein of gold shiver into her hand.

A scrawny paw reached out to take possession, then he snarled at me. 'Your ring too!'

I sighed. It was the only legacy other than debt that I had ever received. I tossed him my Great Uncle's signet ring.

'Thanks, Falco!'

'He knows you!' Helena sounded annoyed.

The villain was obviously some Aventine scavenger, but a stranger to me. I chipped back sharply, 'Lots of people know

175

me, but not many of them would pinch my Uncle Scaro's signet ring!'

Helena tensed as if she hoped I would pull out some hidden weapon, then jump. Vespasian had stopped the Praetorians searching his visitors as a signal of quiet times, but I was not such a maniac as to visit the Palace with a knife up my sleeve; I had nothing to jump with.

Our thief suddenly lost interest. Listening too, I heard why. I caught a whistle I recognized; the scavenger slipped down the entry and vanished with his swag.

A man with a flare tumbled into the alley.

'Who's there?'

'Me – Falco!' Someone else joined him hotfoot. 'Petro, that you?'

'Falco? We've just flushed out that runt Melitus – he get anything off you?'

'Jewellery. Lucky you turned up; I had a sack of gold, too!'

'I'll follow it up. You had a *what?*'

'Sack of gold.'

All the time we were speaking, Petronius Longus had been walking down towards me. Now, in the light of the patrolman's flare, he finally glimpsed a vision of my naiad.

'*Falco!* Now that's downright *perjury!*' he exploded. He gripped his trooper's arm, then brought up the brand like a beacon. From then on, his eyes were ignoring me. In the torchlight Helena Justina shimmered, iridescent as an opal; excited eyes, that challenging expression, and the best set of shoulders in the Capena Gate –

She was the same height as me, so my big, slow friend gave us both four inches. *He* was dressed entirely in brown, with a wooden baton of office twisted through his belt. He wore leather wristguards, greaves strapped to the knee, and a knotted headband round his all but shaven head. I knew he played with children's kittens when he was at home, but he looked grim. Helena edged closer to me; I took the opportunity to slip my arm around her. He shook his head, still rapt in disbelief. Then, all dimpling innocence, the dimwit had to ask, 'I suppose you'll try to tell me, this is your vinegar pot?'

What a vindictive bastard!

Before I could wriggle out of it, Helena broke free of my arm and rapped back in a thin voice: 'Oh that's me! He usually says I make Medusa's snakes look like a pot of fishing worms.'

I bellowed, 'Petronius Longus, for a quiet man you make a lot of unnecessary noise!'

There was nothing I could say to her, so I grumbled at him. 'She's a senator's daughter – '
'Where would *you* get one of those?'
'Won her at dice.'
'Thundering Jove! Where's the game?' he demanded, lifting her hand in his.
'Oh put her down! Titus and Domitian Caesar have both made their poisoned marks on the poor wench tonight – '
Bright-eyed with the discovery of a friend in a predicament, Petro smirked defiantly, then kissed my senator's daughter's hand with the exaggerated respect he normally keeps for handing Vestal Virgins along the Ostian Way. I was struggling to stop him: '*Mars Ultor*, Petro! This is the Camillus girl – '
'Oh, I realized that! If it were one of your Libyan dancing girls you'd have her in some boudoir on her back!' He believed that I had deliberately lied to him about her; he was furious.
'Oh I'll grant you the boudoir – ' I slammed at him through bared teeth ' – though not necessarily on her back!'
Petronius grew flustered. I knew that he would; for him lewd talk was private, between men. He released Helena abruptly so she lifted her chin. She was white as smoked linen. My heart sank.
'Watch captain, advise me please. I want to reach my father's house, can anything be done?'
'I'll take her,' I interrupted, warning him not to interfere.
At that, quite unexpectedly, Helena flung at me: 'No thank you! I've heard your opinion; now I'll tell you mine!' She had lowered her voice but Petro and I both winced. 'You went to Hades and back in Britain; you saved my life; you are the only person in Rome who keeps a lamp lit for my cousin. You do all that, yet you remain foul-mouthed, prejudiced, and full of casual derision – as lacking in good manners as you are in good nature or good will. Most of the things you blame me for are really not my fault – '
'I don't blame you for anything – '
'You blame me for *everything*!' She was wonderful. I could not believe I had ever thought otherwise. (Any man can make a bit of a mistake.) 'If there's one thing, Didius Falco, I shall regret to the end of my days it's not letting you fall in the River Rhodanus while I had the chance!'
She had a way with pleasantries that flayed a man's skin.

177

She was so angry I became helpless, I leaned against the wall behind us, and laughed until I was weak.

Petronius Longus continued to stare in embarrassment over our heads at the wall, but he said drily, 'Regret it even more, lady; even in the army Falco never learned to swim!'

She went whiter still.

We heard shouts. Footsteps scuffled. The trooper on guard at the end of the alley called out in a low voice. Petronius moved forward anxiously.

'Petro, help us out of this dead end?'

'Why not?' He shrugged. 'Let's shift – ' He stopped. 'Lady-ship, I can take you – '

'Back off, Petro,' I interjected sourly. 'The princess is with me.'

'Trust him, lady,' he condescended to say kindly to Helena. 'He's wonderful in a crisis!'

'Oh he's wonderful anywhere,' Helena Justina capitulated reluctantly. 'According to him!'

From a senator's daughter, this startled him as much as it did me.

We all squeezed out of the cul-de-sac into the noisy thorough-fare. His man muttered. We ducked back. Petronius growled back over his shoulder at me, 'They're swarming like honeybees in Hybla. If we cause a diversion – '

'Steer them away from the river,' I agreed quickly.

'Shriek if the lady shoves you in the Tiber, so we can all watch you drown! Lend me this – ' With a swift grin, Petronius unwound Helena Justina from the white mantle that she wore outdoors. He draped it round the smallest of his lads, who pranced out into the traffic followed by appreciative cheers from the rest.

At the Ostian Way crossroad, Petro posted his men on traffic duty. I knew what to expect; everything ground to a standstill within seconds. I glimpsed a raised arm as Helena's mantle flickered white amid the screaming drivers, all standing up on their footboards, hurling abuse at the watch.

In the chaos, we slipped away. To shed its weight while I was looking after Helena, I left the bag of gold for Petronius to take to mother's for me – warning him it belonged to ma, so he had better not risk milking the contents for himself. Then I headed back fast on the way we had first come. Soon we were much too far west, but in quieter streets, the river side of the Aventine, near the Probus Bridge. I brought us south past the Atrium of Liberty, stopping by Pollio's Library to catch a hasty drink from a fountain. While I was about it, I washed my filthy shoes and legs. Helena Justina tentatively began to do the same, so I gripped her heels and swabbed her feet like a very brisk banquet slave.

'Thank you,' she murmured quietly. I gave my grimmest attention to cleaning off her beaded shoes. 'Are we safe now?'

'No, lady. We're in Rome, in the dark. If anyone jumps us they will probably knife us out of sheer disappointment that we've nothing left to steal.'

'Oh don't fight!' she cajoled me.

I did not reply.

I was trying to decide what to do. I reckoned both our homes might be being watched. Helena Justina had no friends nearby; everyone she knew lived further north. I settled on taking her to stay with my mother.

'Have you realized what this is all about, ladyship?'

She read my thoughts. 'The silver pigs are at Nap Lane!' It was the only explanation for her ungracious husband's last-minute legacy. 'His name was in our stolen letter; he realized he was now proscribed. He created that codicil in case he was betrayed by his collaborators, to deprive them of funds in revenge – but what did he imagine I would do with the ingots if I found them?'

'Return them to the Emperor. You're honest, aren't you?' I asked her in a dry tone.

I tucked her feet into her shoes again and began to walk.

'Falco, why are they chasing us?'

'Domitian overreacting? Titus hinted we were suspicious about your legacy. And he may have listened outside the door before he came whistling in. *What's that?*'

I caught a chuckle of sound. A bevy of horsemen swirled out of nowhere. A tall-sided garden rubbish cart was grumbling past empty; I dragged Helena aboard, jammed up the backboard, and we lay, petrified, while the horses dashed by.

Perhaps it was coincidence; perhaps not.

Two hours had passed since we left the Palace; the strain was beginning to tell. I peered out, saw a man on horseback, then ducked so hard I banged myself half-unconscious before I realized I had only glimpsed a statue of some ancient general going green about the wreath. Something snapped.

179

'This cart seems to know where it's going,' I muttered. 'Let's just keep down!'

It was an arthritic waggon pulled by an asthmatic horse, eratically steered by the oldest gardener in the world; I guessed they would not be going far.

We hid until we came to a stable, then the old man unhitched the horse and pottered off home. He left a guttering taper, despite the risk of fire, so either he was utterly drunk or the horse was afraid of the dark.

We were alone. We were safe. There was only one problem: when we looked outside we were in a public garden. It had eight-foot-high railings – and as he left the man had locked the gates.

'I'll cry for my mother,' I murmured to Helena. 'You climb out and fetch help!'

'If we can't get out, no one else can get in . . .'

'I am not bedding down with a horse!'

'Oh Falco, where's your sense of adventure?'

'Where's your sense?'

We bedded down with the horse.

XLVII

In the stall next to the horse was some straw which various ticks and fleas had decided was clean. I spread out my toga, framing an apology to Festus, though that glad spark would have found this a huge joke. In less respectable company, I might have giggled myself.

I unclipped my belt, threw my sandals aside, hurled myself back on the straw and watched Helena Justina straighten my shoes tidily alongside hers. She distanced herself with her back turned, pulling out her ivory hairpins in despair. She dropped the pins into her shoe while her hair untwined in one loosened tangle down her back. I decided against reaching out for a friendly tug. You have to know a woman very well before you pull her hair.

She sat hugging her knees. Without her mantle she was obviously cold.

'Here – our quaint national garment can make a cosy bedspread. Snuggle up and get warm. Hush! Who's to know?' I dragged her back beside me, pinned her with one elbow and rapidly flung the long ends of my toga round us both. 'My own theory is, warming up women was what the founding fathers had in mind when they invented this . . .'

The senator's daughter had landed in my ceremonial cocoon with her head just below my chin. She was too chilled to resist. She shuddered once, then lay stiff as a post in a wattle fence. As soon as she realized she could only escape with a great deal of effort, she fell diplomatically asleep. She does hate fuss.

I lay awake; she could probably hear my brain creaking as I turned over the night's events. I settled into what I now realized was my favourite position for thinking: leaning my cheek against a peaceful woman's head. I had never discovered this before; Libyan dancing girls wriggle far too much.

Dancing girls had actually become a trial to me in several ways. In a manhunt a bare-waisted panicking dancer would be death. They have their place; they give avidly – though they take with equal enthusiasm, as my banker could confirm. Associating with dancing girls had cost me more than loss of face tonight. One way and another, I had had my fill of them.

Once Helena Justina was asleep, I gradually relaxed.

She was no great weight, but I could hardly forget she was there. She fitted perfectly into the crook of my arm, and by turning my head I could breathe warm draughts of the scent which lingered in her hair. Fine, clean, shining hair that resisted the curling irons and soon dropped into smoother folds than maids in charge of fashionable women like to see. She was wearing Malabathron again. Her black swine of a husband must have given her a mighty great pot – unless of course this girl of strange surprises was saving it for me . . . (A man can dream.)

I was too exhausted to achieve much by thinking, even when I felt so comfortable. I nuzzled Helena's scented hair, ready to doze off. I may have sighed, in the slow, sombre way of a man who has failed to solve his problem despite half an hour of thought. At the point when I gave up the struggle it seemed perfectly natural to be lying in a bale of straw with my arm around Helena Justina, and since by that time I had settled close enough to manage it, and since she was asleep, it also seemed natural to kiss her very gently on the forehead before I drifted off myself.

She moved slightly.

It struck me she had been awake all the time.

'Sorry!' M Didius Falco was quaintly embarrassed. 'Thought you were asleep.'

I was whispering, though there was no need since the constant shuffling of his fidgety hooves said the damn horse was still wide awake too. Probably half Rome knew what I had done. I heard Helena murmur in her sceptical way, 'Is a goodnight kiss on the forehead a service your ladies find on your expenses sheet?'

'All I could reach.' I fell back on bluff. 'When I land a lady in a garden stable her kiss is complimentary of course.'

The senator's daughter lifted her head, leaning up on her elbow as she turned, close above my madly pounding heart. Still holding her lightly, I skulked down into the straw, trying to ignore my fierce consciousness of her body lying against me. She must have felt the tightening of my chest. She looked different with her hair loose. Perhaps she was. I had no way of knowing whether I had stumbled upon some new person, or the woman Helena Justina had always been. But I knew the person she was tonight was someone I liked a great deal.

'And how often does this happen, Falco?'

'Not often enough!'

I glanced up, anticipating hard words, but found her face unexpectedly soft. I smiled ruefully. Then, as my smile began to fade, Helena Justina leaned forwards and kissed me.

I had my free hand tangled in her hair to stop her if she tried to move away, but she did not try. After an aeon of blissful disbelief I remembered to start breathing again.

'Sorry!' she teased gently. She was no more sorry than I was. I tightened my grip to bring her back, but found her already there.

Until then my encounters with women had relied on strategic wine jugs and heavy-handed wit, followed by an elaborate ballet I choreographed to arabesque me and my partner offstage into some convenient bed. The experiences of Didius Falco had been less frequent, and far less interesting, than constant allusion may suggest, but to my credit I did usually manage to supply a bed.

Now, without seriously intending it, I was kissing Helena in the way I had been wanting to kiss her for so long I had no idea when the yearning began. She looked at me quite calmly, so I went on kissing her – just as I ought really to have kissed her at Massilia, and every night for a thousand miles before – while she kissed me back until I knew this time neither of us thought it was a mistake. I stopped.

'We're embarrassing the horse . . .' One of the first facts of life a man understands is that you never tell a woman the truth. Yet I told this one the truth; I always had done and I always would. 'Helena Justina, I gave up seducing women.' I held her face between my two hands, keeping back her hair.

She considered me gravely. 'Was that a vow to the gods?'

'No – a promise to myself.' In case she felt insulted, I kissed her again.

'Why are you telling me?' She did not ask why the promise, which was just as well because I did not really know.

'I want you to believe it.'

Very carefully, Helena kissed me. I turned one palm against hers; her cool fingers interlaced with my own. One of her bare feet was making friends with mine as she asked, 'Is this a promise you want to keep?'

I shook my head in silence (she was kissing me again).

183

Various connected circumstances forced me to admit: 'I don't think . . . I can.' It was so long since I wanted a woman so intensely, I had almost forgotten the pain of acute physical desire. 'Tonight I don't want to anyway . . .!'

'Marcus Didius Falco, you are not seducing me,' smiled Helena Justina, as she solved my moral dilemma with the sweetness I had for so long failed to recognize in her. 'I am trying as hard as I can to seduce you!' I had always known she was a forthright girl.

I have no intention of describing what happened next. It is private between me, the senator's daughter, and the gardener's horse.

XLVIII

It was two hours before morning and most of Rome lay asleep. All the waggons and carts had retreated to their berths. Late diners had braved ambush at street corners to straggle home; prostitutes and pimps were dozing on the rushes among their sordid snoring clients; the lights in the palaces and mansions were dim. It was cold enough for a fine mist to have curled among the valleys between the Seven Hills, but when I woke I was warm physically and felt the slow, strong, welling emotion of a man who had convinced himself the girl in his arms would be the woman in his life.

I stayed completely still, remembering. I watched her sleeping face, at once so familiar to me, yet in deep slumber strangely unlike itself. I knew I must not expect to hold her, or watch her sleeping, ever again. Perhaps that was what made me feel I could not bear to let her go.

She woke. Her gaze at once dropped. She was shy – not because of what we had done, but in case she found me changed. Her hand stirred against me, in a somewhat private place; I saw her eyes widen, startled, then she settled again. I smiled at her.

'Helena . . .' I studied her closed, cautious face. A sculptor might have quibbled, but to me she was beautiful. Anyway, if sculptors knew anything they'd take up a more lucrative line of work. 'Nothing to say?'

After a time she replied, with typical honesty, 'I suppose last night was how it is meant to be?'

Well; she had told me something about Pertinax. My answer was equally subdued.

'I imagine it must be.' Which, if she was interested in past history, told her something about me.

I started to laugh: with her, at myself, at life, helplessly.

'Oh Helena, Helena! . . . I learned some wonders about women with you last night!'

'I learned some about myself!' she answered wryly. Then she closed her eyes against my inner wrist, reluctant to let me see anything she felt.

Despite her restraint, or because of it, I wanted her to understand. 'It's like studying a foreign language: you pick up a smattering of grammar, some basic vocabulary, a terrible accent that just gets you understood; you struggle for years, then without warning everything flows, you grasp how it all works – '

'Oh don't! Falco – ' She stopped; I had lost her.

'Marcus,' I begged, but she hardly seemed to hear.

She forced herself on: 'There's no need to pretend! We found a comforting way to pass the time – ' *O Jupiter!* She had stopped again. Then she insisted, 'Last night was wonderful. You must have realized. But I see how it is: every case a girl, every new case a new girl – '

All this was what a man expects to think. In a leaden voice I raged, 'You are not some girl in a case!'

'So what am I?' Helena demanded.

'Yourself.' I could not tell her.

I could hardly believe she did not realize.

'We ought to leave.'

I hated her sounding so unapproachable. Oh I knew why; dear gods how I knew! I had done this to other people. The hardened attitude – so ungracious, but oh so sensible! A brisk departure, in deep anxiety that one hour of passion might be held against you as the excuse for a lifetime of painful commitment which you had never pretended to want . . .

Now here was an irony. For the first time in my life I felt everything I should, everything most women believe they need. The only time it mattered, yet either Helena simply could not believe it – or she was frantically trying to evade me. I locked my grip on her.

'Helena Justina,' I began slowly, 'what can I do? If I said that I loved you, it would be a tragedy to us both. I am beneath your dignity, and you are beyond my reach – '

'I am a senator's daughter,' she interrupted in a busy tone of voice, 'you are two ranks below. This is not illegal; yet it will not be allowed – ' She struggled restlessly but I would not let her go. 'There is nothing for us – '

'Perhaps! Lady, you and I are as cynical as one another about the world. We will do whatever we must, but don't doubt me. I wanted you very badly; I had wanted you for a long time – as

186

much as you wanted me!' I saw her gaze become unsteady. Quite suddenly I hoped, and made myself believe, that her view of me had been better than I thought, not only last night, but perhaps long before. I threw myself into the hope, knowing – yet not caring – that I was a fool. 'And now . . .'

'Now?' she repeated. A tiny smile twitched in the corner of her mouth. I realized she was answering a smile of mine; she was still with me after all. Fighting for her friendship, I watched her melt back to the intimacy we so unexpectedly found last night. More sure of myself, I soothed that tender spot on the nape of her neck where I had undone the catch of her necklace many hours before. This time I dared let myself notice the flutter on her skin where she was touched. This time I understood that she realized how every nerve in my body was aware of her.

For the second time I told her a truth she must have known already.

'Now I want you again.'

XLIX

Afterwards, awe-struck, I felt her racked by half a dozen sobs, releasing tensions which even in her arms last night I had only half realized were there.

'*Marcus!*'

I fell asleep, shedding all other senses as Helena Justina spoke my name.

I had called her my darling. Any self-respecting informer knows better than that. We were both fairly preoccupied at the moment when it escaped, and I told myself that she probably had not heard. But in my heart I knew I hoped she had.

When they eventually unlocked the gates, we walked out past the stiffly sprouting banks of acanthus while the gardeners, with their floppy hats on their big daft heads and their flat dirty feet in the dew, gaped after us. Still, I dare say it was not the first time they had found uninvited visitors nesting in their patch. Before I took her home I bought Helena some breakfast, something hot from a shop. It was a sausage shop. Fortune defend me, you are dealing with a man who once fed a senator's daughter a peppered calf-meat rissole wrapped in a laurel leaf. Fortune defend my lady, she ate it – *in the street*!

I ate mine too, though cautiously, for my mother brought me up very strictly to eat indoors, respectably.

It was dawn along the Tiber, with a pale sun glimmering. We sat in our ruined finery on a wharf by the river and watched leisurely boatmen ply the silvered water. We had a long good-humoured conversation about whether me thinking all gardeners are daft was another example of my pointless prejudice . . . There were wonderful smells of dried fish and new bread. It was the start of a bright day, though the air still hung chill in the shade by the waterfront booths. It seemed to me it was the start of more than a bright day.

We looked a pair of grisly desperados; I was ashamed to take her home. I found a small private bathhouse already open. We went through together; no one else was there. I bought a flask of oil at an exorbitant price, then in the absence of a bath slave, anointed Helena myself. She seemed to like that; I know I did. Then she scraped me down with a borrowed strigil, which was even better fun. Later, while we were sitting side by side in the warm-air-room, she suddenly turned towards me without a word. She held me close, burying her face. Neither of us spoke. Neither of us needed to. Neither of us could.

All was quiet when I brought her home. The worst part was persuading her father's dumb pig of a porter to wake up and let their lady in. It was the slave who had refused to recognize me the evening before. He would remember now: as she went indoors, the senator's daughter turned back quickly and kissed me on the cheek.

I walked from the Capena Gate back to the Aventine.

I walked without noticing my journey. Exhaustion and elation were swamping me. I felt I had aged a generation in a single night. I was utterly happy – benign towards all the world. Although I was so tired, my maniacal grin glittered from ear to ecstatic ear.

Petronius was hovering outside Lenia's laundry, with the pinkish face and limp hair of a man who had been steaming himself in a laundry for a long time. I felt a deep pang of affection, which he did not deserve and would never have understood. He thumped me in the stomach, then looked at me closely. All the strength had gone from my legs but I accepted the thump with only a faint blink.

'Marcus?' he demanded uncertainly.

'Petro. Thanks for your help.'

'Pleasure. Your mother wants to speak to you about that bag of gold. And this is yours, isn't it?' He handed me my Uncle Scaro's ring.

'You tracked down that runt Melitus?'

'No trouble. We know his haunts. I recovered some loot that belonged to your lady – her jewels. I took them round to her house this morning; the people said she wasn't there . . .' His voice faded uncertainly.

'No. She is now. I told her if you managed to return her jewellery a reward would be polite. I suggested something nice for your wife!'

He stared at me. I regarded him with poignant tenderness. What a wonderful friend.

'Look, Falco, about last night – '

I chuckled dismissively. 'Fate!'

'*Fate!*' he exploded. 'What shit's that?' A simple soul; with a sound philosophy! He was heartbroken to find me in this trouble. (He could tell I was in trouble by my ludicrously gentle smile.) 'Oh Falco, you poor excitable devil – what have you done?'

Lenia came out. Behind her the dull boom of the washtubs throbbed before she swung her backside to close the door. After a lifetime of swaggering with armfuls of dirty linen, she did this as automatically as she opened the doors with her foot. Her arms were free now, but her lined forehead told me she had a headache from imbibing too much with Smaractus the night before. Her frock clung to her in twisted folds, eternally damp from the steam. For some reason, she had lately taken to flinging thin scarves back over her shoulders, in a travesty of refinement. She weighed up my condition as impartially as a stain on a bedsheet, then scoffed, 'Soft as cake custard; the fool's in love again.'

'That all?' Petro tried to reassure himself, though as usual when faced with one of my extravagant antics sturdy Petronius did not appear convinced. 'Happens to Falco three times every week.'

He was wrong. I knew now: until that morning I had never been in love.

'Oh my Petronius, this is different.'

'Blossom, that's what you always say!' Petro shook his head sadly.

I gazed from one to the other of them, too tired and too shaken to speak, then turned upstairs by myself.

Love! That took me by surprise.

However, I was ready for it. I knew what to expect too. Some heartless little button of a girl, pretty as glass. No one who would want me (I intended to suffer; I was a spare-time poet). I could cope with that (I could scribble whole rivers of verse). Some bright enamelled button, or a whole string, until I found one whose hard-nosed father I could wear down to a wedding, then sink like any dutiful citizen into convenience and boredom . . .

Knowing Helena Justina would never be convenient. She was a person I could study for half a lifetime with no danger of becoming bored. Had my status been different, I might have regretted not having half a lifetime to spare.

I could not afford it. Not even the button. A man bowed down by my negative bank balance had to brace himself for chasing rich widows of the elderly grateful kind . . .

I walked upstairs feeling certain of all that. I marched up four flights before I changed my mind.

Love was final. Absolute. A horrendous relief. I walked all the way back down again, and went out to a perfume shop.

'How much is Malabathron?'

The perfumier must have been born wearing an insulting sneer. He told me the price. I could just about afford to let her sniff the stopper from the jar. I informed him with a proud stare that I would think about it, then walked home again.

Lenia saw me come back. I smiled in an aloof way that said I would not answer questions, then set off up the stairs.

When I got to my apartment I stood until inspiration struck. I went into my bedroom and dug around in my baggage roll until I found my little silver nugget from the Vebiodunum mine, then walked back down all six flights to the street. This time I went to a silversmiths. The pride of his collection was a twisted filigree strap, hung with tiny acorns all along its meticulous length, which perfectly matched the restrained taste of what I had seen her wear. I admired it profusely, heard the price, and pretended to decide on earrings instead. But I turned up my nose at all his current stock, then produced my piece of treasure and explained what I wanted him to make.

'I suppose,' the smith remarked, 'it would cause you some embarrassment if I asked where you got hold of this?'

'Not at all,' I told him blithely. 'I obtained it working as a slave in a British silver mine.'

'Very funny!' scoffed the smith.

I walked home.

Lenia saw me again. She did not bother to ask any questions, and I did not bother to smile.

My problems were not yet over. I had evicted the hot-wine waiter; my mother was coming to scrub out my balcony. She aimed an unfriendly blow at me with her mop.

I smiled at my mother, a serious mistake.

'You've been with one of your rope dancers!'

'I have not.' I captured the mop. 'Sit down, share a cup of wine, and I'll tell you what the famous Titus Caesar says about your glorious son.'

She did sit, though she rejected wine. I told her how Titus

had praised Festus, laying on the compliments fairly thick. She listened, with no change that I could see, then sombrely requested wine after all. I poured; we tilted cups in his memory. She sipped in her usual way, sitting very upright, as if she merely drank to be sociable.

My mother's face would never age. Only her skin had grown tired in recent years, so it no longer fitted properly on her bones. After I came back from Britain she seemed smaller than before. Her black-rimmed eyes would stay bright and sharp-witted to the day she died. One day that would happen, and though I now spent so much effort fending off her encroachments, when she was gone I would be desolate.

I sat quiet, letting her absorb all I had said.

No one, not even his girlfriend, ever criticized what Festus had done. My mother had received the news, heard his self-sacrifice hailed, ensured decent arrangements were made (by me) for Marina and the child. People talked about him; she never said a word. We all understood that losing that great, gaudy, generous character had swept away the underpinnings of her life.

Now, alone with me, quite suddenly she told me what she thought. When I made the mistake of calling him a hero, her face set even more. She drained off her cup and fiercely banged it down.

'No, Marcus,' my mother said harshly. 'Your brother was a fool!'

And at last she could cry, for Festus and his folly, in my arms, knowing I had always thought so too.

From that day it became accepted that in the presumably permanent absence of my father I came into my full authority as head of our family. To cope with that, ageing a generation seemed a good idea.

L

In the early afternoon I revisited Nap Lane.

Nothing had changed: the rubbish in the alley, the desolate air of neglect, even the sewermen doggedly lowering hods down the same manhole as before. Round the warehouse itself there were men of a military disposition stationed everywhere. Their scratchy-featured captain refused to let me in, though he did so with good manners, which suggested someone whose rank he took seriously had warned him I might call.

That left two courses of action: I could make a fool of myself handing in pots of pink carnations at a certain woman's door, or exercise my body at the gym. Rather than embarrass her, I went to the gym.

The one I used was run by an intelligent Cilician called Glaucus. It was attached to some private baths two streets from the Temple of Castor and had the unusual distinction of being respectable. Glaucus barred professional gladiators and the kind of hollow-cheeked aristocratic youths who yearn with dry throats after little boys. He kept a casual exercise ground where likeable citizens brought their bodies up to scratch with their minds (which were on the whole quite good), then enjoyed pleasant conversation in his bathhouse afterwards. There were clean towels, a small library in the colonnade, and an excellent pastry shop beside the portico steps.

The first man I saw when I ambled into the ball court was Decimus Camillus Verus, Helena's noble papa. He had taken up my jesting offer to introduce him with startling alacrity. Most of Glaucus' patrons were younger men, before they developed paunches and no sense of proportion about how much thwacking of sand-filled punchbags an elderly body can endure; Glaucus believed having fifty-year-old gentry expiring red-faced outside on his steps would discourage other clients. I had spoken to him already and advised him that the honourable Decimus would pay well, in view of which, drilling a tame senator in occasional light sword fencing might be, if not a sensible idea, at least remunerative.

So here my senator was. I gave him a bout with practice swords; I could already see him sharpening up, though Camillus Verus would never have much of an eye. Still, he would pay – not promptly, but who does? – and Glaucus would give him his money's worth in simple exercise, while making sure no casual blade ever nicked his noble hide.

We threw a handball around the yard rather than admit we were too tired, then relaxed in the baths. We could meet here easily, and whatever became of the case, our habit of friendship seemed likely to endure. The gymnasium would provide one place where we could be cronies despite the gulf of rank. His family could pretend not to know about it; mine already believed I had no sense of social tact.

But now we were exchanging news. After we sweated off our grime in the hot-rooms and plunged through the tepid pools, we lay on slabs, enjoying the attentions of the manicure girls while we waited our turn with the huge arm-wrenching masseur Glaucus had filched from the city baths in Tarsus. He was good, which is to say he was horrible. We would come out afterwards like boys from their first brothel, pretending we felt wonderful but really not at all sure.

'You go first, sir,' I grinned. 'Your time's more valuable.'

We both gave way graciously and let someone else go first.

I noticed the senator was looking tired. I asked, and rather to my surprise he said without any hesitation, 'I had a terrible interview this morning with Sosia Camillina's mother – she had just returned from abroad and received the news. Falco, how are you getting on with your investigation? Is there any chance I will be able to tell her soon that we have at least identified who struck the blow? Will the man who killed Sosia ever be brought to book? The woman was very agitated; she even wanted to employ someone herself to take over the case.'

'With respect to me, my rates are the cheapest she will get!'

'And with respect to us,' the senator said rather stiffly, 'my family are not wealthy, but we shall do all that can be done!'

'I thought Sosia did not know her mother?' I probed.

'No.' He was silent for a moment, then finally explained. 'It was all somewhat unfortunate, and I make no excuses for the way my brother behaved. Sosia's mother was a woman of some status, married as you may have realized, and there was never any suggestion that she wished to alter that. Her husband is an ex-consul now, with all that entails; even at the time he was

194

a prominent man. The lady and my brother became friendly while her man was away on a three-year diplomatic tour; his absence from the scene meant that when she became pregnant it would have been impossible for her to pretend the child was their own.'

'Yet she carried it?'

'Refused to have an abortion. Took a moral stand.'

'Bit late!' I scoffed. The senator looked uncomfortable. 'So *you* brought the child up for them, among your own family?'

'Yes. My brother agreed to adopt her – ' I wondered how much pressure Decimus had had to exert to persuade Publius to do that. 'From time to time I let the woman know how Sosia was, and she insisted on giving me money to buy her daughter presents, but it seemed best for them not to meet. That does not make it at all easy *now*!'

'What happened today?'

'Oh . . . the poor woman said a lot of things I could not blame her for. The worst was, she accused my wife and I of negligence.'

'Oh that's unfair, surely sir?'

'I hope so,' he muttered anxiously, evidently much exercised by the possibility. 'Julia Justa and I certainly tried to do our best for Sosia. All my family were deeply fond of her. After that attempt to kidnap her, my wife forbade Sosia to leave the house; we thought that was enough. What else could we do? Were we wrong? But Sosia's mother accuses me of letting her run round the streets like a Transtiberina matchgirl . . .'

He was distressed. I was finding the conversation pretty painful myself, so I did my best to calm him down and changed the subject as soon as I could.

I asked if he had heard any more from the Palace about apprehending the conspirators. Glancing around in case we were being overheard (the surest way to ensure we were), the senator lowered his voice.

'Titus Caesar whispers that certain gentlemen have dispersed!'

This furtive stuff was fun for him but not much practical help.

'Sir, I need to know who, and where to.'

He sucked his lip, but told me. Faustus Ferentinus had sailed for Lycia; he had gone without permission – which is forbidden to senators, who have to reside in Rome. Cornelius Gracilis asked for an interview with the Emperor, though his servants found him stretched out stiff with a sword in his right hand (he was left-handed) before he could attend; suicide – apparently.

Curtius Gordianus and his brother Longinus had inherited sudden priesthoods at a minor temple beside the Ionian Sea, which was probably more punishing than any exile our kindly old tyrant Vespasian would devise for them himself. Aufidius Crispus had been spotted among the seaside crowds in Oplontis. It seemed to me no one who could lay his hands on a private mint of silver would let himself suffer high summer among the smart set in the fashionable villas along the Naples shore.

'What do you think?' Decimus asked.

'Titus ought to have Aufidius watched. Oplontis is only a few days from Rome. If nothing else turns up I'll go down there myself, but I'm reluctant to leave while there's any chance of locating the silver pigs. Has Titus found anything in Nap Lane?'

He shook his head. 'My daughter will have access very soon.'

From the swimming pool to our left came the awkward flub as an overweight hearty with no real diving style launched himself off the side.

'I assume you won't let Helena go there,' I warned him quietly. I ought to have used her full name, but it was too late now.

'No, no. My brother can inspect the place; he'll be advising her on selling off the spice.'

'The building itself still belongs to the old man Marcellus?'

'Mmm. We shall empty it quickly as a courtesy to him, though Helena and old Marcellus are on good terms. He still regards her as his daughter-in-law. She has a knack of charming elderly men.'

I lay on my back, trying to appear like a man who might have failed to notice his Helena's charm.

Helena's father gazed thoughtfully upwards too.

'I worry about my daughter,' he revealed. With a wild pang of hysteria I thought, *the horse has talked*! 'I made a mistake over Pertinax; I expect you know. She never blamed me, but I shall always blame myself.'

'She has very high standards,' I said, closing my eyes as if I was simply sleepy after my bathe. Hearing Decimus turn onto his elbow, I looked up.

Now I had studied Helena so closely, I could see in her father's face physical similarities another man would miss. That stiff bush of hair was all his own, but the direct expression, the tilt of the cheekbones, the slight crease at the corners of the mouth in response to irony, were hers; sometimes, too, she shared inflexions from his voice. He was watching me with

196

the glint of sharp amusement that I had always liked. I felt glad that I liked her father, grateful to remember I had liked him from the start.

'High standards,' repeated Decimus Camillus Verus, apparently inspecting me. He sighed, almost imperceptibly. 'Well, Helena always seems to know what she wants!'

He was worried about his daughter; I suppose he was worried about me.

There are some things a common citizen cannot say to the parents of a highborn, respectable lady. If I declared to a senator that any ground his daughter stood upon became for me a consecrated place, he would not (I could see) feel reassured.

Luckily then the Man from Tarsus approached us with a towel on his arm. I made Decimus have the first massage, hoping his large tip would leave the Tarsan giant kinder towards me. It didn't work; it only fuelled him with a greater energy.

LI

My mother came back that afternoon to tell me I was expected to preside over the huge family party which was going to hog a scaffold at Vespasian's Triumph next day. This promised a real feast of sunstroke, sisters backbiting, and tired children screaming with illogical rage; my favourite sort of day. Ma herself was decamping to share a quiet balcony with three ancient crones she knew. Still, she had brought me a great golden-headed Imperial bream to soften the blow.

'You tidied your room!' she sniffed. 'Growing up at last?'

'Might get a visitor I want to impress.'

The visitor I wanted never came.

As she passed the bench behind me, my mother ruffled up the hair on the back of my head, then smoothed it down. I couldn't help it if she despaired of me; I was in a state of high old despair myself.

Sitting out on the balcony pretending to philosophize, I recognized a light step outside the door. Someone knocked, then came in without waiting. Rigid with anticipation, I was on my feet. In this way, through the folding door, I observed my wonderful mother apprehending a young woman in my room.

It was not the confrontation ma was accustomed to have. She expected mock coral anklets and girlish confusion, not soft drapes in muted clours and those serious eyes.

'Good afternoon. My name is Helena Justina,' declared Helena, who knew how to behave with tranquillity even when facing my parent wielding a bowl of almond stuffing and a twelve-inch boning knife. 'My father is the senator Camillus Verus. My maid is, of course, waiting for me outside. I was hoping for an interview with Didius Falco; I am a client.'

'I am his mother!' stated my mother, like Venus of the Foamy Feet wading in on behalf of Aeneas. (Mind you, I don't suppose

198

pious Aeneas, that insufferable prig, flourished on fish his lovely goddess mother boned and stuffed for him herself.)

'I thought you must be,' replied Helena in her quiet, pleasant way, eyeing my uncooked dinner as if she longed to be asked to stay. 'You once took care of my cousin Sosia; I'm so glad of this opportunity to thank you.' After which, adjusting her veil, she fell modestly silent as a younger woman addressing an older lady does if she has good sense. (It was the first time any woman who knew me had deferred to mama with any show of sense.)

'*Marcus!*' screeched ma, rather put out at being so politely outfaced. 'Business for you!'

Trying to look nonchalant, I strolled into the room.

My mother whipped away the fish plate, then bustled out onto the balcony, diligently respecting a client's privacy. This was no real sacrifice; she could still listen from outdoors. I offered Helena the client's chair while I sat the other side of the table acting businesslike.

Our eyes met. My acting collapsed. She was trying to decide whether I was glad to see her; I was just as cautiously scanning her. At exactly the same moment our eyes lit with self-ridicule – then we just sat, in the silence that says everything, and smiled at each other happily.

'Didius Falco, I want to discuss your bill.'

With one eye on the balcony door, I stretched across the table and just touched her fingertips. A shiver of electricity raised goosebumps on my arms.

'Anything wrong with it, ladyship?'

She pulled away her hands, genuinely indignant. 'What on earth are *Debatable Items*?' she demanded. 'Five hundred sesterces for something you don't even explain?'

'It's just a loose heading some accountants use. My advice is, debate madly and don't pay!' I grinned; she realized it was an excuse to make her call.

'Hmm! I'll think it over. Should I speak to your accountant?'

'I never use an accountant. Half of them can only calculate a percentage when it's their fee, and I have enough hangers-on sharing my stockpot without some bald Phoenician tallyman and his scrofulous clerk expecting to join in too. When you're ready, you'd better talk directly to me.'

I gave Helena a slow frank stare that was meant to remind her of an evening she should forget. I stopped, because my own heart started racing much too fast. I felt as volatile as if I had lost two pints of blood.

I leaned back against the wall with my hands linked behind my head, smiling faintly as I enjoyed the sight of her. She smiled back, enjoying that. I enjoyed her smile . . .

I had to stop this. This was a terrible mistake. All I needed in life was some accessible miss with a flower behind her ear, who would giggle when I read my poems to her. I would never read my poetry to Helena. She would read it for herself, then indicate with underlining where the spelling and rhythms were wrong; I would complain fiercely, then alter it exactly as she had said . . .

'There is something else,' she began. My face stitched itself happily into a wordless, frog-like grin. 'The warehouse in Nap Lane will be released by customs very soon. My father is reluctant for me to go.'

My arms dropped abruptly. 'Nap Lane was the scene of a murder. Your father's right.'

'I really want to look round – '

'Take somebody then.'

'Would you come?'

'Glad to. Let me know when.' I gave her a wicked wide-eyed gleam that said there were things we could do in a pepper warehouse that had spice of their own. Helena looked grave. I cleared my throat sensibly. She rose to leave.

'Tomorrow's the Triumph: will you go?'

'Not for myself – family duty. Let's see about your warehouse after that.'

Climbing out from behind the table I followed her to the door. Leaving it ajar for camouflage, we stepped outside. Confusion: her maid was still waiting on the landing where she had been left.

Some ladies' maids know how to disappear discreetly when a man wants to kiss the beauty they chaperone. In one way, I was pleased to discover Helena's girl entertained no regular concept that her mistress might be wanting to be kissed. At the same time, I was terrified in case the lady did not want it any more.

'Naïssa, walk down. I'll catch you up,' Helena commanded in her calm, efficient voice.

We listend to Naïssa's retreating footsteps until she turned down the next flight. Neither of us spoke another word.

Helena had turned to me with a troubled look. I kissed her hand, at arm's length, then kissed her other hand at half stretch. Swinging her close, I kissed her on both cheeks. With a sigh that

200

answered mine, she fell into my arms, then for a long moment we stood motionless while troubles dropped from us like the single quake of falling petals from an overblown rose. Still holding her and kissing her, I walked her slowly backwards across the landing; eventually, at the head of the stairs, I let her go.

She went down. I watched her all the way to the street. I stood staring for five minutes after she had gone.

She had transformed my day.

I sat back at my table pretending nothing was wrong. My face tingled where Helena had touched me with her hand before she left.

My mother was waiting. She knew there had been plenty of times when I came sauntering back from seeing off a woman with some long-winded pantomime of affection. They came; they went; they threatened no one's peace.

Now mother stomped over to the opposite bench, purse-lipped. 'So that's her!'

My heart turned over beneath a rib. I laughed awkwardly. 'How did you know?'

'I know you!'

I stretched my chin and looked up at the ceiling; I half noticed there was a new bulge where rain was coming in. I thought of Helena Justina as my mother must have seen her, so fine-skinned and elegant in her understated jewellery, with such beautiful manners that she took on her father's knack of appearing diffident, though that strange mixture of moral grit and mischievous humour constantly shone through. Helena Justina, a senator's daughter, talking to me so coolly about fees and warehouses while her eyes sang in silence of the happiness we had shared . . . Everyone knew I was searching (when I bothered, because the search was quite haphazard) for someone like Marina, my brother's girl: an uncomplicated soul with some brains and a pretty face, who could just about keep house and who owned enough friends of her own to stay out of my way. Everyone knew that; I knew it myself.

I stared back at the table, fiddling with escaped tarragon twigs.

'Well!' challenged my mother. 'Do I start baking saffron cakes, or throw on a black veil and wail at Juno's Temple? What happens now?'

'Nothing,' I said, squaring up to the facts. 'She told you who her father is. There's nothing I can do.'

Another angry quirk puckered my mother's mouth. 'Marcus, having seen her, I don't imagine it is up to you!'

Then I gazed at my mother with a long face, while my mother looked rather oddly back at me.

LII

I had nothing to do that evening, so I went to the barber's at the end of our street. I sat out on the pavement while he scraped my chin. I managed to trip up some minor official's lictor and make it look like a genuine accident. The lictor himself was nearly castrated on his ceremonial axe; I felt proud of myself.

I was going to see her again. Who? No one. Just a girl. Just a client. Forget I mentioned it.

The barber's boy ambled up, chewing the end of a Lucanian sausage. He was thirteen, not totally deficient but he managed to make eating a sausage look a complicated challenge for his brain. My sister Maia's children all called him Plato.

'Falco! Lady looking for you outside your house.'

Rarely has a man with a Spanish razor at his throat leapt up so fast.

I hopped over a cockle barrel, dashed round a pile of empty amphorae, and cracked my head on a basket of flowers outside the funeral parlour where hired mourners were getting in voice – not for a wake, but for the next day's Triumph which would close down the city in public holiday. Every musician in Rome would be out distracting the crowds so pickpockets could do their work efficiently.

I saw no lady. No wonder. That fool Plato should have known better: it was *Lenia* who wanted to see me. Lenia, hovering outside the laundry – looking ashamed.

Twenty years of explaining away lost undertunics made a crestfallen laundress such an unusual sight that I realized the cause must be desperate. It was. To celebrate the Emperor's Triumph she was planning an act of reckless delirium: our strong-armed queen of the washtubs was plunging into wedlock.

When people announce their marriages, I try to avoid informing them that they are making a bad mistake. They generally are, but if all the unsuitable pairings in Rome were suffocated at birth by kind friends' good advice, there would be no new generation of civilized men to subdue the world's barbarians.

'Who is the happy bridegroom?'

'Smaractus.'

On reconsideration I gave Lenia the strongest advice I could.

The reason for not bothering is that they never listen anyway.

'Shut up, Falco,' Lenia responded amiably. 'He's worth half a million sesterces!'

For several reasons this news raised a red mist before my eyes. 'If Smaractus told you that, girl, I can promise you he's lying!'

'Don't be a fool; I never asked him.'

'All right, it depends who you seduced. If it was his accountant he's boasting, so halve it. If it was his banker he's being cautious, so double it – '

'Neither. Believe me, I'm not taking chances; I've read his will.'

'Lenia,' I commented sadly, 'there are no depths to which a scheming woman will not sink!'

A strategic alliance with my pernicious landlord could only be part of Lenia's devious business plan. He had his eye on her laundry, that small but steady gold mine, but her own attention was riveted on his hefty real estate. Their lives together would be fortified by the keen nip of greed, as each prayed daily to their household gods that the other would die first.

Many marriages endure for decades on this healthy basis, so I wished her well.

'He'll be living here, Falco – '

'Thought he already was!'

'Just warning you.'

'I don't care what tree that foul bird exudes his guano in – '

'I can't keep him out of the laundry. I thought before the wedding you might carry off your parcel from the vat – '

The original silver pig! The one found in the street, which Petronius and I had rescued afterwards from Sosia Camillina's bank box. I had forgotten all about it; so had everybody else . . .

Hauled up by our mighty Lenia, my pig was soon drying under some seedy temple's weekly batch of soiled smalls. Wiping it with a priest's headcloth amidst a whiff of last Thursday's incense, Lenia asked, 'Did you know that someone had attached a laundry list?'

Petronius and I had left a rope round the pig; fixed to the rope now was a single wax tablet . . .

'Oh dear gods!'

Before ever I took it from Lenia's swollen hand I knew what it was, and whose. I could hear Lenia telling me six months ago, *I let her pee in the bleach vat, then she left a note upstairs . . .* Then, too, I remembered Helena Justina when she was raging at me that first night in Britain. *She said she had told you . . .*

And so she had. Formally enough to be presented in evidence, Sosia Camillina had given me a list of names.

Sosia Camillina, daughter of P Camillus Meto, to M Didius Falco, private informer. On the Ides of October in the second consulship of
Vespasian Augustus, his first as Emperor
T Flavius Domitianus
L Aufidius Crispus
Cn Atius Pertinax Caprenius Marcellus
Ti Faustus Plautius Ferentinus
A Curtius Gordianus
A Curtius Longinus
Q Cornelius Gracilis

I name these men in duty to the Emperor and devotion to the gods.

There they all were. All? All but one, apparently. Above her final sentence was a one line gap. It looked as if Sosia had written an extra name; as if she had written, then at once pulled the flat end of her stylus back through the wax, deleting the line she had just inscribed there with its point.

In this case, I had once told Helena, there could be no loyalty and no trust. Sosia Camillina possessed both. It must have made a heavy burden for a sixteen-year-old girl.

This tablet proved nothing. Just seven men who knew each other; it read like a dinner-party list. Perhaps Sosia had found one in a house she had visited, a note, written out to give instructions to someone's household steward. Sosia had then carefully copied out the names . . .

Seven men, who could say, if we challenged them in court, they had been dining quietly together. Though their real purpose might be not one jot less sinister for that.

And who, then, had been this ugly dinner party's host?

I stared at the faint groove where it seemed Sosia's stylus had erased a further name. My poor Sosia had been bound in law by ties that were not mine. Had she stood here now, fixing me with those great eager eyes that I remembered so vividly, I would have had to maintain her silence with her to the end. But she was long gone. And I still wanted bitterly to avenge her death.

There was one more person involved in this case: somebody so adept at shrinking out of view that I had almost deliberately ignored the obvious link. I thanked Lenia, grasped the ingot in my arms, and struggled with it upstairs to my room. Soon, wearing my best toga, the one that belonged to Festus, I came down again and went out to do what was necessary on Palatine Hill.

LIII

By the time I clambered up to the Palace, I felt so hysterical I expected the Praetorians to arrest me on sight. It was comforting to find that the Emperor's Guards could apparently distinguish a true assassin from a hot but honest man. When I begged to see Titus I was passed in through officials of increasing refinement until a tall secretary, who gave the impression he would not flutter one long handsome eyelash if his mother-in-law caught him buggering the butcher in her backyard, listened and then propped me on a stool with my toga piled neatly in my lap while he walked away into an inner room.

Titus came out.

He made a magnificent sight. He had assumed his full military uniform as commander in chief in Judaea and a confident mood to match. He wore an ornamented breastplate, its torso moulded to heroic proportions, a richly dyed, completely circular purple cloak, and a tunic frogged on every edge with rigid palm leaf braid. Anything he lacked in height to carry this off, he made up in a muscular build. He was ready to go to the Temple of Isis, where he would spend the night solemnly with his father and his brother, before they entered the city tomorrow as victorious Roman generals bringing home their captives and glittering spoils.

Doubt now assailed me. My client had dressed as if to model for the formal statues that would gild his reputation for several thousand years. I did not believe in the power of ceremonial, but I knew that I had come on the wrong day.

I stood up. I handed Titus Sosia's writing tablet, feeling the firm grip of his hand as he took it from me. He glanced in pinched silence at Domitian's name, then ran his eye down the rest.

'Thank you, Falco. This is useful, but nothing new . . .' His eyes seemed remote, his mind half-given to the honours of tomorrow. Even so, he grasped my own hectic excitement in the end. 'What – do you believe it is?'

I pointed out the gap.

'Sir, Camillus Meto's daughter was no scribe. She wrote like a schoolgirl, pressing hard with her stylus. I had to show you the list, but if you agree, at the cost of destroying it – ' I swallowed for I could not easily forgo anything Sosia Camillina gave to me. 'If we melt the wax completely off the backing board, you may find she scraped right through into the wood.'

His glance hit mine; the man was as sharp as a Spanish sword.

'The missing name may still be visible?' Titus Caesar took decisions like the general he was. 'Little to lose!'

He called back the thin secretary. Hollow-shouldered and slightly showing off, this ghoul soon tilted the tablet over a flame, turning his bony wrist to let the drips skitter into a chased silver bowl. He gave it back with a professional flourish.

Titus glanced at the scarred surface, then signalled the secretary to make himself scarce. For a painful moment we gazed at each other, then Titus quietly said, 'Well, Didius Falco, how good an informer are you? Do you want to tell me, before I show you this, who you think it is?'

A military tribune, in the narrow purple bands of the second rank, tripped into the anteroom to meet some official appointment in connection with the Triumph: eyes bright, best boots, inlaid armour burnished to a gleam, and scrubbed from his straight-cut toenails to the red tips of his adolescent ears. Titus did not even look at him.

'*Out!*' he commanded, almost politely, though the tribune bolted without a second glance.

Once again the room was silent. Titus and me . . . Titus still holding the tablet, which I still had not seen.

My mouth felt dry. As an informer I was only middling good (too much of a dreamer and too chary of dubious commissions – the kind that pay); all the same I was good enough. I had vowed never to align myself with the establishment again; yet I gave my own kind of service to my city and the Empire. I would never accept any Emperor's divinity, but I believed in my own self-respect and securing my fee.

So I told Titus Caesar who I thought it was.

'It must be one of the Camillus brothers, Caesar. But I am not certain which.'

LIV

Outside we heard an escort party assembling. Titus strode to the doorway and spoke. The agitation stilled; someone posted a guard.

My abdomen felt sore, as if I had been seriously bereaved.

Coming back, Titus seated me and took his own place on the same couch beside me, laying the tablet between us, face down.

'That poor little girl! Oh, Falco – that whole poor family! Well, it has to be done. Tell me your reasoning, please.'

'Sir, once you think of it, it seems horribly obvious. I'll go back to the start. When the first silver pig turned up in Rome, what happened to Sosia Camillina was deeply relevant; I have always thought that. Possibly Atius Pertinax, in his position as the praetor's aedile, had been able to tell the conspirators where the ingot was hidden. But I now believe that they knew that already – and certainly it was someone close to her who realized that Sosia knew the number to the bank box. So, the speediest way to get into it was to take her there herself – using ruffians to confuse the issue and prevent her recognizing anyone.'

Titus nodded. 'Anything else?'

'Yes. Just before she died, Sosia wrote to her cousin that she had identified the house of a man who was connected with the people who abducted her. I believe that is where she had found this list. The point is, at that time, for her own safety following the kidnap attempt she was confined at home – that is, in the senator's house – though I have no doubt that whenever she wanted, she would still have been given access to her own father's house next door.' Titus shook his head in reluctant acceptance of what I said. 'Caesar, from the moment I undertook this case for you, someone very close has been watching my progress and thwarting every turn. When Helena Justina and I came back from Britain, after months away, someone knew enough to ambush us that very day. I had in fact sent a message from the Ostia Gate – to her family.'

'And so you lost the letter from friend Hilaris?' Titus smiled affectionately as he spoke; honest Gaius, with his pedantic dedication to hard work, had that effect. I smiled too, though simply because I liked the man.

'Quite. I always assumed the two names Flavius Hilaris was sending to Vespasian were Domitian and Pertinax. He would not tell me though. I misunderstood; it's most unlikely the mining contractor Triferus would realize your brother was involved . . . Pertinax, the shipper, must be one of them, but Pertinax had been married to Gaius' own niece. And suppose the other was an even closer relation of his wife's! It must have been painful; no wonder if Flavius Hilaris preferred to stand aloof and let Vespasian decide what to do.'

Without comment on that point, Titus suggested carefully, 'Did you ever consider Hilaris might be implicated here?'

'Not once I met him!' I told him my joke about this case being one where only the public officers were straight; he laughed.

'All honour to the knights,' he exclaimed, applauding the middle class. Then added, fully serious as far as I could tell, 'You ought to consider aiming for higher rank yourself. My father is anxious to build up the lists with good men.'

The property qualification for the second rank is land worth four hundred thousand sesterces; Titus Caesar could not have realized what a ludicrous observation he had made. In some years the Falco income was so low, I qualified for tokens to claim the corn dole for the poor.

Ignoring the imperial jest, I pointed out that for twenty years Flavius Hilaris had been Vespasian's friend.

'Falco, it's a sad fact that when a man becomes Emperor he has to look twice at his friends.'

'When a man becomes Emperor, sir, his friends may look twice at him!'

He laughed again.

Outside the door subdued voices were murmuring insistently now. Titus was staring into space.

'Has Flavius Hilaris been asked to write again?' I asked.

'We sent out an urgent message by signal flare, but traffic is very heavy because of the Triumph. A reply should come back after tomorrow.'

'Do you still need it?'

It was then he finally turned over Sosia's tablet so I could read what it said for myself.

'I'm afraid so,' Titus said.

There were various scratches on the tablet's pale wood; my hunch had been right, Sosia was a heavy-handed scribe. I could trace clear marks, strokes, even individual letters, all the way down the page.

But it was impossible to decipher the missing name.

LV

Titus Caesar folded his arms.

'Well, it changes nothing really. We shall just have to find out for ourselves. Have you any idea which brother it is?'

'No, sir. It could be the senator, who appears so anxious to help your father, but may be doing that to obtain the opportunity to sabotage our efforts. Or equally it could be his brother, who was certainly a close associate of Atius Pertinax. I suppose it could conceivably be both.'

'Falco, how long have you had these suspicions?' Titus asked me curiously.

'Caesar, if you wanted mere speculation, I could have handed you a list a thousand names long six months ago – '

Still gripping his arms across this chest, Titus tipped up that famous Flavian chin. 'Hogging this family's involvement to yourself? You're attached to them obviously?'

'No, Caesar,' I insisted.

We were on the verge of heated argument. No surprise; I had already quarrelled at some time or other with everyone else connected with the case. But Titus, with his strong sentimental streak, abruptly capsized. He threw back his head even further and exclaimed in a sad voice, 'Oh Falco; how I hate this!'

'You hate it,' I told him crisply, 'but you will have to deal with it.'

There was more movement outside. A tribune slightly older than the first, this one in the broad purple stripe of senatorial rank, entered the room. Seeing Titus and me with our heads together he stood quietly; he was obviously held in great confidence, and did not expect a rebuff. Plainly he believed their special day tomorrow took precedence over my own small moment of intrigue. His determined presence recalled Titus to their real order of business.

212

'Is there a problem, sir? Domitian Caesar has ridden ahead, but your father is delaying for you.'

'Yes. I'll come.'

The tribune waited. Titus let him stay.

'We need you to help us identify the remaining conspirators!' Titus urged me. I hesitated. I was too closely connected with people involved to judge the issues cleanly any more. My reluctance was not unexpected, I could see.

'Caesar, the Guards could take this forward for you now. There's a captain I recommend to you who knows something about it already; his name's Julius Frontinus. He became interested when the first ingot was found in Rome; he helped put me on the right track then – '

'A friend?'

'He went to school with my brother.'

'Ah!'

Dealing with a Caesar was unpleasantly civilized. His good manners gave me a sick qualm; instead of escaping I felt hopelessly pressurized.

'Falco, I can't force you to go on with the case, though I wish you would. Look, will you leave your decision just for a day? Nothing is going to happen in the next twenty-four hours. All Rome will be at a standstill. Tomorrow my father will be handing out gifts to people in his pay. You've certainly earned that; you may as well take advantage! Meanwhile, let us both consider what to do. After the Triumph come and talk to me again.' He rose, ready now to answer the call from his staff, yet he did not hurry me.

'These are not my kind of people,' I informed him awkwardly. 'I can round up a thug or a thief and throw him at your feet with a noose round his neck, alive or dead, as you choose. I lack finesse for this.'

Titus Caesar lifted an eyebrow sardonically.

'A cornered traitor is unlikely to respond according to strict court etiquette. Didius Falco, my father has had a letter from Flavius Hilaris, applauding your physical endurance and mental agility; he's spent three sheets of first quality parchment singing your praises! You have managed when it suited you to deal on your own aggressive terms with anyone who stumbled in your path, yet it does not suit you now?'

'Sir, very well. I'll honour my contract, identify who organized the plot – '

'And find the silver pigs!'

'Sosia Camillina suspected where they were. I believe she was right all along.'

'Nap Lane?'

'Nap Lane.'

'Falco,' Titus was thoroughly exasperated now, 'I cannot keep my men in Nap Lane any longer! They have work elsewhere. The warehouse has been virtually stripped down and reconstructed several times. The value of the contents is a serious complication for the officer in charge. The lady you act for has been promised that my officers will leave – '

'Then let them,' I suggested with a faint smile. 'And let me tell Helena Justina that your men have been recalled to other duties as from tomorrow, the day of your Triumph. It might be useful if that news was to be broadcast amongst her family . . .' I did not explain why, but like other intelligent men he enjoyed a conversation that left him work to do.

'Nothing is going to happen so long as my soldiers are perching on the pigs? I agree. You may tell Helena Justina the warehouse is available. I will ask the Praetorians to inspect the place informally from time to time – but Falco, I rely on you!'

I left the Palace on the northeast side, coming down to the Forum on the Clivus Victoriae. All the streets, normally so dark at night, were ablaze with the flickering light of torches as dim figures worked to adorn their porticos with garlands. Gangs of public contractors were erecting stands. The gutters ran with a constant chuckle of water as mud and debris were sluiced from one island block to another. Squadron after squadron of soldiery went marching past on their way to the great muster at the Plain of Mars. Citizens who would normally lock themselves into their shops and houses after nightfall hovered in groups outside, reluctant to leave the expectant atmosphere. Already the city hummed.

I sent one of my nephews with a note to Helena Justina. I said the spices were now hers but I could no longer make myself available for her proposed warehouse spree. I did not tell her why. By the time breaking my promise became an embarrassment, she would understand; meanwhile, I guessed she would assume I had decided to avoid her.

Perhaps I should.

I had never written to Helena before. Now I would probably never do so again. No doubt once she knew what I had done

214

on Palatine Hill, the honourable Helena Justina would be only too keen to avoid me.

I told my nephew to wait for any answer, but she sent none.

That night I visited Petronius at his house. His wife, who takes a dim view of me at the best of times, was not at all pleased; she wanted him to spend time with their children to make up for having to waste all the hours of the public holiday keeping watch for shopbreakers along the Ostia Road.

I told Petro what I believed was now afoot and he promised to stake out the warehouse with me when I tipped him the word. I left him on his hands and knees being ridden like an elephant by his three tiny girls. His wife gave me a black pudding when I departed, I think as a present for leaving them alone.

I wanted to get drunk. Luckily for Petro's wife I hold the philosophy that you can be drunk at any other point in a case, but never when you know at last who it is you are looking for.

When I went up to the Palace I had thought it was all over. The cases you hate most never seem to end.

LVI

I took all of my sisters and a dozen small children to watch Vespasian's Triumph. For that alone my soul deserves quiet rest in Elysian fields.

I managed to miss the tedious march of the consuls and senators by the simple trick of having overslept. (Even with the city in ferment, up on the sixth floor I could doze deep into the morning as peaceful as a dove's egg in a stone pine nest.) Out on the Campus Martius the army drew up in parade, while Vespasian and Titus took their places on ivory seats in the Portico of Octavia to receive the troops' acclaim. When this shout tore the skies, even an Aventine sleepyhead leapt out of bed. While the Imperial party pecked at breakfast under the Triumphal Arch, I sorted out my holiday tunic, peacefully watered the flowers on my balcony, and combed my hair. I hummed on my way northwards, passing through the garlanded arcades, into a wall of sound.

It was a lively day, warm and bright, with a lift in the air. A bad day for bunions; by the time I strolled out there was standing room only. All the temples had been thrown open, and the baths were closed; incense, smoking on a thousand altars, grappled with the whiff of half a million people perspiring in their holiday clothes without a chance to bathe all day. Apart from one or two dedicated housebreakers slipping through deserted alleys with discreet sacks of swag, everyone who was not in the procession was watching it. There were so many gawpers packed along the processional route that the marchers and floats could hardly crawl along.

My brother-in-law Mico (the plasterer) had for once been put to use. They sent him out at first light to erect a scaffold just for us in front of some unwary citizen's private house. There was not really room for a scaffold, but when the aedile's troops saw the entire Didius family installed on a day's hampers, all

216

eating squelchy melons and wearing country hats, with their noses already stuck well down their gourds of wine and their throats full of ready abuse, the troopers accepted a slice of melon each then shambled off without trying to tear the scaffold down.

Luckily, by the time I arrived the senators had passed, so the trumpets and warhorns were being carried by, their towering bell-like mouths just level with our heads. Victorina and Alia mouthed obscenities at me. The rest of the family covered their ears against the din and decided not to strain their vocal chords complaining I was late.

'Do you remember,' Victorina reminisced in a loud voice, as the blaring ranks of trumpeters reached a momentary gap, 'that time at the Triumph for the Conquest of Britain when the Emperor's elephants frightened Marcus so much he was sick?'

It had nothing to do with the elephants. I was seven. I was sitting cross-legged on the floor beside a tray of Persian sweetmeats that were standing in the shade. All I could view of the British Triumph were other people's legs. That whole afternoon I munched my way through three pounds of honey-fried stuffed dates, until my little lips were tender from licking off the salt and my aching belly decided to revolt. I never even saw the elephants . . .

Maia threw me a hat. Of all my sisters, Maia displays the most consistent good nature towards me – with the single exception of the fact that it was Maia who did me the honour of importing into our family my brother-in-law Famia. This Famia was a chariot-horse vet for the Greens – and I would have found him a specimen of crass mediocrity even if I had not inclined quite strongly to the Blues. In fact I disliked all of my sisters' husbands, which was one reason I hated family gatherings. Being formally civil to idiots and wastrels was not my idea of a festive day. Apart from Galla's husband, whom Galla had temporarily thrown out on a rubbish heap, these despicable characters came and went in the course of the day, and my only consolation was that their wives treated them even more poisonously than they treated me.

And it was a long day. After heralding by the trumpets, we had the spoils of war. Titus was right, nothing like it had ever been seen anywhere in the world. It was a year since Vespasian seized the throne, six months since he came home himself. Plenty of time for the Palace to organize a spectacle, and they had. For hour after hour we were treated to representations of

217

Vespasian's Judaean campaign: deserts and rivers, captured towns and blazing villages, armies wheeling over baking plains, siege engines invented by Vespasian himself – all teetering by in vivid tableaux on floats that towered three- or four-storeys high. Then, amid the aching creak of solid drumwheels and the smell of newly painted canvas as it cracked in the sun, stages with painted oars on their skirts blundered and dipped through the streets like high-crested sailing ships. I liked the ships best; sailing on dry land seemed perfect to me.

On it went. Row after row of bearers in crimson uniforms and laurel wreaths marched through the city from the Plain of Mars, past the theatres where crowds crammed the outer walls, through the Cattle Market, round the Circus, up between the Palatine and the Caelian, then on into the Forum by the Sacred Way. They brought banners and hangings in rich Babylonian stuffs, painted by fine artists or encrusted with jewelled embroidery. Swaying on palanquins, statues of the city's most cherished gods were carried by in festive dress. And flaunted in such quanitities that it became almost meaningless, came treasure by the ton: not only the rich gold and jewellery excavated from the rubble of devastated Jerusalem, but priceless marvels extracted with steely diplomacy at Vespasian's command from cities in the wealthiest corners of the world. Loose gemstones were tumbled in mounds on litters just as they came, as if all the mines of India had hiccupped overnight: onyx and sardonyx, amethysts and agate, emeralds, jasper, jacinth, sapphires and lapis lazuli. Then followed, on stretchers in casual heaps, the gold crowns of conquest, diadems spiked like glittering sunbursts, coronets set with monstrous rubies and great sea pearls. After that more gold, until the streets flickered with the glow of it as the molten tide flowed on towards the Capitol in one slow, swollen meander of heroic extravagance.

I remember that towards the afternoon the noise dimmed – not because the crowds were hoarse (though they were) or losing interest (they were not), but as if folk could no longer contemplate this lavish show of Empire with the simple exuberance that first brought them to cheer. Applause no longer seemed enough. At the same time, the endless marching feet pressed past with increased pride at the climax of this, the main part of the procession: the treasures from the sacred Temple at Jerusalem – the strange seven-branched candelabrum, a golden table weighing several hundredweight, and the Five Scrolls of the Jewish law.

'Festus should be here!' Galla whimpered, and they all sniffed. (The wine gourds were well drained by this point.)

There seemed to be a pause. Maia and I jumped all the children down to street level and marshalled them by families to the nearest public latrine. We took them back and filled them up with water again before they died of dehydration and excitement.

'Uncle Marcus! That man's got his hand up that lady's skirt!' Marcia. What an observant child. This sort of embarrassment had been happening all day. Her mother Marina said nothing; worn down by Marcia's constant piping indiscretions, Marina rarely does.

'Picking that lady's pocket, I dare say,' I remarked recklessly. Maia exploded. 'Gods, Marcus, you're so lewd!'

Dazzling white animals, with flowers round their horns, were led by on crimson streamers by light-footed priests from all the sacred colleges. Flute players escorted them in a swirl of incense fumes, while dancers exultantly cavorted in handsprings wherever there was room. Acolytes carried golden censors and implements for the sacrifice.

'Uncle Marcus, that man's there! That man who stinks!' A face in the crowd. Well, a smell.

I saw him as soon as she shouted. He lounged against a portico pillar across the street. His long face, sallow skin and thin disgusting hair were unmistakable: the hot-wine waiter I found in my room after my British trip. It struck me at last that it was no coincidence Smaractus found a spare tenant when I was away. That rank piece of pungency had been planted, planted to watch me. He was watching me still. Unclamping a two-year-old who was sitting on my shoulders, I whispered to Maia that I was leaving her in charge while I slipped off to see a man about a racing tip.

I don't think our Maia has ever forgiven me; one way and another I never got back.

LVII

I crossed the street under the toes of the first ranks of the captives from Judaea. Seven hundred prisoners, specially selected for their impressive stature to be brought overseas and displayed by Titus in his victory parade. They were smothered in expensive robes to hide the bruises where soldiery had assaulted them on the journey; as I tumbled over the pavements before they ground me down, I could smell their fear. They must have known it was part of the Triumphal ceremony that before the Emperor made sacrifice on Capitol Hill, he would pause until word was brought that his enemies had been ritually executed in the Mamertine Jail. For all these poor blighters could tell, all seven hundred of them faced the noose, not just one token leader of their revolt.

A certain Simon son of Gioras had in fact been selected for strangulation today. Already getting their pecker up to thrash him in the kidneys as they dragged him out of the line at the Gemonian Steps, the prisoners' escort flailed viciously at me as I scurried across the road just in front of them. I barely made it intact to the crush on the other side. The waiter had spotted me coming and was squeezing off towards the Sacred Way. Packed as the street was, he had no difficulty persuading citizens to allow him a space to ooze by. Without the advantage of his personal fragrance my task was stickier, but frustration with this filthy case was giving me an edge; I elbowed people mercilessly out of my own way.

I trailed him all along the street that used to go north, under the shadow of what we called the Upper Palace, through part of the grounds of Nero's Golden House. We hit the Sacred Way. On the corner by the Temple of Vesta, with its mock thatched roof and lattices, the crowds craning their necks for the approach of Vespasian and Titus had clustered so thickly there was only one way my quarry could turn – into the Forum on its southern edge. We were hemmed back against the public buildings as the prisoners overtook us. We were both struggling now. Our only way to move was to be eased along by muscular contortions in the crowd, like a recent dinner undulating inside a snake.

There was no hope of concealment as from time to time the waiter glanced anxiously back. He bludgeoned across the front of the Julian Courts, and I sweated after him. On the processional way I could hear the stamp of twenty-four members of the college of lictors, the escort for the Emperor – presumably all in red tunics and shouldering their bundles of staves, though they were hidden from my view by the press of the crowd. Vespasian himself was coming now. The excitement rose, and with it my desperate mood. I tried to fight my way forwards, yet to do anything but stand still and applaud Vespasian like everybody else was virtually impossible. By the Temple of Saturn, I had made up no ground on the waiter and as I turned, distracted by the racket of the Emperor's chariot, I finally lost sight of him for the last time.

I let him go. Life was too precious to waste. Fighting to keep my feet, I found myself on the steps, almost where I had been standing on that summer day when Sosia Camillina ran towards me and all this began.

There I stood, squeezed breathless, while the Emperor in whom she so dearly believed rode up to meet the senate at the Temple of Jupiter, to celebrate his victory as a champion of the city and dedicate himself in his role as Chief Priest to the peace and prosperity of Rome. Four powerful white horses dragged his mighty chariot into the grateful roar of the crowd. The old man stood in his richly embroidered robes, beneath a golden oakleaf wreath held over his head; it was the Crown of Jupiter, and too heavy for a mortal man to wear. On his sturdy arm lay the laurel bough he would place in the lap of the gods on Capitol Hill; in his great firm hand he carried the traditional ivory sceptre with its eagle taking flight. The public slave whose task was to murmur reminders of the Emperor's own immortality seemed to have given up. There was no point. Vespasian was a grim old cynic; he knew.

Slowly the gilded triumphal chariot thundered by. Vespasian looked, as he himself said afterwards, as though he was calling himself a fool to have wasted a day on this endlessly crawling parade. I did not cheer, but despite myself I laughed.

After him, Titus. Titus in a second great chariot, looking as if his heart was going to burst. Finally Domitian, the junior prince, handsome as mustard on a prancing white horse.

They had done it. They were here. Three Sabine provincials no one had ever heard of until last year had, with good luck and some merit, made themselves dynastic princes in Rome.

I turned away. Behind the three Flavians, the full mass of the army now came marching in: line after line of standard-bearers, trumpeters, baton-wielding officers in tall crimson crests, augurs, engineers, then the endless ranks of footsloggers six deep, swinging along in the easy tramp that had taken the legions effortlessly throughout the world. Regulars piled through the streets in cohort after glittering cohort, followed by their exotic auxiliaries – swarthy-faced archers in shimmering scale armour mounted on swift ponies, then heavier cavalry, ominous today in chased golden face masks that made them quite expressionless as they shook their feathered spears in unison.

There was going to be a long wait while the Emperor climbed the Gemonian steps on his knees, then more delay while he made formal sacrifice at the Temple of Jupiter on Capitol Hill. Turning back the way I had come would be impossible for another hour. I decided to circle right round the Palatine and weave back to the others along the Caelian side. This would enable a discreet check of certain premises on the way.

I followed the line of the Cloaca Maxima, the Great Sewer, built five hundred years ago to drain the marshes round the Forum and the river side of the Aventine. My road soon brought me among the spice markets, where I came upon a watchman guarding the manhole where sewermen still plugged away daily under Nap Lane. They were not here today. On a public holiday no one works; only watchmen sometimes watch, if they want somewhere quiet to get drunk. This watchman had guzzled his way through one raw skinful and was taking a nap to encourage him for more.

So far nothing unexpected. Yet at the head of the alley I spotted a girl I vaguely thought I knew.

'Naïssa?' It was Helena Justina's constantly abandoned maid.

She had made up her face with borrowed paint in honour of the day. She had done it in poor light so in broad sunshine the final effect passed beyond enhancing her features to a vivid glaze of colour; it gave her an unnatural, astonished stare.

'Where is your lady, girl?' I demanded anxiously.

'In her father-in-law's warehouse. I was frightened to go any further; she told me to wait here.'

'It's just a warehouse, nothing sinister; you ought to have gone in with her!'

'What shall I do now?' Naïssa queried nervously, widening her fantastically painted eyes.

'Whatever she told you, Naïssa!' I instructed unsympathetically, while my mind raced.

Having informed Helena Justina yesterday that I was not free to go to the warehouse, I knew I ought to abandon my present plan. I wanted very badly to see her, but turned away. Now I had accepted that at least one of her close relations was involved in the conspiracy, facing her was hard to contemplate. Yet all the time I kept remembering that the warehouse was where Sosia had been murdered. To leave Helena alone there would have been even more difficult.

'Are you Didius Falco?' Naïssa asked, with a glimmer of recognition in her eyes. I stopped. 'She told me to go to your house with this – '

She was holding something out. It was wrapped in a scarf, but the weight felt familiar as soon as it dropped into my hand.

'Was there a message?'

'No, sir.'

Already I realized something serious was happening. I said urgently to the maid: 'Go back and watch the Triumph with the family again. Tell Helena Justina's mother, as discreetly as you can, that your lady is under my escort now. Her father should be attending the sacrifice, no need to bother him yet. But if Helena does not reappear by the time of the celebration dinner, go immediately to the senator and tell him where we are.'

The next time I began to walk it was rapidly down Nap Lane. As I went, I unfolded Helena's scarf.

What I held in my hand then was a bracelet of British jet, fashioned in interlocking pieces like whale's teeth. It was the bracelet that Sosia Camillina once gave to me, which had been stolen from me on the doorstep of the senator's house.

LVIII

Sometimes a case consists of a progression of facts that lead you from one to another in a logical sequence; with these an informer who has any sort of brain can do all the work himself, at his own pace. Sometimes it is different. All you can do is stir the mire, then keep prodding so pieces of flotsam float to the top, while you stand there and watch for some putrid relic to emerge and at last make sense. Something had swirled into view now; the only problem was, it must be Helena who had stirred the mire. But if Helena had found this bracelet where Sosia found her list of names, it made sense. And it meant Helena Justina now knew who the last conspirator was.

To keep it safe, I buckled the bracelet onto my belt.

When I walked into the alley some things had changed, some were exactly the same. Rank weeds lolled against decaying doorposts where fungus gleamed like shrimp roe; further on, new chains flaunted bright padlocks on businesslike new doors. It must be a place where property ownership constantly changed, shifting with the storms of commerce, be they blown up on the ocean by the gods in their wicked mood, or manufactured in the Emporium by speculating men.

At the Marcellus warehouse there seemed little alteration on the outside. In the lane a broken down waggon which I remembered had been shunted along a couple of yards; I was surprised it could be moved. I noticed the difference because there was a manhole with its cover off where the clapped-out vehicle had stood before in apparently permanent decay. The yard gates were closed, but unlocked. I walked in on hurried feet.

When I came here looking for Sosia, the Marcellus warehouse had appeared almost abandoned. Since then, the sea routes to Alexandria had reopened, and evidently several triremes laden to swamping-point had made the trip for Pertinax while he was still alive and operating in trade. This was obviously a working unit now. A line of carts stood against the yard wall, and when I approached the warehouse door I could smell the difference from five paces away. Someone had left a great key in the outside lock. The twelve-foot door gave with a creak, though I had to lean against it with my whole bodyweight to heave the monster ajar.

What a place! Now that Pertinax and his partner Camillus Meto had been using it again, the atmosphere was magical. But the dead silence told me nobody was here.

The pepper warehouse was a square, high, cluttered space, dimly lit from far above. Even now it was still less than half full, but on that warm afternoon the varied aromas of the rich goods inside hit me at the entrance like the whoomph of a well-sealed steam-room at the baths. Once my eyes focussed in the weird light I could see bell jars of root ginger standing in shadowy rows like pharaohs' statues lining the route to the tombs in some silent city of the dead. Sacks were piled in the centre of the floor stuffed with cloves, coriander, cardamoms and cinnamon bark. One entire wall was lined with wooden stalls where I plunged to the elbow in peppercorns, black, white and green. I stuffed half a handful – worth a year's salary – into my pocket absent-mindedly.

She was nowhere to be seen. I walked steadily up a long aisle of baskets and kegs to the back of the building, then returned. My eyes watered slightly. I stood in that dizzy fug of aromatic scents, like a man drowning in medicinal balsam.

'Helena!' I spoke her name, but not loudly. I waited, straining to find her presence, but I could tell she was not there.

'Helena . . .'

I walked out into the glare of the yard. Someone had been here. Someone had left the key. Someone intended coming back.

No one was in the yard. I stood looking again at the line of waiting carts. They were quite substantial. Spices were normally transported in panniers slung on mules.

I walked to the gate. Naïssa had gone. Nothing else had changed. I walked back to where the watchman had just woken up enough to look up at me in bleary happiness.

'I'm looking for a girl.'

'Good luck to you, sir!'

By now all the world was his friend. He insisted I share his next bottle, so I sat on the ground beside him while I tried to decide what to do. Sharing his bottle involved sharing his company, both of which explained why the watchman had been drinking alone, for his company was unendurable and his wine worse. Drinking seemed to sober him up, so to take my mind off his tedious personality and the foul taste of his liquor on the roof of my mouth I enquired after progress in the sewers. I should have known better. It turned out he was an opinionated orator who started to cackle on, imparting grimly-held theories about incompetent management by the aediles who ran the public works. He was right, but that did not make me keen to hear his views. I bit at a peppercorn, cursing myself.

'This work has been going on for almost a year. Why so long?' If I had been a lucky man, he would have answered he was only the watchman and had no idea; men who lecture you on local government are never so honest or so brief. After a slurred treatise on the art of sewer maintenance, wildly inaccurate on engineering facts and positively intolerable once he started drawing diagrams in the dust, I found out that quite simply the patched cracks consistently reappeared. The job was troublesome. The fault lay two hundred yards down Nap Lane. None of the self-important occupants would agree to have their yards dug up, so all the concrete had to be barrowed here then slung along in baskets underground . . .

'Can't they use a manhole nearer the spot?' I asked.

He answered with the logic of the truly drunk, that there wasn't one.

'Thanks!' I said, tipping down the brim of Maia's hat over my face.

I knew without moving that I had found the silver pigs.

We lay there, side by side, – a hopeless drunk with half his belly showing, and his companion under a country hat – while I got used to this idea. Somehow I felt no surprise when brisk footsteps approached us from the main street direction and passed by, striding down the lane. I lifted Maia's hat a crack above my nose.

I saw a man I recognized go in through the warehouse gate.

There was just time for me to hop down the lane and flatten myself inside the clapped-out cart before he burst back out like an exploding lupin seed. He must have discovered the same key that I found, still in the lock. I kept well down, and heard him walk straight to the false manhole that had been hidden beneath the wrecked vehicle until it was moved. He seemed to pause, listening; I tried not to breathe. I heard him strike a sulphur match. He swung himself down the iron ladder, while I slid to the floor crabwise and approached the hole, circling around so that my shadow fell away from it. I stood back until the faint clang of his shoes had stopped ringing on the ladder, then I waited a few seconds longer in case when he reached the bottom he looked up.

No one in sight: I scrambled up and shinned down the ladder myself, silently planting the arches of my feet on the metal rungs.

There was a small chamber to turn in, from which an excavated passage ran under the yard wall. It was high enough to walk without crouching, and smooth underfoot. Everywhere was thoroughly lined with mortar, and quite dry. Enough light came from the manhole to fumble my way to a heavy open doorway where I stayed, secure in the outer darkness of the passage, to observe the man I had followed as he spoke to Helena. It was the younger Camillus brother, her uncle Publius.

What I still did not know was whether he had come as a villain, anxious to secure his loot – or whether, like me, he was an innocent, merely curious citizen.

LIX

Publius and Helena held a lamp each. Beyond these tiny orbs, which glowed upon their faces with sick translucency, gloomed a black rectangular mass.

'So you're here!' Camillus Meto exclaimed, with the mild astonishment of a man who had imagined a young girl would want to watch the Triumph. From the acoustics as he spoke I gathered they were in a small chamber, densely packed. 'Did I startle you?'

Neither seemed particularly alarmed; I was. I could hear my heart knocking like an airlock in a narrow bronze water-pipe.

Helena Justina had been standing quite still in the under-ground room as if lost in thought. She must have heard her uncle's footsteps, but she showed no surprise. She spoke to him cheerfully, like any relative. 'Look at this! The saffron vault keeps a good secret. I wondered if the soldiers would have found it. Obviously not!'

'You knew about this place? Did Pertinax bring you here?'

'To show me the perfumes, several times. We were married then, of course. His dry cellar, with a secret door, where the most costly spices could be locked away. Such a simple trick, having the entrance in the lane outside – I never believed him when he said it was safe . . . I've found some other lamps – '
She began lighting them with a spill, then they both stared.

It was a low vault, with slabs of rough-hewn stone forming shelves where ceramic jars and glass vessels stood like elixirs in an apothecary's shop. Here, apart from the dried saffron filaments from bright Bithynian crocuses which gave the cavern its familiar name, Pertinax and Publius Meto had secured their precious oils, safe from the excise and from any light-fingered warehousemen of their own. You could not smell the saffron for the much more concentrated perfumes which haunted the place with their enclosed, ambrosial scent. But Helena and her

228

uncle did not notice those. Filling most of the floorspace was a sombre block, chest-high, which chilled the memory of an ex-lead-mine slave: silver ingots by the score stood stacked in the gloom, as regular and tight as turf blocks built into a military wall.

I could see Camillus Meto was watching his niece.

'Is Falco here with you?'

'No.' Her voice was hard.

He laughed shortly, with an implication I objected to. 'Cast you off?'

Helena ignored the remark. 'A down payment on an Empire!' she marvelled in her old, bitter way. 'Falco would have liked to see this. Such a pity he found out that three quarters of this eerie booty no longer contains any silver at all.'

'Clever old Falco!' Publius said quietly. 'I can't see the Praetorians knocking at seaside villas in Pompeii and Oplontis, trying to sell them cheap lead water pipes!' He seemed more positive than I remembered him before. 'What were you doing here all alone when I came in?'

'Thinking.' She sounded sad. 'Thinking about Sosia. I wondered if this vault was where she died. She knew it was here; she visited once with Gnaeus and me. She may have come, knowing that it was a secret place – '

With an abrupt movement Sosia's father set his lamp on a shelf and folded his arms, gazing round bleakly as lines deeply incised his face.

'It's too late to make any difference!' he stated, in a strained voice. He wanted to stop her. For his sake, so did I. He could not stand here and face it. His voice had the harsh break I remembered from Sosia's funeral, as if he were still fretting to avoid the fact of her death, brusquely rejecting anyone who reminded him.

Helena sighed. '*Fair, reverent and dutiful*; father read me your eulogy. He was so upset – '

'He copes!' Publius rapped.

'Not so well as he did. Father said to me recently, he felt he was drowning in a whirlpool – now I see this I understand!'

'What?' I saw Publius' head come up.

Helena Justina demanded almost impatiently but with a tinge of bitterness, 'Isn't it obvious?' She straightened her shoulders, then declared in the taut voice I had only heard her use when insulted to the heart by me, 'Pertinax may have provided the warehouse with its secret vault, but he had not the brains to devise a plot so devious. I assume it is my father who organized all this.'

As she gestured angrily towards the bank of ingots, Camillus Meto stared at her. They and I contemplated the consequences of what she had suggested. In a Roman scandal none of the family escapes. Unborn generations, judged by the honour of their ancestors, were already condemned by this act against the state. The disgrace of a senator would drag down all his relations. His loss of honour afflicted the respectable and the innocent too, including his brother and his sons. Publius would be permanently scarred. The good-hearted lad I had met in Germany with Helena would find his career blighted before it was under way; his brother in Spain too. Far away in Britain this curse would fall unhappily on Aelia Camilla; through her marriage, even onto Gaius. And here – on Helena.

Her uncle threw back that oddly ordinary head and commented in a heavy voice, 'Oh Helena, Helena! I knew of course; I had known for a long time. I was not sure whether you had realized!'

I thought, if he *was* in the plot himself this man was acting extraordinarily well. If he was, Helena must know. But in that case, the lass was lucky I was here. Facing up to him alone was desperately dangerous . . .

LX

'What are you proposing to do?' Camillus Meto asked his niece in a cautious tone.

'If I can, put things right.' She spoke very crisply, without a second thought. That was Helena all over. I loved the poor deluded girl for her straightforwardness!

A tickle ran across my foot so insistently I lifted my leg and shook, though I knew that in this arid hole no creature was likely to live. The darkness pressed coolly on my prickling skin. The passage lay buried in thick silence, though far away I could hear a remote, single note of applause as the Triumph continued at the Capitol.

In the faint light of half a dozen small oil lamps, Helena Justina was half turned away, though I knew her so well I could tell her moods from the inflexion in her voice. She sounded wan, as she always did if she felt troubled and alone. I could *not* interpret whether she had confided the truth to her uncle, or was testing him. As for him, he looked like a man whose emotions were either very shallow or so deep you could never hope to fathom them.

'I would have expected you to suppose your father was too respectable!' he commented.

Helena sighed. 'Isn't that the point? The family rely on him to do everything that is noble. But when I was in Britain I had a long talk with my aunt. Aelia Camilla told me a great deal to explain all this. How Grandfather Camillus lived in Bithynia, partly to save money when the family's financial resources were running low. How he nursed his wife's dowry for twenty-five years in order to find funds to qualify father for the senate – '

'So how do you and sister Aelia account for this?' Publius enquired, sounding intrigued yet with the usual slight sneer in his tone.

'You know papa.' Helena spoke gravely. 'Not one of life's firebrands! Perhaps the strain of carrying responsibilities which

231

he felt were above his talents drove him to some wild political gesture. If our Gnaeus, using his position as a son-in-law, applied any kind of pressure papa might be vulnerable. Perhaps Gnaeus used blackmail. My father then struggled to stave off family disgrace – as he did so, becoming inextricably drawn in. While I was still married, perhaps he hoped somehow to protect me. Every man has his weakness, Falco would say.'

'Ah Falco again!' Publius now adopted the note of thinly disguised contempt he had always used when dealing with me. 'Falco has ridden dangerously close. If anything is to be salvaged from all this we shall need to deflect that young man.'

'Oh I've tried that!' Helena Justina gave an oddly narrow smile. A cold fist clenched in my stomach; an involuntary tremor ran down the back of my thigh.

'I thought so!' scoffed Publius candidly. 'Well, this heirloom is an unexpected bonus for you. What will you do with it then, run off with friend Falco?'

'Believe me,' Helena snapped fiercely, like the girl I first met in Britain, 'Didius Falco would not thank you for suggesting that! His one aim in life is to shed me as soon as he can.'

'Really? My spies tell me he looks at you as if he were jealous of the very air you breathe.'

'*Really?*' Helena echoed sarcastically; then she snapped back vigorously, 'And what spies are those, uncle?'

Her uncle did not answer her.

It was then, contemplating what Helena might possibly be about to reveal of her private feelings for me, that fright and yearning tore me apart so much that I was racked by a catastrophic sneeze.

There was no time to back out down the passage, so I adopted my most nonchalant face and slid out into the vault.

'Your green peppers are top quality!' I congratulated Helena to camouflage the reason for the sneeze.

'Oh Falco!' I hoped I detected a gleam in her expression, as though she welcomed me, yet she sounded quite angry. 'Whatever are you doing here?'

'I understood you had invited me.'

'*I* understood you had declined to come!'

'Luckily for you, when the third five-year-old kicked my shins with his tiny iron-shod boot, family duty began to pall. Is this where Atius Pertinax used to keep his petty cash?'

'It's a saffron vault, Falco.'

'I must make a note to build one in when I design my country villa! Any chance of me palming half a pint of Malabathron? I want some for a special girl I know.'

'Only you,' remarked Helena, 'could offer to flatter a woman with a present you had stolen from her first!'

'I hope so,' I agreed cheerfully. 'With any luck I'm the only one who knows which really suits you best.'

All this time her sneering uncle had been watching the two of us, and I had more sense than to imagine he was hoping to learn anything from my seduction technique.

'Young man,' he accosted in his thin voice, 'why exactly have you come wandering in here?'

I beamed at him, as guileless as a village idiot. 'Looking for the silver pigs!'

Now that I had found the ingots, I crossed to examine them and introduced myself, as any lead mine slave would, by giving them a friendly kick. I hurt my toe, but did not care; at least I knew for certain this ghostly mass was real. As I bent to rub my foot my hand hit a small object hidden against the leaden stack. I held it up: it was a plain brass inkwell, its contents long ago dried up. All three of us looked at it but none of us spoke. I put it in the pocket of my tunic slowly, then shivered in my holiday cloak.

Helena Justina spoke up with a hint of dramatic urgency: 'You are trespassing, Falco. I want you to go.'

I turned. As our eyes met, I felt the sudden familiar lift in my spirits. I felt certain, too, that we were partners sharing a charade.

Now there was three of us in the vault, a new tension had taken effect. It felt like belonging to a geometric problem where certain fixed elements would enable us to draw the figure if we followed Euclid's rules. I smiled at her ladyship.

'I finally worked out that a few barrels of nutmeg were not enough to keep bringing down the roof of the Cloaca Maxima. Lead bars would though! The political plot has foundered; so the ringleader probably intends the ingots for himself. I've also worked out that he'll make for the pigs and then make off. There's a neat row of heavy-duty waggons in the yard that I reckon are due to leave laden with silver after curfew tonight. When he comes for them, here I am.'

'Falco!' cried Helena, apparently in outrage. 'It's my father – you cannot arrest papa!'

'Titus could. Still,' I commented drily, 'in cases of treason we spare senators the inconvenience of a public trial. His honour

233

can expect to receive a warning note in time to fall tidily on his own sword in the privacy of his very select home – '

'There is no evidence,' Helena argued.

Sadly I disagreed. 'A great deal of circumstantial evidence has always pointed direct to Decimus. From his first volunteering to assist his friend the praetor, through to the way you and I were ambushed, and on to an unsavoury man who was planted in my rooms during the period when your father was so conveniently paying my rent . . . As a matter of interest, ladyship, why have you never mentioned the existence of this vault? What are you intending to do – let your father make good his escape with what silver there is? Very loyal! I'm certainly impressed!' She stayed silent, so I turned to her uncle, still playing the ingenuous part. 'Bit of a turn up for you, sir? Your highly placed brother named as Domitian's paymaster – '

'Shut up, Falco,' Helena said, but I went on:

'And madam here, who *so* admires an Emperor who will do the paperwork, yet seems magically eager to allow her noble father to diddle the Mint . . . Helena Justina, you know you can't do it!'

'You know nothing about me, Falco,' she muttered in a low voice.

I whipped back, perhaps more intensely than I meant: '*But oh my soul, I wanted to find out!*'

I was desperate to get her away from here before things started getting rough – as I had no doubt they soon would.

'Sir, this is no place for a lady,' I appealed to her uncle. 'Will you instruct your niece to go?'

'That is her decision, Falco.' His mouth compressed slightly in his practised, indifferent way. He had a strangely static face; I guessed he had always been self-sufficient, private to the point of being odd.

I was standing with my back to the cold bulk of the stacked lead bars, with Helena to my left and her uncle on the right. I could see he knew that whatever I was saying to her, I was always watching him. I tried again.

'Listen to me, ladyship. When you and I were in Britain you said Sosia had told me who the conspirators are. So she did.'

'Then you lied to me, Falco!'

'Not knowingly. But I know now, that before she died she identified the men involved. Titus Caesar is in possession of the evidence. So will you do as I say, Helena, I beg of you? What has happened here, and what happens today, need be nothing to do with you – '

Publius Camillus Meto finally broke in: 'Wrong, Falco!'

Helena Justina was hugging her light mantle against the chill which lapped our skin. Wearing his toga, as a man of any standing would on a public festival, Publius held his arms folded just above his waist, like a soldier on a mission reassuring himself subconsciously that his dagger and his sword were still to hand. He was looking directly at me as he searched to discover the truth of what I really knew. I lifted an eyebrow, encouraging him to go on.

Then he said in a voice that became creamy with vindictiveness: 'If you were properly informed, you would realize Helena Justina has been at the centre of this scheme since she was married to Pertinax!'

Odd how your mind works sometimes; before I even turned back to her, I had accepted that what he said was true.

My head spun. Our eyes met. She made no attempt to deny it. I ought to have known. With my brutal luck, I had bound myself to her wholeheartedly and until now had never doubted the lady's honesty!

As she watched me accept it, I saw the contempt in her face. I had trained myself never to react visibly, yet I realized everything I felt for her had become all too obvious in my face. I could not change my expression. Simple distress held me rooted where I stood against the ingots, unable to accuse her, unable even to speak.

Then blackness exploded at the back of my skull, and among the blackness penetrating lights.

LXI

Nothing she had ever said was true. Nothing she had ever done was real . . . I was unconscious but I still saw her stark face, frozen at that moment when she watched me realize.

I was recovering my senses enough to know I was lying on my face, while someone – Camillus Meto himself – was tying up my arms and feet. He had made quite a good job of it, though he had made the mistake of not trussing the two lots of rope together as I would have done myself. If he left me alone, I might manage to obtain a degree of mobility.

Odd how your mind continues working even in unconsciousness. As I came round, I could now hear an indignant voice asking the questions I ought to have demanded immediately: *if it was Helena, why did she tell me Pertinax owned the contraband ship? Why did she give Titus Caesar the conspirators' names? Why did she send me Sosia's bracelet today?* . . .

I must have groaned.

'Keep still,' Meto grunted.

I had always suspected that bland exterior might conceal a jaggedly clever man. He had selected the one statement that would devastate me; then clubbed me with the pommel of a sword, which I could now see lying near. Trying to distract him I started to mumble, 'I haven't felt so stupid since an army training officer told us the session was over, then ran at us with his drawn weapon as we left the exercise ground . . . The lesson was, never to trust your opponent until he was carrion – ' On second thoughts I added innocently, 'Or until you have him very securely tied up!'

Standing directly above me Meto apologized insincerely. 'Sorry!'

Really, there was no pretence any longer. And I had no doubt; the moment he had struck me down he acknowledged his own guilt.

236

'Where's Helena?' I demanded.

'I've got her outside.'

I tried to keep my voice level, but that news left me frantic. What had he done to her? What *would* he do to her?

'People will start looking for me, Meto!'

'Not yet.'

'Did you have to say that about her?' I was violently angry.

'It only matters if you cared for her – '

'Oh no!' I interrupted gratingly. 'It only matters if she ever cared for me!'

Laughing, he picked up the sword. 'Well, Falco, if she did you bungled it!'

'Oh I bungle everything!' I admitted with regret.

But I knew a horse who could have sworn an affidavit that that was untrue.

I lay still. I had an idea Camillus Meto might be the type to kick me in the ribs; mine had suffered enough on this case and still pained me as it was. While I was a slave I had braced myself for constant mistreatment, but now I had convinced myself that was over I could feel uncontrollable panic rising at the mere threat.

A low whistle sounded at the end of the passage. I heard Meto walk towards the door. He exchanged a few words just outside, then reported without coming back in, 'My men are here to remove the silver pigs. Don't try anything Falco – remember the girl. I'm taking her with me, so neither you nor my brother should do anything that causes us to be pursued!'

He went out. I lay trussed on the floor. One careless emotion had cost me the case. So far I had lost the silver, lost my lady, lost a villain and probably before the day was out I would kiss farewell to my miserable life.

It seemed a long afternoon. Someone rolled me aside, then shadowy figures filtered out the marked bars from the pile, working methodically to extract those that were stamped. As they staggered to and fro removing them, I recognized among the group the two jellybrains who had kidnapped Sosia. Neither showed any interest in me.

When their task was complete the groaning labourers left the vault, leaving me and the remaining bars of lead in the pitch dark.

I sensed slight vibrations. Then I guessed that the cartloads of silver had rumbled away overhead, taking the risk that the disruption caused by Vespasian's Triumph would enable them to slip through the deserted streets in daylight, despite the curfew laws. The faint hope I had nurtured, that the patrol of Praetorians Titus promised me would turn up while the carts were still here, evaporated; no Guards would be free until the Emperor was back in his palace tonight, and even then there was a fair chance those listed for duty would prefer to celebrate . . .

Petronius Longus always said in any case that the Praetorians could not catch a flea.

I wondered thoughtfully where Petronius Longus himself was at this moment . . .

I had ended up lying on my back. I began to rock sideways, swinging more and more until with a groan I turned onto my front. Blood surged painfully back into my arms. With my face in the dust, I cursed a few times for form's sake, then bent at the knees with my feet in the air and grabbed for my ankles with my bound hands.

After this lively fiasco had continued for some minutes, for once my luck turned: my violent contortions shook free the knife I had hidden down the wide backpiece of my left boot. I felt it skitter down the side of my leg and heard it drop to the floor.

I cursed again, with greater feeling, as I straightened with an excruciating wrench.

I started to skate about on the floor, searching for my knife. When at last I located the thing my real troubles began. I wriggled sideways, then half onto my back, until after several desperate attempts I managed to nab the knife between the fingers of one hand.

I could probably have managed to cut through the rope round my ankles without losing much of my leg, but unless I had been an acrobat that took me no further to freedom since my hands would remain inaccessible behind my back. Luckily the men who dragged out the ingots had been so exhausted by the time they had finished that they had left the door fractionally ajar. Slithering and bumping I managed to find it from memory, aided by its draught. I wedged the handle of my dagger between the door and its frame. Holding one shoulder against the door, I began the task of cutting through the binding on my hands.

This clever game resulted in much Falco agitation and two cut wrists.

It took a long time and several bouts of apoplexy, but eventually I managed to break free.

LXII

The noise of the Triumph was more subdued, but still distracting, when I emerged.

The yard was of course empty, but I decided to look around. I crossed stiffly to the great door, listened, heard nothing, so squeezed discreetly in. I stopped by the door while my eyes grew accustomed to the shimmering cinnamon haze.

They were still here! Helena Justina, the dimmed light of my battered life, looking almost as jaded as I felt, was sitting on a bale; she seemed unharmed, though she had been tied up. The reason her slippery uncle had not yet absconded was immediately apparent; he was helping himself to sackloads of her top-class peppercorns. Pertinax had been his partner, so I suppose Meto reckoned half fell due to him. He glanced up and spotted me.

'Tut, sir! I can't let you rob my client!' I cried.

For one brave instant as Helena looked round what passed between us was no more than lovers' shared reproach, as if her sense of betrayal gnawed as painfully as mine.

'Oh gods, Falco,' she uttered miserably. 'Don't you ever give up?'

My legs were shaking and my fingers sticky with blood. I had one eye fixed on her uncle and he had his fixed on the sword; it lay across a barrel equidistant from us both. You could tell he was middle class; he was so careless with his tools.

'No point lying still in the dark until some villain is ready to slip his blade between my ribs – ' Meto was setting down the basket of peppercorns he had been filling with a scoop. He had seen I had a dagger in my hand. I added gently, 'I use the word villain advisedly of course.'

Without letting my gaze fall I began to unbuckle my belt. Wrapping the buckle end round my left fist, I let the leather slide through the jet bracelet which I brought into his view.

'You seem curiously nostalgic, sir! Take this, for instance:

240

Sosia Camillina's piece of jet – ' He stiffened. Then I dropped the quiet question: 'Why did you take it? Why did you keep it? Was it triumph over me, or pity for her? A trophy or a genuine memento?' When he made no answer I hurled at him, 'Or guilt? Publius Camillus Meto, *did you kill your own child?*'

Helena gasped.

'Don't be a fool!' Meto exclaimed.

I had shaken him. I had shaken her. Saying it aloud, I had shaken myself.

'Did Pertinax?' I bellowed, to harass him. In fact I knew who had.

'No.' His reply was low.

'But you killed him!'

'Don't be ridiculous – ' I saw him begin to resist. 'Falco, your own meddling killed my daughter – '

It was Helena who interrupted fiercely, suddenly joining me: 'Don't blame the buffoon for the whole pantomime!'

'Domitian killed your daughter.' Sparkling with malice I weighed in for myself. 'You know that very well. You may have been horrified – I do believe you were – but you could say nothing about it because that would incriminate you. Domitian killed her. His initials are on the inkwell you saw me find in the saffron vault. Domitian killed her; my guess is he was there alone. He acted in haste when he realized she must recognize his famous face. Someone – him? you? Atius Pertinax? – carried her body from the vault up here, probably not expecting the Aventine watch to appear; the Aventine watch and me – ' I heard a catch in my own voice.

'Marcus!' Helena exclaimed.

I knew then for absolute certain, he had lied to me. Helena Justina was *never* in the plot.

My eyes went to her.

Publius had begun to move.

'Who found that bracelet?' It had him mesmerized; his advantage was already thrown away.

'I did, uncle!' He was stopped by Helena herself. 'I found it today in your house. Oh Juno, you make me so angry! You think other people are completely insensitive! *You* kidnapped Sosia; *your* name was in the letter Uncle Gaius wrote to Vespasian. Today I watched you calmly stand here and let me blame papa – papa who has spent twenty dreary years covering up your disgrace! My aunt Aelia Camilla told me the truth – your wild youth in Bithynia, that was too wild and went on far too

241

long to be simple exuberance! Your public career in Mauretania that ended so abruptly for reasons that were never explained! Exiled from one province after another, and now from Rome! Political speculation, social scandal, riot, shady business deals, women – *Sosia!* Her mother the wife of a consul-designate, the husband so inconveniently abroad; you would rather the child had been exposed on a midden – but as always, father decently stepped in. Father's life has been a misery – you even inveigled him into marrying me to a man he disliked so you could persuade Pertinax to help import the silver!' I had heard her rant before, but never with the passion she was demonstrating now. 'You think nobody can know – '

'Even Sosia knew,' I slipped in. 'Your name is on the list she gave to me. Condemned to a common informer, Meto – *by your own child!*' I saw no reason to tell him that Sosia scratched his name out.

He looked from Helena Justina to me, then laughed softly as he had never done before. It showed that momentary handsomeness I had noticed before at Sosia's funeral; I could see how when he wanted to bother he must have drawn the women.

'Excellent team!' he applauded us. It was true. That was what we had always been. In this case we had formed a true partnership. We were fighting him together now. 'Made for the middle rank,' he scoffed. 'Not for me. Life with a high moral tone, and so little else! Trapped among third-grade tax collectors, freed Imperial secretaries, the Admiral of the British Channel Fleet! Hard work on a mean salary or struggling in trade. No ceremony abroad, no style or power at home – '

If this was his social grievance, it was not one that impressed me. I growled at him, with the full venom of a tired man from an Aventine tenement, 'You never lacked; you had comfort and leisure all your life. What do you want?'

'Luxury and influence!' he admitted without flinching.

Helena Justina suddenly stood up. Her voice rang clear.

'Then take the silver. Let it be my gift for my poor beleaguered father. Take it. Go away and never trouble him or any of us again.'

It was a brave gamble and I understood now what my clear-principled lady had earlier been trying to achieve. Like her father, she was trying to salvage her uncle's reputation, even on his terms. She was swamped in a tangle of family loyalties beside which the petty wrangling of my own relations seemed positively jolly.

'Your conscience-racked father has nothing left for me – '
Publius began.

It was a decoy. At the same moment, both he and I swung
forwards towards the spot where Helena Justina helplessly
stood. She knew she was in danger. He saw me anticipate and
sprang instead for his sword. I saw him change course and
zig zagged after him.

LXIII

Almost as soon as I launched at him I realized he could fight. In some shady part of the Empire he had learned tricks a middle class gentleman ought not to know. Fortunately for me I was not middle class.

The fight was vicious, worsened because Meto was the type who believed it distracted his opponent to snarl a great deal and to clash weapons whenever he could, whether the blow he was landing served any purpose or not. I didn't mind that. I was soon making noises myself as we gasped through the aisles of pepper and spice, hitting barrels and bales until we were both straining for breath. I was glad Helena Justina had the sense to keep out of the way.

I fought the senator's wayward younger brother up and down in that gloomy scented place for half an hour. As we crushed the rich contents of Helena's heirloom under our scrabbling feet our eyes streamed. Publius must have been approaching fifty, but he possessed the family height. His expressionless demeanour made him unnerving; there was nothing to work on, nothing to play off, no automatic responses I could tickle along, then delude.

He had the better weapon with a longer reach, though that was the least of my worries; I had practised this combination for years with Glaucus at the gym. Meto had practised too, however. Wherever he had trained, they believed in shearing hamstrings and prodding thumbs in eyes. At least I had prepared myself to keep him at a distance by lashing out with my unfurled belt, then, when he battered in too close, winding it round my forearm like a gladiator to ward off his lunging blade.

He was fit. I was tired. We had pounded up past Helena for the third time, with me avoiding the danger of meeting her anxious eyes. I knew I must appear to be struggling – quite a normal sight in her view – then her uncle relaxed, my concentration flickered – and suddenly he knocked up the dagger from my hand. I sprawled frantically after it, throwing myself headlong, then spidering sideways with grit spiking my palms and knees as I fell at full stretch onto my knife.

I was still on the floor, flat out, ready to roll over with my arm up, but knowing it was probably too late. Helena Justina had been standing so still we were both forgetting her. Her uncle came running with his sword high, letting out a terrifying screech. As he rushed, even though she was bound, Helena flung all her weight against a barrel I had at one point pushed her behind. The keg toppled. Its contents gushed out, bouncing and skidaddling for yards across the hard-baked warehouse floor.

No time to thank her. I got one knee under me and pushed myself to my feet. Splaylegged, I swarmed across the stricken keg. Meto exclaimed. He faltered as the tiny iron-hard balls beneath the tender arches of his well-kept feet rocked him over on his insteps. My own horny pads wore boots with triple soles a good inch thick. I kicked out to scatter the nutmegs as I scrambled forwards, then before he could recover I ducked under his guard and smashed the pommel of my knife against his wrist. He dropped the sword. To make sure, I barged him with my shoulder away from it.

Helena Justina immediately captured the sword.

'Stay!' The bastard moved. 'Over!' I choked. 'Don't move. It's all over – '

'Not bad,' he gasped, 'for a . . . tousled tyke from the Subura slums!'

'Nothing to lose – *don't move!*' I knew the type. This one was going to give me trouble right to the slamming of the door to the cells. 'Don't push me, Camillus!'

Helena demanded quickly, 'Falco, what now?'

'The Palace. Vespasian can decide.'

'Falco, you're a fool!' Publius exclaimed. 'Share the silver with me; the spices too, and the girl, Falco – '

I was angry then. Once he had disposed of her to suit his own low purposes, when he had married her to Pertinax. Never again.

'Your nice niece has terrible taste – but not as terrible as that! The play's over. The Aventine watch are blocking the Ostia Road searching everything that moves there from a grandmother's shopping basket to a camel's hump. Petronius Longus won't miss an illegal waggon train. That silver's your death warrant – '

'You're lying, Falco!'

'Don't judge me by your standards. It's time to go.'

Sosia's father – and he was Sosia's father; I think he knew I could never forget that – made me a wry gesture, open palmed, like a gladiator who has lost his arms acknowledging defeat.

'Let me choose my own way.'

'What,' I scoffed, 'death with that high moral tone you so despised in life? A *middle class* traitor – too honourable to hang?'

'Oh Marcus – ' Helena murmured. And at that moment I first heard the great door creak. 'Allow a man his civic rights,' she begged. 'Give him the chance; see what he makes of it. Let me give him the sword – ' She had done it before I could stop her, that fine clear-eyed face open as day. Of course he had it at her precious throat at once.

Camillus Meto had no more honour than a stinging nettle and the lass had brushed too close. He scrunched one hand deep into the soft body of her hair, flinging Helena to her knees. She took on a grey look. One move from either of us and he would slice her like a smoked Spanish ham.

I ordered him steadily, 'Let her go – ' as I tried to keep his eye.

'Oh Falco! Your real weak point!'

'No, sir – my strength.'

Helena did not struggle or speak; her eyes were scorching me. I took a step.

'No closer!'

He was standing between me and the door. It gave him the best light, but I had the best view.

'Behind you, Camillus!'

'Oh gods!' he sneered. 'Not that world-worn trick!'

I raised my voice: 'Partner! You took your time!'

Helena cried out as her uncle hurt her, twisting her hair in a merciless grip that was aimed to distress me. That was his mistake. I was keeping my eyes on him, because of Helena, but at the end he heard the furious footfalls rush.

He began to turn. I shouted: 'Yours!'

Then Publius moved; I leapt, and spun Helena away.

I buried her face, turning her, forcing her head down against my chest.

Before it was over she stopped struggling; she understood. I released her very gently, then held her close while I cut the ropes binding her, before I let her look.

Her uncle was dead. Beside him, in a pool of blood a sword: not his own. Beside that, his executioner.

The senator Decimus Camillus knelt on the ground. For a moment his eyes were closed tight. Without glancing up he asked me dazedly, in the voice he used when we were cronies at Glaucus' gym, 'What does your trainer tell us, Marcus? *To kill a man with a sword takes strength, speed – and a real desire to see him dead!*' That was indeed what honest Glaucus generally said. It had been a good strong blow with his whole heart behind it, but I would never tell him that. 'Oh my brother, Hail and Farewell!'

Still holding his daughter with one arm, I approached and offered the other to bring him to his feet. Still clinging to me, Helena fell on his neck. I embraced them both together. For that moment we three were equal, sharing our deep relief and pain.

We were still standing together when the Praetorians arrived. Petronius Longus appeared in the doorway, pale as milk. Behind him I heard the trundle of the waggons being returned.

There seemed to be a lot of noise. People of rank took charge, things became confused. Men who had played no obvious part in the afternoon's events congratulated themselves on their handling of the affair. I walked slowly outside, feeling my eye sockets as hollow in my face as an actor's mask.

The warehouse was being sealed, with the body still inside. The yard gate was being chained. Decimus was escorted off to explain at the Palace; I watched his daughter being led to a sedan chair. We did not speak. The Praetorians knew an informer – even the Emperor's informer – has no business with the daughter of a senator. Meto had gashed me; she had my blood on her face. She wanted me, I knew she did. She was bruised, she was shocked, I could see that she was shaking; yet I could not go to her.

If she had made the slightest sign I would have pushed all the Praetorians aside. She never did. I stood at a loss. The Guards were taking her home.

It was night. Rome simmered with bad deeds and unholy cries. An owl shrieked above the Capitol. I heard the mean lilt of a sad flute piercing the city streets with man's injustice to woman, and the gods' injustice to men.

Petronius Longus stood at my shoulder without speaking a word. And we both knew, the case of the silver pigs was effectively closed.

LXIV

This was Rome; there were formalities.

That same night, while Vespasian entertained the favoured and fortunate at his own banquet in the Palace and all Rome dined by families and voting tribes elsewhere, I was hauled up to the Palatine for an interview with his son. Titus Caesar, famous for his graciousness, congratulated Camillus Verus, Petronius Longus, me. The senator was too deeply shocked to object. Helena Justina stood in silence beside her mother, both heavily veiled. Even so, Helena was as morose as a dead jellyfish, I could tell.

Speciality of the day was intended to be granting M Didius Falco the gold ring: four hundred thousand sesterces and promotion to the middle rank. A generous gesture from a young Caesar who liked to do good deeds.

M Didius Falco, famous for ungracious behaviour, lived up to his reputation with careless ease. I thought of what it meant – not simply the land and the rank, but the kind of life they enabled me to live. Like Flavius Hilaris, ploughing a useful furrow in his own way – so passionately – and enjoying quiet, comfortable houses with a wife he dearly loved; the life of my choice among people I liked, where I knew I could do well.

Then I remembered Sosia. Sosia who was dead, and now had not even her father to ask the gods to treat her tenderly. I announced to Titus Caesar: 'So that's your contract bonus! Keep it, Caesar. I never earned it; I was hired to expose the man who murdered Sosia Camillina – '

With the cheers of all Rome still ringing in his ears, Titus was in a bonny mood that day, but still capable of wincing a little at me. There were few officials present, but I had done him the favour of not specifying Domitian by name. It was not a name I ever wished to speak.

'Didius Falco, Vespasian has personally closed that account!' Titus observed carefully.

'In my ledger it will never be closed,' I answered the metaphor coldly.

'Probably not! I understand that. Believe me, we all mourn for that sad girl. Falco, try to be understanding in return. Rome, now, needs to believe in its first family. Emperors must make their own rules – '

'That, sir, is why I am a republican!'

I was aware of shocked movements, though Titus himself did not stir. He gazed at me thoughtfully, then appealed to the senator. With an effort, plainly caused by grief and exhaustion rather than any antipathy to me, Decimus attempted: 'Marcus, for my daughter's sake – '

But I told the senator bluntly that his fine-spirited daughter deserved better than a bumped up, bought off, newly bribed-to-silence audit clerk.

He took it fairly well. He probably agreed; I'll guarantee his wife did. If that had not been his own opinion when I started to insult him, it ought to be now. To complete the process I snarled at the finish, 'Senator, don't let your judgement be warped by one heady moment!' Then I turned.

I walked straight to his daughter, in the public audience room. Thank the gods she was veiled. I could not have done it if I had had to see her face.

'Ladyship, you know how it is: every case a girl, new case, new girl! All the same, I brought you home a souvenir to turn your finger green: *Ex Argentiis Britanniae*. The grateful gift of a lead mine slave.'

I had given Helena Justina a silver ring. There would be no other opportunity to see her, so I had fetched it from the silversmith tonight. Engraved inside was one of those cheap jewellers' mottoes that mean nothing or everything depending on your mood: *Anima Mea* . . .

I knew I was hopeless. I rejected her – in public – then laid this burden on her solitude. It was not my fault. The smith had had no instructions, so he put whatever he felt like; once I had seen it I could not bring myself to have it changed.

And after all, the motto was true: *Anima Mea, My Soul*.

I lifted her hand, closing her fingers down firmly on my gift. Then without looking at any of them, I left.

LXV

I went to the Embankment. Up past the shuttered shapes of the puppeteers' booths onto the deserted promenade.

This was where I walked once with Helena Justina. It was a place where I went sometimes, by myself. Now it was dark, but I wanted the dark. I hunched into my toga, listening to Rome at night, fighting back my panic at what I had done.

I stood completely alone in that high place above Rome. A wind was blowing chilly. From the distance came intermittent strains of music, the stamping of sentries' feet, wild gusts of laughter and occasional sinister cries.

When I was calm again, which was when I was very, very cold, I came down.

I went back to the Palace. I asked to see Titus again. It was now very late. In the corridors tall shadows veered, while the few attendants I could find were gossiping and looked up, startled, when disturbed by my white-faced ghost.

No one seemed to find my presence odd. No one seemed to mind. Sometimes it is like that in official places when the night squad comes on duty; so little happens normally that they are glad of a change in routine.

They passed me in through various apartments dripping with drapery to a rather plain anteroom I had never seen before. Someone went into an inner room where I heard my name spoken in a low, incurious voice. After a moment a cheery old cove came out in his slippers, followed at a placid amble by the man who had brought me in, who then disappeared. The old cove scrutinized me.

'Both the young Caesars are tucked up in bed. Will I do?'

He wore a rumpled purple tunic, with no belt. He was a big, solid man about sixty years old, square-built and healthy, with a deeply lined forehead and an open stare. Somehow his very lack of ceremony lent his presence weight: over the years he

251

had grown used to carrying men with him through sheer personality. He did it well. Damn the bastard from his great toes to the thin hair on his head, I liked him at once.

I knew who he was; the Emperor, Vespasian.

I thought it was best to answer politely that he would do.

He gazed at me with amused indulgence, then motioned me in. He had been working in a small area, made cosy with well-placed lamps. There were two neat piles of correspondence undergoing his attentions. It looked a disciplined scene. It was the sort of office I should like to work in myself.

'So you're Falco. You look a bit peaky. Want a cup of wine?'

'No thanks. I'm just a bit cold. Please don't trouble.'

'Oh it's no trouble!' he roared cheerfully. 'There are unlimited cup-bearers and flagon-pourers waiting up the corridor for a chance to show off their stuff – ' I still shook my head. Rather to my surprise he continued rattling on. 'Bringers-in and takers-out. Each of them some sort of exalted specialist. If you want one, they can probably produce a slave to pick the fluff out of your navel, complete with a fluff-picker's apron and a pearl-handled fluff-picking tool!' He seemed to have settled down.

'Nice relaxing retirement, sir,' I chivied him gravely, 'coming into all that!'

'I stopped relaxing when I saw the wages bill,' Vespasian said bitterly.

He turned those deep eyes on me and I realized, I could have handled Titus, but not him.

'I heard about your antics over the fee!'

'I did not mean to insult you, sir.'

Vespasian was silent. It seemed to me the look of strain for which he was so famous could easily be the effect of years in public places trying not to laugh. He was not, however, laughing now.

'What you insult is your own undoubted intelligence!' I like a man to be frank. Just as well. 'So what,' enquired the Emperor more mildly, 'is this latest piece of pantomime about?'

So that was when I explained to Vespasian what I had come here hoping to achieve.

I told him the tale and I said I was sorry; I begged for a second chance as a clerk. He asked why; I said her; he said no.

I said *what?* Then he said no again.

This was not what I expected, not what I expected at all.

After that Vespasian offered me a job. It was my turn to say no. I pointed out he disliked informers and I disliked Emperors; we were hardly well matched. He explained that he did not dislike the informers as such, only the work that they did. I confided that I felt much the same about Emperors.

He looked at me for a long time, though did not seem particularly upset.

'So this visit is about the Camillus girl?' I said nothing. 'Falco, I don't believe in unsuitable liaisons across the ranks. A senator's daughter has a duty to respect the honour of her family. I'm considered old-fashioned,' the Emperor commented.

I could hardly avoid knowing, since it was the talk of Rome, that Vespasian himself had kept house for years with a freed slave who had first been his mistress forty years ago. It was said, though it seemed unlikely, he had even brought this loyal old body to the Palace with him now.

'Sir, with due respect, I won't interrogate you on these matters, so I don't expect to have to answer for myself.'

I think he was offended this time but after a second he grinned. 'Titus says she seems a sensible wench!'

'I thought so,' I snapped back, 'until she tangled with me!'

'My old friend Hilaris,' Vespasian protested, refuting this, 'would strongly disagree. I never argue with Gaius; it leads to too much paperwork. He thinks well of you. What am I to tell him now?'

I looked at the Emperor and he stared at me. We reached an agreement; it was my own idea. He just sat there with his arms folded until I came out with it. He would put me on the list for the second rank; he would do it when I produced the qualifying money myself.

I had committed myself to earning – and *saving* – four hundred thousand pieces of gold.

Before I left I insisted on one other thing.

'I want you to see this.'

I took out the inkwell I found in the saffron vault; it came from my pocket in a scatter of peppercorns. The Emperor turned it over in the palm of his great hand. It was an ordinary inkwell, a simple shape with a retaining ledge inside to prevent spills. On the base was neatly scratched: *T FL DOM*, the initials of Vespasian's younger son.

Before he could speak, I took it back.

'Since it won't be needed in court, I'll keep this as a memento of the case.'

To do Vespasian justice, he did let me take the thing away.

I went home.

As I descended from the Palatine, Rome in the dead of night lay all round me, like a series of deep black pools between the faint lights on the ridges of the Seven Hills. So I turned my footsteps through the sleeping streets and at last came back into the familiar squalor of my own places, and the grim apartment where I lived and to which I had once brought a girl called Sosia Camillina.

It was the worst day of my life, and when I walked into my office I realized that it had not ended yet. The folding door opposite stood open. As I entered, a shaft of cold air moved subtly within the room. There was somebody out on my balcony lying in wait.

LXVI

My mother never came so late. Petronius was suspicious of the open air at night. I decided there was no chance whoever was lurking out there could be anybody I might wish to see.

I had bought some pottery lamps with my early fees from the senator, so I lit them all now for the first time to make it obvious that I had come to stay. Keeping one eye on the balcony door, I peeled off my clothes, poured myself a bowl of water, and washed all over until the smell of wealth and decadence was gone from my cold skin. I walked into the bedroom, making a lot of noise, found a clean tunic I was fond of, then combed my hair. It was still too short to curl.

All this time whoever it was went on waiting outside.

I wanted to go to bed. I went back into the main room, picked up one of my lamps, then steered my tired legs out onto the balcony. I was utterly exhausted and completely unarmed.

The air was soft, and faint noises of the city in the dark rose occasionally with that odd sharpness you get sometimes as sounds reach the sixth floor.

'Now there's a sight!'

She was standing by the balustrade staring out, but as soon as I spoke she turned around: eyes like warm caramel in a creamy almond face. The gods only know how long she had been there; or what doubts assailed her confidence while she waited for me to come home.

'Sosia wrote to me about your view.'

'Not the view,' I said.

And went on looking at Helena.

She stood there, and I stood here, she in the dark and I with my lamp, neither of us certain any longer if we were friends. Distressed moths began to zoom in from the night. One day we would talk about what had happened, but not now; there was too much to re-establish between us first.

'I thought you would never come. Are you drunk?' I had called at several all-night wine shops on my way home.

'I'm sobering rapidly. How long have you been waiting?'

'A long time. Are you surprised?'

I thought about that. No. Knowing her, I was not surprised.

'I thought I would never see you again. Lady, what can I say?'

'Now you've spat in my eye in public, perhaps you should call me Helena.'

'Helena,' I murmured obediently.

I had to sit down. Levering myself onto the bench I kept for dreaming out of doors. I groaned with weariness.

'You want me to go,' she offered awkwardly.

'Too late,' I said, echoing another day. 'Too dark. Too dangerous . . . I want you to stay. Sit by me, Helena; sit with a man on his balcony and listen to the night!' But she stayed where she was.

'Have you been with a woman?'

It was too dark for me to see her face.

'Business,' I said.

Helena Justina turned away, looking over the city again. There was a tight band squeezing my ribcage from the side where I damaged myself in Britain right round to the side I was not hurt at all. 'I'm so glad to see you!'

'Me?' She turned back fiercely. 'Or just anyone at all?'

'You,' I said.

'Oh Marcus, wherever have you been?' This time when she asked there was a different catch in her voice.

I told her about the Embankment, and I told her about Vespasian.

'Does that mean you're working for the Emperor?'

I was working for her.

'I'm working for myself. But he agrees that if I save up the money to qualify, he'll include me in the lists as second rank.'

'How long will it take?'

'About four hundred years.'

'I can wait!'

'That's if I never eat, and I live in a barrel under the Fabrician Bridge. I won't let you wait.'

'I'll do what I want!'

256

Helena Justina rubbed her hand over her eyes and as her temper rasped I realized she was as tired as me. I held out one hand; at last she came. She perched alongside; I laid my arm behind her to shield her from the roughness of the wall. She sat stiffly, leaning a little away from me. I tugged back the mantle she wore over her head, and when I stroked the warm softness of her hair suddenly she closed her eyes. I knew now that meant yearning, not distaste.

Tucking in a loose strand that belonged folded back above her ear, I told her quietly how I had always liked the way she twisted up her hair.

'While I was waiting,' Helena reported frostily, pretending to ignore that, 'I saw off three chits in indecent frocks who had heard you might be rich – ' I reached for her hand; she was wearing my ring. I expected that. Though not to feel it on the third finger of her left hand. 'Your mother came.' The reassuring clasp of her fingers answered mine. 'She thought someone should stay; she warned me that you would troop in eventually, cold and tired and drunk and miserable as Cerberus. She thinks you'll come to no good.'

'She thinks I need a good woman.'

'What do you think?'

'If I found one, I'd disappoint her.'

'You might disappoint each other. Or – '

'Or,' I agreed carefully, 'we might not! My darling, that isn't the point.'

After a moment Helena began again,

'You once said, if you loved me it would be a tragedy. But what if I love you?'

'I'll forgive you, if you can forgive yourself!'

She opened her mouth to speak, but I stopped her, laying one finger gently against her lips. 'Don't. I can't bear that. You've seen how I live. I could never bring you here. You know what my prospects are – virtually nil. I can't insult you with promises. Better accept how things are. Better say nothing, lady. Better run while you can – '

'It's too late.' Helena Justina repeated my previous words bleakly.

I released her and covered my face.

The moment passed.

A huge moth plunged into my lamp. He lay on the table, not even singed though stunned. He was two inches long and shaped like a catapult bolt, with strong mottled brown wings, folded close. He looked as dazed as I felt.

I stood up, lifting him delicately in the hem of my tunic; you can be a brave man but not enjoy the struggles of a live moth in your naked hand. Helena put out the lamp.

I placed the moth on a flower in my window box. He staggered slightly then stood docile. I left him there to fly off or take his chance with becoming a pigeon's breakfast in the morning. For a while I stood looking over Rome. The moment had passed, but her words would remain with me. As I worked alone, whenever there was privacy and quiet, Helena's words would be there.

'Marcus!' she begged.

I turned back to her steadily. There was barely enough light from the lamps indoors for me to make out her face. It didn't matter; I knew everything about her. Even hunched in sadness with her confidence gone, the sight of her caused a deep throb of panic and excitement within me.

'You know that I shall have to take you home.'

'Tomorrow,' she told me, ' – if you want me to stay.'

'I want you to stay!' I stepped across the balcony.

The senator's daughter gave me a look that said she knew what was on my mind, and if the thought had not existed in the first place it would be there now; it was that sort of look. I was near enough to reach down for her with one arm around her waist. Then I swung her up, locked against me while I let myself start to remember how it felt to hold her close. We were both wary but she seemed quite co-operative, so I picked her up. Helena Justina weighed slightly less than a government ingot; not quite too heavy to handle, though difficult to steal . . . A man could carry her over his threshold and still not lose his silly smile; I know, because that is what I did.

It was so long past curfew the noise of delivery carts was finally beginning to quieten. It was far too late for me to take her home, or for anyone from her father's house to collect her from me. Tomorrow morning everything I knew of life would start again. Tomorrow I would have to take her back.

That was tomorrow. Tonight she was mine.